Cupid's darts will land where they may,
Especially on this, good Saint Valentine's Day.
May *your* lover's vows ever prove true,
Bringing nothing but joy your life through.
        from *Lovers' Vows,* by Meg-Lynn Roberts

This delightful little rhyme embodies the spirit of Valentine's Day, and sets the tone for our romantic collection of holiday stories. Valerie King sends her hero and heroine on a chase around the countryside and on a quest for love, Meg-Lynn Roberts pens a Valentine play in which a couple realizes that life truly does imitate art, and Jane Toombs rejoins lost souls into a loving and everlasting embrace.

Three stories of love and romance to brighten the heart and mist the eyes, stories to tickle the fancy and soothe the soul, stories to remind you that true love has, and always will, bring together lovers throughout all of time.

ZEBRA'S REGENCY ROMANCES
DAZZLE AND DELIGHT

A BEGUILING INTRIGUE   (4441, $3.99)
by Olivia Sumner

Pretty as a picture Justine Riggs cared nothing for propriety. She dressed as a boy, sat on her horse like a jockey, and pondered the stars like a scientist. But when she tried to best the handsome Quenton Fletcher, Marquess of Devon, by proving that she was the better equestrian, he would try to prove Justine's antics were pure folly. The game he had in mind was seduction—never imagining that he might lose his heart in the process!

AN INCONVENIENT ENGAGEMENT   (4442, $3.99)
by Joy Reed

Rebecca Wentworth was furious when she saw her betrothed waltzing with another. So she decides to make him jealous by flirting with the handsomest man at the ball, John Collinwood, Earl of Stanford. The "wicked" nobleman knew exactly what the enticing miss was up to—and he was only too happy to play along. But as Rebecca gazed into his magnificent eyes, her errant fiancé was soon utterly forgotten!

SCANDAL'S LADY   (4472, $3.99)
by Mary Kingsley

Cassandra was shocked to learn that the new Earl of Lynton was her childhood friend, Nicholas St. John. After years at sea and mixed feelings Nicholas had come home to take the family title. And although Cassandra knew her place as a governess, she could not help the thrill that went through her each time he was near. Nicholas was pleased to find that his old friend Cassandra was his new next door neighbor, but after being near her, he wondered if mere friendship would be enough . . .

HIS LORDSHIP'S REWARD   (4473, $3.99)
by Carola Dunn

As the daughter of a seasoned soldier, Fanny Ingram was accustomed to the vagaries of military life and cared not a whit about matters of rank and social standing. So she certainly never foresaw her *tendre* for handsome Viscount Roworth of Kent with whom she was forced to share lodgings, while he carried out his clandestine activities on behalf of the British Army. And though good sense told Roworth to keep his distance, he couldn't stop from taking Fanny in his arms for a kiss that made all hearts equal!

A Valentine Embrace

VALERIE KING
MEG-LYNN ROBERTS
OLIVIA SUMNER

ZEBRA BOOKS
KENSINGTON PUBLISHING CORP.

ZEBRA BOOKS are published by

Kensington Publishing Corp.
850 Third Avenue
New York, NY 10022

First Printing: January, 1995

Printed in the United States of America

TABLE OF CONTENTS

Valentine Chase

by
Valerie King

On with the dance! let joy be unconfined;
    No sleep till morn, when Youth and Pleasure meet
To chase the glowing Hours with flying feet.

—Lord Byron

One

"You are sadly mistaken, Hope," Meg Woodville stated firmly as she carefully withdrew a pair of white silk stockings from her chest of drawers of burnished mahogany. Letting the stockings dangle in the air, she finished her thought, "Your brother is not in love with me. Not by half."

Hope grimaced, her hazel eyes disbelieving. "Then why have I seen you in his arms a half-dozen times or more—and kissing him, too?" she queried.

Meg felt her cheeks grow warm as she averted her gaze from the precocious young lady and rolled the stockings up into a loose ball. She did not have an answer for Hope who was keeping her company while she packed her bags. She did not even have a tolerable answer for herself to explain her scandalous conduct of the past several years.

She was in the bedchamber which had been assigned to her during her stay at Threshwick Hall, county seat of Viscount Castleton. She had completed her duties as governess to Hope Staveley, sister to the viscount, and was now preparing for her departure on the noon mails. Hope no longer had need of Meg's tutelage since today, on St. Valentine's Day, the young woman was celebrating her eighteenth birthday.

Meg wore a serviceable carriage dress in the empire style made high to the neck and long to the wrist of a warm, brown wool. The color, though of itself quite ordinary, contrasted beautifully with her auburn curls, peach-colored complexion, and vivid green eyes. As she continued to remove her clothing from the chest of drawers, she chanced to glance at her reflection in the mirror and saw features returned to her which her friends and relations had years ago promised would create for her a marriage of brilliant proportions. Her face was oval, her features delicate, her green eyes wide and luminous, her lips bow-shaped.

But Meg had never wanted brilliance in a marriage, she had only wanted love, and love had so completely eluded her! She turned back from the mirror, repressing a sigh and continued packing for her long journey.

A large, unwieldy trunk was stationed beside her wardrobe and a well-worn portmanteau lay open on the bed. Hope sat curled up in a most unladylike position on the bed just beyond the portmanteau, gowned in light blue velvet. She wore a shawl of prettily embroidered blue merino wool which was ready to fall from her shoulders as she swung one of her yellow kid gloves about in a circle. February in Derbyshire was a month requiring serious attention to an ever present chill in the air. Both ladies were dressed with the awareness that snow would likely see them through the remainder of the month and beyond.

Hope gave her dark brown curls a shake, and addressed her original concern. "From the moment you crossed our portals, Meg—that is, Miss Woodville—"

At that, Meg turned to Hope and smiled. "Meg will do very well. I have wanted for some time to count you as a friend. I only hope that once I am settled in Somerset you will prove a better correspondent than ever you were a student."

Hope grinned in response. "I promise I shall. Oh, Meg, I shall miss you so very much—you've no idea! But pray attend to me for if you don't I vow you will be making the worst mistake of your life. As I was saying, from the moment you crossed our portals, you and my brother have smelled of April and May. You know you have! Oh, why won't you put off your journey until after my birthday ball? Perhaps if Geoff was to dance with you—to hold you in his arms—he might realize you are leaving forever and then he would take you onto the terrace and kiss you and beg you to become his wife. Pray reconsider your decision! Stay! You must stay, at least for the ball!"

Meg Woodville could not bring herself to look at the young woman who had been her particular charge for the past three years. Her heart was already too full of missing her—and Threshwick Hall—to possibly do more than crumple into a heap of unhappy tears at the sight of the young lady's pleading eyes. She pretended, therefore, to busy herself with packing her portmanteau, rolling up another pair of silk stockings, and carefully tucking them between the folds of one of several expensive, though rather worn, French chemises. "So you are to be incorrigible to the last," she returned, forcing a smile as she moved to her wardrobe. "You continue to press me to stay, when you know I am engaged for a position in Somerset. You insist your brother holds me in some affection though every action of his bespeaks the contrary. And you are so romantic that you are convinced one dance will undo the mischief of three years of brangling."

Only then did she dare to meet Hope's imploring gaze, glancing at her from over her shoulder.

Hope shook her head and dropped the glove beside her knee, the yellow kid becoming a pool of butter on the red velvet bedspread. "I think you are being foolish beyond permission to leave now when this evening you could be attending my ball and at least attempting to engage Geoff's affections! Why can you not put off your departure until tomorrow? I can't see that it will make one whit of difference to your new employer."

From her wardrobe, Meg carefully withdrew a gown of sprigged muslin. "Well you are not Mrs. Macclesfield with five daughters underfoot—and by all accounts each quite as impossible as the last. She is in desperate need of my services—she did not mince words in her correspondence with me, on that score I assure you. Since I have told her she can expect me tomorrow, to arrive even one day late would be thoughtless in the extreme!" She folded the gown carefully and laid it in the bottom of her deep trunk.

"What a poor creature she must be if one day will send her into the boughs! Already she seems to be a veritable crosspatch. I heartily recommend you do not go to Somerset. You should stay here and permit me to find you a post nearby. Though if I were to be married soon—" She broke off with a gleam in her eye.

Meg glanced at Hope and chuckled. "My darling girl, is everything always so simple to you? Never mind, don't answer that. I already know what you will say—that I complicate matters by giving them too much thought."

Hope smiled faintly in return. "Well you do, you know," was her quiet answer. A shade of silence rested between the ladies for a moment. In a subdued voice, Hope queried, "Has—has my brother bid you farewell?"

At that, Meg felt her throat constrict. How odd that the mere mention of the man with whom she had argued steadily for the past three years should cause tears to smart her eyes. From the wardrobe she withdrew a soft, lavender cashmere shawl which she had repaired twice in the past month alone. The exquisite shawl had belonged to her mother. The shawl was a soft remembrance of a beloved parent who had died ten years prior. She smoothed her hand over the fine, soft wool and shook her head. "No," she responded slowly. "I expect—that is, I am certain he is busily engaged with Mrs. Keyworth reviewing the details of tonight's *fete.*"

She heard Hope give a snort of disgust. Another brief silence ensued. Meg returned to her portmanteau. As she folded the shawl in a tidy square and laid it over the chemises, Hope said, "Well, since I can see the pair of you are determined to remain stubborn, there is only one thing for me to do—I wash my hands of you both and will now turn to my own amusements. Oh! Did I tell you that I received another delightful valentine from Mr. Alfreton? The last of seven-in-all—one sent each day for the sennight preceding my birthday. Do you think it a good omen that I was born on St. Valentine's Day? I do. I am convinced my life—my *married* life—shall be full of love and romance. And Mr. Alfreton is so very poetical. I know you do not like him above half, but oh, Meg, sometimes when I am near him, my heart soars!"

Meg watched her own hand shape itself into a claw and crumple the fragile threads of the lavender shawl with her fingers. The only reason she could leave Derbyshire at all, without the smallest twinge of conscience that she was abandoning Hope to the wolves, was because she knew Lord Castleton would be taking his sister to London within the sennight for her first Season. The impressionable young lady needed to be away from Alfreton's wretched, persistent, and utterly clever pursuit of the young heiress.

Fortunately, Hope appeared to be dazzled by the thought of the success she was likely to enjoy among the *beau monde* so that Meg trusted Hope's future would take care of itself. But to hear the young woman in raptures over Alfreton's valentines brought a chill to her governess's bones. For one thing, she knew Alfreton would follow his prey to London—indeed, to the ends of the earth, if necessary.

She glanced at Hope and tried to remember the hoydenish girl she had met on St. Valentine's Day so long ago. Hope had been chasing an errant goose through a muddy peach orchard when Meg had first caught sight of her. Her skirts had been splattered with mud, and a serious smear all across the back of her gown indicated how frequently Hope had fallen down in her efforts to conquer the recalcitrant goose. Even though her charge was now curled unladylike upon the bed, she had matured into a lovely young woman, her velvet gown clinging to a womanly shape, her round hazel eyes fringed with thick black lashes, and the last of youthful, round cheeks having long since given way to high, elegant cheekbones. Her rich brown hair was drawn up into a knot atop her head and laced with a blue velvet ribbon. She wore a gold locket about her neck which Meg knew contained well-executed miniatures—one of her brother and one of herself.

She felt a deep sadness threaten to overwhelm her as

she regarded Hope. She loved her as she would have a sister—perhaps even a little as a mother since nearly ten years separated them in age. And today she was leaving on the mails for a new post. Her mission with Hope was complete. But had she accomplished enough with the young woman? Her apparent *tendre* for Alfreton caused Meg to doubt her success. Yet Hope was now fully grown. And if Meg had not been able during the past three years to convey to her charge how improper, how thoroughly ill-judged an alliance with a man of Alfreton's stamp would be, then there was little she could say to the apparently besotted young woman now that would make the smallest difference.

So, instead of attempting to brangle with her over the fortune hunter, she said, "Mr. Alfreton is a delightful companion and a man of great abilities. I would only hope that one day you might meet someone very much like him, only a great deal closer to you in age, once you are fixed in London this spring."

Hope's hazel eyes welled up with tears. In a whisper, the young lady returned, "I shall never meet anyone like him—never! There can only be one Mr. Alfreton." As a tear rolled down her cheek, she uncurled her feet, slipped to the floor from the tall, four-poster bed and hurried from the room. In her wake, she left behind her yellow kid glove and her shawl of embroidered blue wool.

Meg picked up the glove and the shawl and pressed them to her bosom. Hope was wrong, Meg thought ironically. There were many, many gentlemen just like Mr. Alfreton, ready to pounce upon the sensibilities of an innocent in order to gain the advantage over a fortune. She sighed. Was it possible Alfreton had actually been able to engage the child's affections?

Meg sighed deeply, wondering if she ought to speak to Castleton about the incident and warn him that if appearances proved correct it was entirely possible that for some reason Mr. Alfreton had actually been able to win Hope's heart. The mere thought of having to say something so abhorrent to Castleton caused her to shiver and she set the notion aside completely. Such a warning coming from her would only provoke another quarrel.

Her packing partially complete, Meg left the confines of her bedchamber and, using the servants' stairs, made her way to the kitchens where she began bidding all the employees of Threshwick Hall a tearful farewell. The nether regions belowstairs were a-bustle with activity for Hope's birthday ball. Even so, the servants stopped in their preparations to wish Meg a safe journey to Somerset. After receiving a fulsome embrace both from the housekeeper, Mrs. Keyworth, and from Cook's heavy arms and ample bosom, as well as from the remaining female servants each turn, and after shaking hands with the butler, Ashby, and Threshwick's numerous footmen, she returned with brimming eyes to her bedchamber.

Another hour passed as she completed the final packing of her portmanteau and her unwieldy trunk. When she was nearly finished, she caught sight of a missive half-buried in a bowl of fragrant pink, white, and red rose-petal potpourris. The letter was an odd shape and as she approached it she realized the paper had been cut in the shape of a heart.

A valentine!

How her own heart began hammering hard against her ribs!

A bold *M* was slashed across the front.

A masculine hand, surely!

Had Castleton placed the valentine in her chamber after watching her descend the back stairs?

She felt a warm blush of pleasure rise on her face. She touched her cheek with trembling hand. Perhaps he wanted her to stay, to continue in his employ. Perhaps he needed her to escort Hope about London, to chaperone her during her first Season. Perhaps his affections had become engaged afterall. Was it possible he was in love with her?

What absurd thoughts! Castleton in love with her! How utterly ridiculous. She had become as fanciful as Hope.

She picked up the valentine and let her fingers drift across the smooth, expensive paper. She turned it over in her hands and saw the hard, misshapen pool of red wax. Castleton's familiar seal was reflected in the wax!

Her heart again picked up its cadence. A valentine from Geoffrey! Meg tried to remind herself of all that had transpired in three years and how completely impossible it was that Geoffrey Staveley, fifth viscount Lord Castleton, could love her, but still her heart pounded in her breast. Her mind became snagged upon an old memory. Like muslin caught on a thorny brambleberry vine, she could not disengage the quick visions which raced through her brain.

She had arrived at the village of Catmose, situated three miles north of Threshwick Hall, on the day she was expected to arrive—on St. Valentine's Day three years ago. She knew from seven years' experience as a governess that those from whom employment was sought did not tolerate tardiness—even if a coach became snowbound overnight! So she had arrived in Catmose—on the proper day, but two hours beforetimes, and was awaiting the appearance of Castleton's coach to take her the remainder of her journey to Threshwick Hall.

She remembered thinking that of all the counties in which she had been employed, Derbyshire was by far the loveliest. Even in February, with the brisk of winter still shrouding the land in snow, she knew every delight of nature was hers to enjoy with each turn of the season. The land was full of diversity, of gentle hills, thick stands of forest, great stretches of rolling farmland, yet all punctuated by rivers and streams, shrub-laden dells, intriguing caverns, brooks that disappeared underground, and an occasionally sharp, jutting tor. Each tor carried a history and along the way her traveling companions, more familiar with the terrain than herself, had happily recounted for her the local legends of the tors. Each legend, perhaps uncoincidentally, always involved some poor maid who had, out of intense despair, launched herself from the very pinnacle of the tor—unrequited-love playing the part of the faithful culprit. The people, the land, the legends had captured her heart instantly.

So it had been that with a light snowfall dusting her green bonnet, her fur-lined green velvet cape and the tops of her sturdy half-boots of brown leather, she experienced a sensation of wonder as she waited outside the Catmose Inn and surveyed the busy High Street, the steep rise of the church spire above the line of lovely brown, stone cottages, and the tree-studded hills beyond. How special the day had felt as though today her fortunes were destined to change. It was, after all, St. Valentine's Day.

She remembered seeing Castleton approach from a great distance. Initially he had only been a lone figure on horseback, a stranger, his back straight in the saddle, his greatcoat splayed behind him across his horse's flanks, his hat low on his head. She could see he was a man of some importance by the way he carried himself, by the quality of his fine black horse, by the manner in which he was deferred to by the many villagers who passed by him with doffed hats, inclined bonnets, polite bows, and elegant curtsies.

His consequence in the village of Catmose notwithstanding, Meg could not help but note that he was an unusually handsome young man. His cheeks were ruddy from the cold of course, but the striking line of his jaw, his thick black brows, his fine, aristocratic nose and firm chin all combined to blend into a most pleasing masculine face.

She could not keep her gaze from him. She felt drawn to him, by his elegant countenance, by the charm of his face, and perhaps not less so because she could see that for all his polite demeanor in acknowledging his neighbors along the street, he was a trifle overset. His brows were drawn together as though some puzzling thought dogged the heels of his mind.

When he caught sight of her, she knew she ought to have averted her gaze, but somehow she couldn't. For one thing, an arresting look, as he watched her, immediately took the place of his former distress. Afterward, a warmth crept into his hazel eyes and a smile touched his lips which served to increase the charm of his features.

She smiled in return, which she was certain she should not have. But she had smiled nonetheless, and he had guided his horse directly toward her, never once averting his gaze from hers. In some strange manner, she felt as though he was speaking to her heart by the boldness of his gaze, forcing her to recognize her many forgotten hopes and dreams.

The closer he drew toward her, the more clearly she seemed able to see within her own heart and mind. She

understood in that moment that ever since her parents'
deaths, which had left her penniless, she had been alone
and that however much she had tried not to, she had
despised her solitary state. Deeply buried desires—all
the dreams of her girlhood—rolled over her in a crashing
wave, her dreams of one day enjoying the companionship
of a husband, of delighting in a home of her own, of
taking pleasure in holding her babes in her arms. All had
been lost ten years prior when her dowerless, orphaned
state had sent the man she loved, of necessity, pursuing
his fortunes in the army quite apart from her.

Of course the stranger before her represented in his
countenance, in the cut of his clothes and in the quality
of his horse the future which death had stolen from her.
And he could not have known that his presence opened
a very deep wound. But so it had.

She did not comprehend what began to overtake her
as she watched him. It was as though all ability to think
had disappeared. She could only feel. She felt an overwhelming sadness that love had eluded her for most of
her young adult life. She was seven and twenty and had
never known the completeness of a man's love, a man's
arms about her, his kisses, tendernesses spoken in her
ear, a future planned together. Gazing into the stranger's
hazel eyes, she felt the loss so keenly that when he dismounted, still holding her gaze steadfastly, and he approached her, she found herself unable to thwart what
she knew to be his quite ignoble intentions.

His horse blocking his movements from the traffic beyond, he had walked straight up to her, had taken strong
hold of her arm, and without speaking even a single
word, had taken her in his arms. He kissed her full on
the lips, a warm, sensuous kiss which had weakened her

knees dreadfully. She remembered having feebly tried to push him away with a closed fist, but the next moment she scandalously surrendered to his assault and to the forgotten dreams which had so suddenly overtaken her. She leaned into him, forgetting about propriety and about her position as governess in Lord Castleton's household.

How warm his kiss had been on her snowy-cold lips, giving rise to many passionate longings which rippled through her like the gentle waves of a pond disturbed by a boat's oar. His arms surrounded her fully as he held her closely to him, his feet planted apart and set firmly in the snow. February was forgotten and in Meg's heart spring bloomed vibrantly, the heady scent of roses thick in her senses, the promise of an abundant summer richly given in each touch of his lips upon hers. She was young again, and free to bask in the sun without worry. Her heart left its restraints and floated into a sky of the deepest blue.

Would that he kiss her forever!

In slow stages however, as he persisted in his embrace, reality returned to her along with the shocking knowledge that she was behaving in an unconscionable manner. She began at last to push him away, murmuring her horror at her own conduct.

"I—I should not have—I cannot conceive of why I permitted you—oh, do pray, release me."

When at last he drew back from her, tears of frustration and mortification were already burning her eyes. What had she done? She looked up at the stranger. Who was this black-haired hazel-eyed man? Was he acquainted with the inhabitants of Threshwick Hall? Would she be turned away once her conduct with this man became known to Lord Castleton? A terrible panic rose in her heart. What had the stranger meant by accosting her as he had? Had she somehow unwittingly encouraged him? Would he keep silent only to seek her out again, to accost her again?

He had searched her eyes for a long moment, confusion appearing to reign as strongly in his mind as it was in hers.

Then the truth of his nature asserted itself. A certain sardonic expression overcame his face. "I perceive you are a stranger to Catmose," he said curtly. "May I bid you welcome? I am Castleton."

At that, she felt her cheeks drain of all warmth, her panic turning to sheer terror and causing a dizziness to assail her. She stumbled sideways as he turned on his heel and returned to his horse. Before remounting his glossy black stallion, however, he had saluted her, effecting a sweeping, facetious bow. She felt sick with dread.

He was her employer! She had permitted her employer to kiss her and worse, she had responded so thoroughly to his embrace!

"I see you are overset," he called to her from astride his horse. "Too late, I think, to effect a maidenly protest. Good-day."

There had been just such an angry edge to his voice, that some of her shame left her in that moment. She sensed that his anger was not directed toward her, and this knowledge gave her sufficient strength that before he had wheeled his horse about she had been able to return his compliment by dropping a deep, mocking curtsy and letting her cape flow about her in a wide circle as she sank into the snow.

His scathing glance as he disappeared around the corner of the inn was her reward. But what had he expected her to do? To succumb to a fit of the vapors merely because he said, *I am Castleton?* Then he had known nothing at all of Margaret Louise Woodville!

When a few minutes later, Castleton's coach arrived to take her to Threshwick Hall, she climbed aboard with less trepidation than perhaps she ought to have felt. Perhaps it was her greatest flaw but there was always this part of her that would rise up and engage battle when it was offered to her—and Castleton had indeed thrown down his gauntlet, even if he had not been aware of it! She could do nothing less, therefore, than pick it up, savoring the moment she would face him once she arrived at his home.

He had been furious when she had presented herself as his sister's next governess. She knew he had wanted to cast her from his door, but how thoroughly she had tossed his gauntlet back in his face when she had said, "Are you afraid, m'lord, that you will not be able to restrain yourself in my presence? I assure you, I shan't have the least difficulty. Your subsequent bow, after having assaulted me, told me everything I would ever need to know of your nature to be assured I would never permit you to kiss me again."

His nostrils had flared. His hazel eyes had sent sparks showering her green bonnet. He had engaged her then and there without batting an eye! And . . . he had kissed her since, just as Hope had said, probably half a dozen, scandalous times. And each time not without affection, or a sensation at least on her part that she was tumbling in love with him. But it would seem that for some reason, they always fell to brangling afterward.

Now, as she held the valentine in her hand, she could not help but wonder whether in each of his assaults his heart had ever been engaged. Perhaps now she would learn the truth of Castleton's sentiments toward her. Perhaps he loved her after all.

But just as she carefully eased the seal off the paper, the door suddenly burst open. She jerked her head in astonishment toward the intruder and saw to her amazement that Castleton had just broken into her bedchamber.

The thunderous expression on his face did not permit her even the smallest hope that the valentine was full of vows of love and undying affection.

His gaze snapped toward the valentine and his compressed lips gave her to understand quite clearly that the missive was not from him after all. Her heart sank and her temper rose, just as both had done from the first of her acquaintance with Lord Castleton.

She could not restrain, therefore, addressing him in precisely that manner she felt he deserved to be addressed. "How kind of you, m'lord," she began facetiously, "to have broken down my door. Now I will not be required to expend the energy required to open it when I am ready to depart!"

"Stubble it, Miss Woodville," he responded harshly, his fists on his hips, his stance wide and angry. "I see you received one, as well." He held up a similar missive, then returned his fist to his hip. "I expect you have an answer for this piece of mischief for I don't hesitate to tell you I hold you accountable! You were always so certain you knew precisely how to handle a filly of Hope's spirit and the devil—I believed you! Now see what all your coddling has come to!"

In deep frustration, he flipped his valentine in a spin toward the window.

Two

Meg watched Castleton's valentine spiral to the wood floor where it landed propped against cherry-red velvet draperies. She was utterly bewildered. She shifted her gaze to her own valentine and with a sense of foreboding, opened the heart-shaped paper and quickly read the hurriedly scratched missive.

Words grabbed at her.

Long attachment.

Most attentive gentleman.

An unwished for elopement!

The final sentence of the horrendous valentine was so very much like Hope that had the situation not been so desperate Meg would have laughed. *I seem to have misplaced one of my gloves of yellow kid. Would you find it for me, Meg? There's a darling. And, oh, of course my woolen shawl of blue merino has disappeared as well. Wish me joy with Mr. Alfreton. I am utterly* aux anges. *Good-bye.*

"Oh, no," Meg groaned as she whirled around and sank onto the edge of the bed, one hand flying to her cheek, the other holding the letter tightly in her lap. She looked up at Castleton. "She has eloped?" she queried in utter disbelief. "I don't believe it. I—I can't believe it! And certainly not with such an absurd creature as Peveril Alfreton. Not our Hope!"

"Yes, *our* Hope. I trust you are satisfied with the results of your quaint philosophies?" He mocked her, mimicking her, *"But Castleton, you pleaded so fervently, if Hope is not permitted the frequent visits and attentions of Mr. Alfreton she will in all probability form an irrational attachment to him. She is of just such an unsteady temper that were you to forbid her to see Alfreton, she would likely elope with him."* He moved toward her, standing over her in a menacing fashion, his hazel eyes boring into her. "Now see what your clever scheme has achieved—Hope has eloped with that scoundrel, just as I knew she would once I began to permit him to run about my house. What a simpleton I have been. Even now she is undoubtedly married to the damned fellow!"

Meg glared back into hazel eyes and refused to be brow-beaten by her former employer. Asserting her practical turn, she stated, "Well I know for a certainty that she cannot possibly be married to Alfreton yet. For one thing, she was here in my bedchamber," she paused to glance at the small ormolu clock on her dressing table, "not an hour and a half ago. She can't have gotten to Gretna Green by now. Such a journey requires *days!* The only other possibility for such a young lady would be Paris and I know Alfreton hasn't a feather to fly with— Paris would be out of the question!"

"You forget a Special License. And if you think for a moment that Alfreton has not had one secreted away in his coat pocket for the past six months you are sadly mistaken."

But this Meg dismissed with a wave of her hand. "There is not a clergyman in Derbyshire who would marry them and well you know it! She is by far too well known for miles about to be in danger of that. Besides, Hope is of such a garrulous disposition that she would reveal her elopement before the clergyman had opened his prayer book. No, she is not yet wed, even if Alfreton had enough sense to procure a Special License beforehand." She frowned and opened up the valentine again. "Besides, right here she has told us where they are even now—how very much like Hope to jeopardize her own elopement— she says they will enjoy an early nuncheon at the Two Swans Inn. We must follow after them," she said rising from the edge of the bed, sweeping abruptly by him as she moved to stand before her wardrobe.

"You do not believe she has tricked you?" he asked, incredulous. "I am convinced she means to set us off on the wrong scent by leaving behind such a blatant clue as to her intended whereabouts."

Meg withdrew her fur-lined green velvet cape from the wardrobe along with her faithful, green velvet bonnet. She shook her head. "Hope is many things, but she is not clever at schemes and deceptions. Mark my words, she is at the Two Swans even as we speak. If we hurry, we might even catch them." She settled the bonnet over her auburn curls and was tying the bow beneath her ear in a hurried movement when she realized Castleton had fallen silent and was staring at her, his lips slightly parted, his brows drawn sharply together.

She paused with her fingers still on the bow and queried, "What is it?" for he had a peculiar expression on his face. She supposed he was finally beginning to realize the horrendous nature of the scrape into which Hope had just tossed them all especially since he didn't seem to hear her. "Castleton?" she queried again.

But Castleton couldn't hear her. His gaze had become
fixed upon the smooth emerald velvet of Meg's bonnet
and upon the pretty green satin ruching beneath the brim.
He was remembering the circumstance upon which he
had first seen her wearing the elegant confection. His
mind reached backward in time and it was as though he
was riding down the High Street of Catmose again,
catching sight of a beautiful young woman standing beside the Cat and Mouse Inn. He would never have known
her for a governess since she gave the distinct appearance
of a woman of ability and fortune. Her clothing was quite
fashionable, a fur collar rising up from within the confines of an elegant green velvet cape. Over auburn curls,
just peeping from beneath the brim, she wore an exquisite matching velvet bonnet, dusted prettily with white
snow. He thought she might have been a widow for she
stood alone, unguarded by either the attentions of a servant and, however lovely she was in appearance, he could
see she was not in the first blush of youth.

A widow, he had concluded. A widow in Catmose.
Given his temper of the moment, his anger that he had
just discovered his beloved Isabelle—the woman he had
meant to make his wife—in the arms of another man,
the prospect of a beautiful young widow just come to
Catmose pleased him enormously.

She had been a warm vision for such a snow-laden day,
her auburn hair a beautiful contrast to creamy skin and
vivid emerald eyes. Her features were perfection—a
straight nose, gently-arched brows, her mouth a delightful
bow shape ready to be kissed. She watched him approach
with neither a reproachful stare nor a maidenly blush.

Faith but she had been beautiful, standing patiently in
the snow, waiting for what he did not know. He had been

completely mad in that moment as he dismounted his horse. He had walked up to her, a strange notion having become fixed in his brain that he would prove to himself by kissing her how changeable all women could be. He would assault her as passionately as the Squire's son had kissed Isabelle. Then he would know for certain what he had just learned, that ladies were fickle, their hearts bending at will to whatever man chanced to accost them of the moment.

So he had taken her in his arms and held her fast, this stranger, this widow, this companionless lady, whoever she was. She had struggled a little, but he had persisted until he had felt her arm slip about his neck. How right he had been afterall as she returned kiss for kiss!

Women were not to be trusted.

He had intended to release her instantly and toss her aside with a quick denouncement of all of womankind. Instead, much to his astonishment, another sensation entirely had engulfed him—of a longing so intense that all thoughts of vengeance for the moment dissipated like warm breath in icy air. The snow all about him seemed to disappear and summer was richly upon him as the warmth of the woman's body against his seemed to penetrate the thick, black wool of his greatcoat. A splendid heat drenched his heart, like the warmth rising from moist grass beneath the sun's rays. He saw a new life open up before him, of love and passion and kisses as sweet as the nectar of the honeysuckle. He tasted of her nectar as she clung to him, possibilities, endless in their wonder and pleasure, exploded in his mind one atop the other. For a long moment, Isabelle was forgotten, and his sad heart had been born anew in the arms of the stranger.

But the kiss had ended, the truth of his day's discov-

eries rolled back over his mind and dove deeply into his
heart, all obliterating the sweet enjoyment of the moment.
Anger engulfed him. He released her. She had appeared
overcome with bewilderment, with mortification. He
backed away from her, bowing low to her, mocking her
with his exaggerated courtesies. She had responded by
curtsying deeply, her green velvet cape blanketing the
snow around her as she returned his sardonic gesture.
Riding back to Threshwick Hall he had wondered over
and over who she was and how many men she had permitted to accost her as thoroughly as he just had. Her
curtsy had at first angered him, but after a moment he
couldn't keep from smiling to himself. She was bold. He
began to consider the future with a woman he now believed must be a widow. Perhaps a long affair. He rev-
elled in the moment he would meet her again, and in the
prospect of again forcing his attentions upon her.

Learning she was Hope's new governess had filled
him with shock and dismay. The rage he had felt that
she had dared to come to his house after she had learned
of his identity nearly sent him into a fit of apoplexy. But
she had endured his thorough reproach of her character
with a lift of a brow, clearly unimpressed by his tirade.

He still didn't know why he had permitted her to take
up her post except that from the moment she had found
herself in the presence of a man who had just kissed her,
she had held her own, to a nicety, against his quite brut-
ish will.

"Castleton!" Meg called sharply to him. "Whatever is
the matter? You appear as though you've seen a spectre!"

Castleton gave himself a shake, his vision clearing in
slow stages for the memory clung to him tenaciously.
"Not a ghost, precisely," he said quietly. He realized that

the reliving of the memory had given Meg sufficient time to see the same velvet cape settled about her shoulders and every button secured.

He comprehended her intentions and barked at her. "You may take off your bonnet and your cape—or better yet, keep them on, only see that you clamber aboard the mails at the proper hour. I will go after Hope. She is no longer your concern!"

Meg merely lifted a familiar brow and replied, "Don't be such a nodcock, Castleton. If you were to go after them alone, and actually chanced to find them, your temper would undoubtedly get the better of you, and Alfreton would be dead before the cat could lick her ear! Where then would you or your sister be? Don't even ponder the prospect of arguing me out of my conviction! I know you far too well to permit you to pursue Hope alone. However, if you choose to persist in thwarting me I shall have Cheadle harness a team to your town coach and follow in the wake of your curricle!" She stared hard at him, placing her hands on her hips in defiant reflection of his own belligerent stance.

He narrowed his eyes and glared. "Damn and blast, Meg Woodville! I know that if I forbade you to make use of the coach, you'd find some way of following after me. Has anyone ever told you you are by far the most stubborn female to have been born in Albion?"

"Yes," she responded baldly. "You have. A score of times and I am still unimpressed. Now which shall it be? Are we to journey together, or must I make use of the farm horses if necessary?"

He gave a snort and turned brusquely on his heel. "Suit yourself," he retorted. "You always do."

But he had not moved quickly enough, and she saw

as he quit her bedchamber the glimmer of a smile on
his lips. Was he as indifferent to her as he appeared?

Meg retrieved his valentine from the floor by the window and stuffed both horrific missives into her reticule.
She picked up her fur muff and headed toward the stables. Ten miles in Castleton's curricle, with a fresh, quick
team in harness, would likely see them at the Two Swans
within the hour. If only they would be able to stop this
absurd elopement. But what if Hope was truly in love
with the fortune hunter?

That was a question she chose to ignore. All that mat-
tered for the present was finding Hope before marriage
vows had been exchanged.

"Well, there is nothing for it!" Castleton stated cryp-
tically. He had been silent for the first five miles of the
journey and by the frown rippling his brow, Meg knew
from long experience that he had been examining his
conduct with her. It was his way. She was not surprised
therefore when he said, "I do beg your pardon, *yet again,
again for the hundredth time,* for my harsh words earlier.
I was overset. Hope, well, she was always headstrong.
You were very right to insist upon accompanying me. I
believe you have always understood my temper."

"Yes, I have," Meg responded without hesitation.
"And I do accept your apology." Clutching the side of
the curricle, which was moving swiftly along the lane,
she lifted her chin as she turned toward him. Catching
his gaze, she smirked, ever so slightly.

To her intense enjoyment, a brief flight of anger rushed
over his face, before he harrumphed and chuckled all in
one breath. "Vixen!" he exclaimed. He then called to his

horses, sensing that their pace was slackening. He clicked his tongue and gave a slap of the reins on their backs.

When he had reestablished the spanking pace which had characterized their journey from Threshwick Hall, he turned to give her a hard, penetrating look but remained silent.

"What is it?" she queried.

Before answering, he reverted his gaze to the well-travelled, dirt road, crusted with ice and snow, and again encouraged his horses along. When at last he spoke, his voice carried a serious tone which surprised her. "It is no concern of mine," he began, "and you may tell me to go to the devil if you like, but all these years you have never told me how it was you became a governess. Lord knows I've pressed you often enough, but now that you are leaving, will you satisfy my curiosity and tell me all? And do not pitch me that gammon about having had the privilege of entering the profession of your choice for I never did believe that whisker. For if you call trailing after my sister and trying to teach her how not to muddy her skirts and how to refrain from shouting in a drawing room a profession, I will reconsider my belief that you are a woman of exceptional abilities and intelligence."

Only when he had finished did he glance down at her.

Meg heard his compliment and felt her heart warm beneath his praise. She was reluctant to meet his gaze, for fear he would comprehend how pleased she was, and instead took to studying the drystone wall, layered prettily with snow, which bounded the highway to her left.

"Will you not tell me, Meg?" he asked gently, again slapping the reins against the horses's flanks. The use of her Christian name, which he always employed in those moments when they were alone and for some reason were not brangling, again brought a warmth rising in her heart. He continued, "Do I pry so deeply then?"

Meg turned toward him yet again and fluttered her gaze across his face for the barest second. She was afraid that if she met his gaze squarely, she would lose her ability to reason and would tell him things she did not want him to know. Pretending to be entranced by the Derbyshire countryside as it flew by, she replied, "I will not insult your intelligence by telling you how much I adore the task of polishing the etiquette of my charges. But do not think for a moment that, though my profession is not my first choice, I in any manner despise it, for I do not, I assure you. And Hope I count as a friend now, a very good friend. She was always encouraging me to find a husband when I took her to the assemblies in Derby. But I'm 'fraid I lost heart for that pursuit many years ago. That I needed to earn my keep is not an infrequent occurrence for daughters of many genteel families. And that, my lord, is all I mean to tell you about how it came about I first took up a post as governess."

He was silent apace as the drystone wall gave way to a vista of snow-laden fields and distant hills ending in a jutting tor. "Didn't bring your young man up to scratch, eh?" he responded at last.

Meg found her temper rising instantly as she shot him a reproachful glance. But when she saw the sympathetic twinkle in his eye, her anger subsided.

He chuckled. "You were always one to rise so readily to the fly, m'dear. Besides, you gave me the answer I hoped for. You see, I have always wondered whether or not love had ever touched your heart. You're very secretive, you know. Never permitting anyone to see more than what you wish them to see."

Meg found herself surprised. "Is that how I appear to you?" she queried. "As though I guard each thought and each memory and discreetly reveal only what I wish?" She wondered if this was true.

"You are the soul of discretion, and a little bit more."

"I am surprised you would think so when upon my arrival in Catmose, I permitted you—a complete stranger!—to kiss me. And that, in full view of any gapeseed wishing to stare!"

"That was a long time ago. I should not have accosted you."

She turned toward him. "No, you should not have!" she stated readily. With much pleasure, she watched his jaw stiffen and his color darken.

He again slapped the reins and turned to hold her gaze. "Well, you were not precisely the soul of propriety yourself and—oh, the devil take it! Caught again! Good God, I am nothing more than a halfling where you are concerned."

She smiled fully upon him. "At least you were always honest, Castleton. And for that, I—"

"—If we are to be friends, you must call me Geoffrey, or Geoff if you prefer."

Again, a peculiar warmth floated about her heart. She turned her gaze back to the countryside. The snowy field had given way to a brief stretch of woodland, of beech trees and a scattering of pollarded oaks. Snow surrounded the tree trunks in a white tapestry of crusted mounds, laced with brown, withered leaves. Winter was not yet over. She glanced up at the sky and saw that the clouds were darkening. It would be snowing soon. Too much snow and they would have to curtail their pursuit of Hope altogether.

She thought about Castleton—about Geoffrey—and his opinion that she was guarded with him. She supposed she was, if for no other reason than that they were both quite adroit at setting up each other's backs. But if she had not been forthcoming, neither had he. It had behooved each of them to guard their revelations.

But it wasn't necessary now, she thought. After all, she would be leaving soon. Perhaps not today as she had planned since Hope's immediate future was of primary concern, but tomorrow, certainly. She took a deep breath, therefore, and said, "His name was Charles. He was an officer with a brilliant future before him. I had no dowry and he couldn't support a wife and children on officer's pay. Our parting was simple, forthright, and much-needed, but he took my heart with him. I was given to understand some years later that he married a suitable woman of modest fortune and that he distinguished himself at Waterloo. They reside in Kent." Speaking of him brought distant memories drifting close to her heart. The first year after parting from him had been deeply painful. Each year that followed inevitably less so. But what surprised her now was that she was unable to recall Charles's features to mind. How curious! Was her love dimmed so fully now?

"I see," Castleton returned quietly. "Then you haven't a dark, forbidding past which Hope was certain you possessed?"

Meg chuckled. "Was there ever a more romantic young lady than your sister? No, I am afraid I may disappoint you, but there it is. We loved one another, but we were also sensible. I was denied love and marriage because of a lack of fortune. But do not think I repine. I am not so romantic. Neither was my mother who encouraged me to always assess my situation with common sense along with a realistic comprehension of the society into which I happened to be born. I have tried over and over to impress upon Hope the need to do the same. You cannot imagine how distressed I am that for some reason I was unable to fix the same notion in her head. This flight! Oh, Castleton—that is, Geoffrey—you cannot know how oversetting it is to be pursuing her on this absurd elopement!"

"You must not blame yourself," he said magnanimously, especially in light of the fact that an hour past he had blamed her entirely. "If Hope has not heeded your strictures, then she must learn from experience. And if she has wed that rogue, I'm 'fraid experience will prove a severe taskmaster."

Meg shuddered and gripping the side of the curricle harder still, commanded Castleton with a single phrase. "Spring 'em!" she cried.

Castleton obliged her and with a shout and a crack of his whip, urged his horses into a full gallop.

At the Two Swans, Meg stood in the doorway of the parlor brushing snowflakes from her shoulders and muff. Her gaze became transfixed by the sight of the chamber which had not changed one whit since she had last visited the inn. Her heart began beating strongly in her breast. Fear and wonder rose sharply to vie for supremacy in her mind.

Geoffrey had kissed her here—a second kiss. Why had

she forgotten it? But then that was two years past. A
long time ago.

Three small windows to her left were flanked by flowery, chintz curtains of blue, yellow, green, and pink
which permitted the gray winter's light to spill onto a
rectangular, oak dining table of ancient scrolled lines to
the left of the stone fireplace. Four polished chairs of
the same heavily grained wood graced the table. On the
opposite side of the fireplace, whose massive hearth was
lit with a large, tidy fire, sat two winged chairs which
trapped the heat by their position and shape into their
shiny bellies of horsehair. A coaching scene, showing
four mettlesome chestnut horses harnessed to a gleaming
yellow post-chaise was proudly displayed on the mantel.
Meg's gaze was drawn back to the table and in her mind's
eye she recalled in vivid detail how the evening had begun and progressed.

The laughter returned to her, endless, teasing, familiar,
laughter which had flowed among Hope, Castleton, and
herself for hours. A snowstorm had held them captive.
By eleven, however, Hope had begun to yawn and shortly
afterward Meg had seen her tucked between the sheets.
But Castleton had begged her to rejoin him in the parlor
before she retired for the evening. How readily she had
returned to him unwilling for the evening to end.

They had continued talking for hours with a snow-
laden wind rattling the shutters and buffeting the walls.
The fire had roared in the hearth that night beneath the
attentive and capable hands of the inn's landlord. The
candles guttered and guttered again.

She had sipped a glass of brandy. Castleton had done
the same. She had not wanted to leave. Oh, but she did
not want to think of the rest of it! She gave herself a

shake, removing one hand from her muff and letting it dangle beside her. Footsteps in the taproom outside the parlor helped to break up the unwelcome reverie. The door opened and when a cold buffet of air flowed over her, she turned to see Castleton enter the parlor. He closed the door and began stamping his feet.

She looked at him for a long moment while he busied himself removing snowflakes from the shoulders of his greatcoat and from the tops of his glossy top-boots. To her surprise and her dismay, her heart began straining toward him. She felt a sudden and quite powerful longing for him, but why? Perhaps it was the memories the Two Swans Inn had provoked in her mind? Or was it possible, somehow in the midst of their brangling, he had found passage to her heart? Mentally, she touched his face wanting to memorize his features lest she forget him as she had forgotten Charles.

How different everything might have been had she not been Hope's governess. If she had resided near Derby and had met Castleton first at one of the assemblies instead of at Threshwick Hall, perhaps then they would have been polite and kind to one another. Perhaps then, they would have tumbled in love. Perhaps he would not have kissed her until he had properly requested her hand in marriage.

If only she had not been the dowerless daughter of a fine and excellent, though quite penniless, parson.

If only . . .

Perhaps . . .

How absurd that her life had come to this—futile musings and wishings.

"Hope was here!" Castleton cried. "The landlord confirmed it. And of course that curst Alfreton was with her! Not more than an hour past, too! Damn and blast!"

How grateful she was that he had spoken for his firm voice and his anger served to dispel the remains of her ridiculous, gloomy and utterly worthless reflections. Giving herself another strong shake, she responded in kind. "We should go then. Immediately. I promise you I am not in the least fatigued!"

"But which direction?" he asked. He tore his black hat from his head which sent a few remaining snowflakes flying about the chamber. One touched Meg's cheek. He crossed the room to the fireplace in long, impatient strides. "There are no less than three roads which all wend their way north. Is Alfreton going to be clever or stupid? Two of them would take him well out of the way, but would eventually see him to Chesterfield. And the branching of the lanes is too far from here for anyone to have noticed their direction should I even wish to inquire—which I don't! It's bad enough to be trailing after my sister anyway, but under such a circumstance, I'd rather the whole countryside did not know what she was about!"

Meg could see he was sorely distressed. When he cast himself into one of the winged chairs, she moved to stand near him, her gaze fixed on his profile. He stared straight ahead and turned his hat in his hand. Impulsively, she put her hand on his shoulder and to her surprise he overlaid her hand with his own and sighed deeply.

"We shall find them," she said gently. "It's only a matter of a little diligent effort. As for the countryside, I don't give a fig what anyone thinks, nor should you. I had much rather have Hope returned safely and unwed while risking the ill opinion of a set of rustics who having nothing whatsoever to do with Threshwick Hall, than to have her leg-shackled to that scoundrel. If you like, we could hire another cart and I could travel down one of the roads and inquire after Hope, while you took another lane and did the same."

He looked up at her and shook his head. "A lady travelling alone? I don't think so, but I appreciate your considerate offer."

Meg smiled at him, thinking that when he chose, he could be quite an agreeable companion. She slid her hand off his shoulder and drew a chair forward from the dining table to sit opposite him. "What shall we do then?" she queried as she seated herself. "If you wish, you could make your decision by spinning me around in a circle and whichever lane I end up facing shall be our lot." She smiled encouragingly at him.

Castleton returned her smile, some of the tension he was feeling easing up as he held her gaze. She was deuced pretty in that bonnet, he thought distractedly. Of all her features, her finest was her smile. She had nice, even teeth and the last time, the only other time, they had been in the Two Swans Inn he had remembered enjoying her smile all evening. He recalled having purposely decided that night he would make her smile as much as he could. Never had he laughed so much as during that evening. Hope had retired early and he had begged Meg to keep him company through the storm. He had teasingly told her he had a severe fright of snowstorms, a remark which had brought her smile again to her lips and a great warmth swelling over his own heart.

They had talked for hours and sipped sherry or was it brandy, he could not quite recall. She had finally risen to retire for the night. He didn't know what had prompted him to do so, but he had taken her in his arms. This time there was no greatcoat of his or thick fur-lined cape of hers to hinder the press of their bodies. How soft she was in his arms, the fine velvet of her gown clinging to her womanly shape. He held her close and slid his hand the length of her back. He had searched her mouth, plundered her mouth and thrilled to the gentle moan which had issued from her throat at his persistent kisses and thorough embrace.

Meg watched the gleam in Castleton's eye and knew what he was thinking, what he was *remembering*. She was drawn back to the memory as well of that shared evening and kiss. She had felt in his arms as though she was descending into a place of great warmth and safety from which she never wanted to return. She had given herself fully to the enjoyment of his affection, only begging to be released when she knew that because of the lateness of the hour, the headiness of the wine, and the intimacy of the parlor, she was in terrible danger of succumbing to the richness of her newly birthed passion for him.

He had released her, of course. He was a gentleman.

But the unkind words he had spoken to her afterward . . .

Meg rose from her chair suddenly, as the remainder of that trying moment flooded back to her. His words had been a cruel taunt when she had drawn back from him. They came to mind as sharply as if he spoke them even now.

Do you always kiss with such abandon?

She had been mortified at the implication of such a question. Ashamed. She had fled the parlor with tears burning her eyes and constricting her throat. She had heard him call after her, but her shame gave flight to her feet and she was up the stairs before he could stop her.

Meg was so full of the pain of remembering and of

Castleton's daggerlike query that she could hardly breathe. She wished above all that Hope had not chosen to take nuncheon at the Two Swans today in her flight to Gretna Green.

She rose from her chair and moved to stand before the window, her cheeks warm with embarrassment as they had been over two years ago.

"Meg," Castleton called to her. "What is it?"

"I—I am concerned for Hope," she lied.

She heard him rise from his chair, his footsteps resounding along the wood floor as he crossed the chamber. She felt his hands on her arms. "I never meant to hurt you that night," he said. "I don't even remember precisely what it was I said to you, or why you were so distressed. If I hurt you, I'm sorry for it. Clearly my words were ill-judged. I had meant to tell you how much I enjoyed kissing you. I was in awe of how readily you fell into my arms."

"You intimated I was accustomed to enjoying the attentions of many gentlemen."

"Well, weren't you?" he asked.

Meg drew in a sharp breath, anger flooding her. How could he think such a thing of her? Had he not known her now for three years without comprehending her character even a trifle? She was reminded yet again precisely why it was that no matter how many times she might wish to fall into his arms or upon how many occasions she might wonder if she loved him, she always succeeded in brangling with him. For some reason, Castleton had gotten it fixed in his brain that she was accustomed to kissing whenever and whoever it pleased her to kiss.

Resigning herself to the fact that he would never change in this opinion, and that his opinion would always rankle, she turned around to face him and straightened her shoulders. Forcing a laugh, she replied, "Whether I enjoyed the attentions of a score of men, I shan't reveal anything to you. And now, do forget that day. I assure you until we arrived here, I most certainly had."

His hands slipped away from her shoulders. A frown creased his brow as he studied her face. "Why is it I have the sensation you are mocking me?"

Meg wanted to rant and rail, to call him an absurd, addlepated gudgeon. She even opened her mouth to speak but fortunately at that moment a scratching sounded upon the door and a moment later, the landlord appeared bowing obsequiously to Castleton.

Meg gasped for in his hands he held a familiar, heart-shaped missive, perhaps not as large as the ones she and Castleton had received earlier, but heart-shaped nonetheless.

"I do beg thy pardon, m'lord," he began in his peculiar Derbyshire dialect. "But m'wife handed me this odd letter and said I were to give it to thee, that thy sister had left it in the parlor."

Castleton strode toward the landlord. "Thank you," he said as he retrieved from the landlord what proved to be a valentine indeed.

When the landlord had bowed himself out, Castleton quickly broke the seal and began reading the contents.

"Good God!" he cried. "You will not credit this. Do but listen. This valentine had been intended for Alfreton. *My dearest, my darling, my beloved Alfreton, now that we are to be husband and wife, I shan't withhold even the smallest gesture of my love and affection for you. Deep within the caverns, I have had one of my servants place a gift I purchased for you in Derby at Christmas.*

I could not give it to you then because my brother would have been very angry. Isn't it wonderful we no longer need to be concerned about his opinions? I love you ever so much. Once you find the gift, only then can we continue on to Gretna. Once we are wed, I promise you I shan't have the least difficulty in acquiring my dowry as you so sensibly suggested. I shall buy you many gifts before the honeymoon is over."

Meg was horrified and Castleton apparently not less so as he crumpled up the valentine. "Has he so bewitched the child!" he cried, his cheeks red with anger. *"She* will buy *him* many gifts! We must find them, Meg, because if we do not, I shall hunt him down—married to my sister or not—and slay him with my own hands."

Meg searched her mind quickly and responded. "Hope must be referring to the caverns to the northeast of here—they were always a favorite with her. That would be the third lane! Have the horses put to, at once! Perhaps if Alfreton was to spend some time searching for Hope's gift, we might catch them within the hour!"

Three

The most easterly roadway leading to the caverns took the curricle through the worst of Derbyshire lanes. The partial melting of a recent snow had left the road rutted with crusted mud and the new snow made the whole of it a deception to the eye. Meg found herself time and again bumping shoulders and legs with Castleton, especially since regardless of the condition of the lanes he moved the horses along at a fretful pace.

After one particularly bruising collision, he slowed the horses a trifle and bid her move quite close to him so that their bodies were joined at the sides. He then commanded her to slide her arm about his waist while he did the same. Holding the reins in one hand and holding her tightly with the other, very soon whatever bumps the lane presented saw them enduring the jolts as one. Her discomfort on that score was considerably diminished, but she found her distress on an entirely different plane increasing.

The strength of his arm about her as he protected her forced her mind into the future. She thought of Mrs. Macclesfield and her five daughters—the youngest was but seven. In all likelihood she would be spending the next eleven years raising the woman's children. Of course there would be a myriad of pleasure in seeing the girls emerge into fine young women—she had most certainly enjoyed watching Hope transform from a decidedly hoydenish girl, game for every lark, into a young lady who could with very little effort behave appropriately and with considerable grace during even the dullest of social occasions.

But Meg had always wanted a family of her own, her own children to encourage out of barbarity and into civility. Why was it she wondered, that Castelton's arm about her waist, and the firmness of his arm as it angled across her back, made her question her future so very much?

As the lane stretched out a little and offered very few holes in which the wheels could jump in and out, she glanced up at him. Despite, and perhaps because of, his obvious faults, Geoffrey Staveley was all man—from the strength of his arms and the muscled tautness of his legs, to the deep line of his cheek and firmness of his jaw. There was nothing soft about him. She felt a familiar yearning increase in her heart as she watched him concentrate steadily on the lane ahead.

"We are almost arrived," he said, aware she was looking at him. "Don't fret yourself. We can't be far behind them."

She looked away from him aware that because the lane was smoother now there wasn't the least reason she should continue holding him fast. That he did not release her brought her a sweet sensation of contentment. For a mad moment she wished she could stay with him forever, this close, this fixed upon a common objective. Again, the wretched thought occurred to her that it was quite possible she was in love with him, and had been for a long time.

But his opinion of her character—all because she kissed a veritable stranger upon her arrival in Catmose—was abominably low. How could he respect her? Why should he behave differently toward her? Why else would he have stolen so many kisses from her since?

She had been foolish beyond permission from the first and well she knew it. If Castleton regarded her with contempt, she had only herself to blame.

So be it, she thought, straightening her shoulders. She had made a mistake, several in fact, and now she must endure the consequences.

She released him upon this thought and he did not prevent her.

A few minutes later, they arrived at the caverns but found them deserted. The sight of fresh carriage marks in the muddy snow near the stream which ran adjacent to the caves, however, encouraged Meg that they had not erred in judgment. "They have been here!" she cried, gesturing toward the entrance to the caverns.

She glanced up at Castleton and found him staring at the cave with a curious expression on his face. "I became so panicked," he said in a whisper. "You've no idea how badly you scared me."

"What are you talking about?" she asked, puzzled. "Not of Hope or Alfreton, I perceive."

"No," he responded in a low voice with a shake of his head. He looked down at her, his hazel eyes narrowed, a faint smile on his lips. "You were always a great one for knowing precisely how to taunt and tease me. I only wonder that I did not lose my temper that day."

Meg caught her breath. He was sitting too near her for comfort and the expression in his eyes was causing her heart to quicken. How easily his nearness could persuade her into conduct she knew was wrong. Good God! If he tried to kiss her, she knew she would permit him the liberty yet again! What was wrong with her?

"You wore the most delightful gown of an embroidered white muslin, all covered with pretty red cherries and green ivy leaves. Every time the wind swept through, the hem of your gown would float up and dance all about you. Then we went into the caverns."

"Oh," Meg breathed, sighing deeply. She wished he had not brought to mind that wondrous summer's day, especially when she was trying to keep her heart and mind in strong check given how closely he sat beside her, given how recollections of the Two Swans Inn and now the caverns were culling forth memories she knew ought to be forbidden to her forever.

She had all but forgotten that summery day. Was it only eight months past? "I behaved unconscionably," she said as her cheeks grew warm beneath his steady gaze. What was he thinking? He must be remembering how she had secreted herself in a small space behind a formidable stalagmite and how he had searched for her for half an hour, calling her name. Only when she realized he was indeed sorely distressed—that the tenor of his frantic calls to her revealed he believed she was hurt or worse—only then had she jumped out at him and pulled on his coattails.

He had endured several emotions all at once giving a cry of delight that she was safe, uttering a curse that she had played off one of her tricks upon him, and then issuing a brief lecture on how she ought not to endanger herself in that manner again.

She would have argued with him on this last score, but apparently his first emotion overtook the others. He caught her up in an embrace that had all but squeezed the air from her lungs. "You are safe," he had breathed into her hair, her ear and all along her neck, until she was shivering with delight. Then his concern and compassion had suddenly transformed and his lips had been upon her neck, her cheeks, her lips. He kissed her for a very long time, and again she had succumbed to his embrace, to the feel of his lips upon hers, to the strength and warmth of his arms holding her fast.

This will not do, she thought distractedly. The more these memories crowded in upon her, the less she was able to think clearly. She blinked several times and her eyes began to focus again on Castleton.

Oh, dear! His expression had changed. She knew that particular look. She had seen it in Catmose, at the Two Swans, and at the caverns. A shiver coursed down her neck and side again as though his lips were touching her. He leaned close to her, she parted her lips. "No," she breathed in faint protest as she placed her hand upon his chest. Yet, all the while she wanted him to kiss her again. She was hopeless. Utterly, completely, hopeless. A birdwitted ninnyhammer, nothing more! He was nearly upon her now. . . .

"Be thee Castleton?" a voice called out sharply.

Meg recoiled in horror at having been caught by a stranger nearly in the act of kissing. How was it neither of them had known someone was about?

"Yes," Castleton had responded brusquely. Meg could not keep from stealing a glance up at him and saw that his cheeks had darkened.

"I thought 'twere thee," the country man said. "I remember seeing thee at market day, Christmas past. I'd not be disturbing thee save that I've a letter for thee. 'Twere left 'ere by thy sister. I hoped thee would be along. She's quite young to be about with a man, alone, wi'out a servant."

The expression on the farmer's face, as he approached the curricle and handed a familiar, heart-shaped missive to Castleton, bespoke a fatherly concern. He then tipped his hat and strode quickly on his way.

"Thank you, my good man," Castleton called over his shoulder. "But tell me, how long ago were they here?"

The farmer replied, "A half hour, not more."

"Thank you."

The farmer disappeared down another lane.

Castleton lifted the broken seal. "From Alfreton, this time, addressed to Hope," he stated. He perused the valentine then exclaimed, "Good God, what drivel!"

He handed the valentine to Meg, and set his horses to, again encouraging them quickly to a smart pace. Meg opened the valentine and read the contents through. The words had been written in Alfreton's sprawling hand and signed by him. There could be no two opinions on that score. But something about the contents, about Alfreton referring to Hope as "A Spring of Eternal Delight," gave her pause. Hope had upon many occasions turned her hand to poetry as most young ladies were wont to do. One of her earliest efforts had been entitled, "Spring of Eternal Delight." Alfreton might have written the love letter, but another curious notion entered Meg's brain which she did not readily dismiss. There was something about the style of the valentine that spoke to her of Hope's temperament. But why would Hope have constructed the message then had Alfreton copy it onto a valentine? Unless Hope was scheming. But what would Hope think she might accomplish by leading her brother about the countryside? Wear down his opposition to the match? Hardly.

Meg shook her head and tucked the valentine into

her reticule. She was unable to credit that Hope was
involved in anything more complicated than a scandalous elopement.

At a crossroad, which met with the King's highway a
mile southwest of the caverns, Castleton drew his curricle to a halt. "Which way now, Meg? Does this latest
absurd valentine leave us the smallest clue as to where
our charming couple was destined?"

Meg shook her head. "The poem rambles and the only
phrase which refers in even the smallest way to a physical location is something like, *A spring flowing steadily
from the earth.* What do you make of that?"

Castleton shook his head. "There are many springs in
Derbyshire, but none nearby and I know this vicinity as
well as I know my own lands."

Meg considered the crossroads. The one to the left
would lead back to Threshwick. The one straight ahead
to a vale in which were situated several farms. To the
right, the town of Matlock.

Meg stared down the road and said. "How far is Matlock from here?"

"Not far. Five miles, I think."

"Matlock Bath. The waters are constant in temperature
year round. Do you suppose this could be a reference to
eternal springs?"

"By God, you've the right of it! I'm sure of it!" He gave
a sharp call to his horses and within a few seconds the
curricle was moving briskly down the King's highway.

They arrived in Matlock feeling travel worn, especially
since for the last quarter mile they had been forced to
follow a rambling flock of sheep into town. Castleton
stopped at the Three Bells Inn where he hired a fresh team
and saw his own prime cattle bedded in comfortable stalls

until he could send for them during the next day or so. While he was gone, Meg ordered a hearty nuncheon for them both. Regardless of the unhappy circumstance of their flight, she was hungry and suspected Castleton was even more so.

When he found her in a private parlor seated before a table spread with cold beef and chicken, a hot pigeon pie, broccoli, peas, carrots, sweet-smelling fresh-baked bread, a bowl of fruit and steaming coffee already poured into a cup at his place, the dark expression on his face lightened instantly.

"Bless you, Meg! I didn't know how hungry I was until I smelled this fare. I am grateful beyond words."

"You are most welcome, but don't think I haven't considered myself in ordering a nuncheon—you come the crab more readily when you are feeling peckish, you know!"

He smiled crookedly as he began filling his plate. "You know me far too well for me to do more than beg pardon for every cross word I've ever offered you out of my hunger." He then cut a slice of beef and wasted no time in sliding the thin, flavorful meat into his mouth.

She smiled at him and chuckled. "Are your horses in tolerable condition? That stretch of road leading to the caverns was wretched indeed."

"They are a stout pair and suffered no injury. But it will do them well to rest here for a couple of days."

Several times, the question of where they were to begin their search in the sprawling town rose to her lips but she bit back the words. Castleton was enjoying his meal, and she thought it likely that introducing the subject would only cause both of them to suffer an increase of anxiety. As it was, the thought of Hope being leg-shackled to Alfreton served to diminish her appetite. She therefore steadily forced the nourishing meal down her throat, especially since they could not possibly know where the remainder of the afternoon would see them.

When they completed their meal, Castleton inquired of the landlord of Hope's presence in the town. Meg was surprised, yet somehow not overly much, when the landlord frowned at Castleton, then bid him stay for a moment. "I know this may seem odd, but Miss Staveley was here and I believe she left something in her wake. One of the maids found it—a silk shawl, I think."

Castleton watched the man leave and scowled at his retreating back. Hope had certainly become forgetful on this journey, he thought. A suspicion bit at his brain, causing him to turn swiftly about. Was he being led on a wild-goose chase? What if this was a ruse designed to lead them so fully astray that the elopement was all but insured because of it?

He moved to stand in front of the window and stared at High Street which was crowded with coaches, horses, dogs, and children well-wrapped against the snowy day. A bleating ewe waited by the milliners, distressed at having become separated from the rest of her flock. The caterwauling was a pleasant sound on a cold February day. He glanced up at the sky and saw that a certain leaden appearance was now darkening the afternoon and promising another heavy snowfall before evening.

Where was Hope? he wondered. Was it possible this was one of her tricks, leading the pair of them about the Derbyshire countryside, perhaps to divert attention from her true destination? Yet, by all appearances, Hope and Alfreton were just ahead of them. If not to divert attention, then, to what purpose was Hope taking them to so many familiar places? How strange she would have chosen the Two Swans, the caverns, Matlock?

He realized with a start that he had kissed Meg at the Two Swans and at the caverns. Was this part of Hope's purpose? Yet he had not kissed Meg at Matlock. In fact, at Matlock—he gasped and turned toward Meg. She was standing near the doorway watching him. He knew she was remembering, just as he was, for her complexion was quite pale, and her face pinched with anxiety.

"I'm sorry," she said quietly, her words filling the strained distance between them.

He shook his head. "You've no reason to apologize," he returned gravely. "The blame is mine alone."

He turned back to the window, his gaze settled upon the sill which showed a slight film of dust. His mind pulled him inward, revealing in picture after unforgettable picture the horrible events which transpired after the kiss at the caverns.

When he had released Meg, after kissing her so thoroughly and with such sincere affection, he had been horrified by his conduct. He knew he was not in love with her, nor had he any intention of offering for his sister's governess. But to have kissed her so passionately would surely have given Meg cause to have expected a proposal of marriage.

He didn't know what to say to her, so he kept his tongue.

Retracing his steps to the entrance to the caverns with Meg in tow, he found Hope awaiting them. She immediately began pressing him to take her to Matlock where she wished to enjoy the baths. He agreed readily, grateful in that moment that his sister was along since he found himself in such an awkward predicament. So, having set-

tled Hope next to him that he might not have to endure
having Meg pressed against his side during the journey
to Matlock, he began to tease Meg, to taunt her, as was
his custom.

She answered in kind, never once losing her compo-
sure. Never once did she give the smallest indication that
she was troubled either by his words or by his conduct
in the caverns.

Somehow the teasing turned to something unkind and
they began to brangle. Yet no matter how sorely he provoked her, she never gave ground. He admired her for that.
He wondered if she knew how much he admired her.

When they reached Matlock, however, he went beyond
the pale and made a truly wretched reference to the kiss
they had shared. *I suppose you have shown many of your
beaux the delight of the caverns,* he had said, only daring
to hint at the kiss since Hope was fixed between them.
She had glared at him knowing full well his intent. She
had ordered him to stop the curricle at once. He obeyed
her request, but before the horses came to a complete
halt, she had begun descending the carriage. Somehow
the skirts of her prettily embroidered gown of cherries
and green ivy had become caught beneath Hope, Meg
had stumbled in her movements and had fallen backward
onto the cobbles, her gown tearing, her head striking the
stones of the street very hard. He had almost driven over
her, as well, but Hope—thank God for her quickness!—
had given a hard tug on the reins and had prevented
Meg's sure death.

Meg had been surrounded by people instantly who carried her into the inn. When he had seen the curricle and
pair taken to the stables, he had entered the parlor only to
find her white-faced, lids closed, her breath shallow.

Only then had the enormity of the accident been driven home to him. For several weeks following, their relationship had been strained and formal. Time had eventually healed the trauma of the moment, but any former easiness between them had all but disappeared in the ensuing months, until today. Perhaps it was because she was leaving that he had felt less reserved in her presence. All he knew of the moment however was that he had nearly killed Meg that day, and for that reason he had made every effort to control his temper since.

He did not know Meg had joined him until he felt a gentle hand upon his sleeve. "I am sorry for having lost my temper that day," she said. "I always felt you blamed yourself overly much for my taking a tumble on the cobbles."

He looked down at her and covered her hand with his own. "I provoked you sorely! I was so cruel to you. Will you ever find it in your heart to forgive me?"

"Geoffrey," she whispered. He remembered her speaking his name when he kissed her in the caverns. The sound of his name on her lips now was like a balm to a wound which he did not even know he had been suffering. She continued, "All these years, had I risen less readily to the fly, had I shown some ability not to give answer for answer, perhaps we could have rubbed along tolerably well together instead of always being at daggers drawn."

Castleton stared at her. He had heard her words, but found he couldn't quite agree. Strong words filled his mind, but could not find their way to his lips. *But I wouldn't have enjoyed the past three years nearly so much had you been timid and observant of every pro-*

priety nor had you risen less readily to the fly. Faith,
but I miss you, Meg!

He wanted to speak these words aloud, but his throat
kept closing up. He found himself cursing Hope for having turned eighteen today. He wished she was but ten or
eleven so that Meg would be required to remain at
Threshwick Hall another seven years at least, to spar
with him, to see that his meals were sent timely to him
no matter where he was on the estate, to look at him as
she was now with her beautiful green eyes sparkling in
the winter's light.

He again found himself leaning toward her, drawn to
her, down to her, his gaze fixing upon her lips like so
many times before. What was wrong with him that he
always felt this way when he was near her and looked
into her eyes. Had she bewitched him?

But again, a voice intruded. "Here is the shawl,
m'lord, and there seems to be something wrapped up
within it."

"A valentine!"

They had exclaimed the words together. Castleton
crossed the room quickly, retrieving the shawl and another valentine from the landlord. When he had gone,
Castleton turned to Meg and queried, "Do you suppose
we have been sent on a wild-goose chase?"

"I had begun thinking so when we turned toward Matlock. But to what purpose?"

Castleton wanted to say he thought he knew, but was
reluctant to do so. "I think there is only one way we
shall ever know—we must follow Hope's lead through
to the end of this absurd chase."

"Geoffrey," Meg whispered again as Castleton crossed

the chamber to join her by the window. "Dare we hope she has no intention of wedding Alfreton?"

"As to that, I cannot say," he responded, breaking the seal on the valentine. "It's possible she has led us astray in order to set us off the scent. For all we know, she could be halfway to Gretna by now."

"Perhaps we should return to Threshwick then," she suggested.

"First we shall see what my wretched sister has written in this latest missive of hers, or poem, or whatever it proves to be!" With heads bent together, and the wintry light from the window flooding the valentine, they quickly perused the heart-shaped letter. *By now I suppose you have guessed that I have tricked you both. But don't think I don't mean to have Alfreton. By now, we are probably already arrived at Aunt Elizabeth's home and you know how fond she is of me. I shall be Mrs. Alfreton by the time you reach The Cottage which is where you shall find me if you are quick about it. Aunt Elizabeth will be delighted to see you!*

"Impossible!" Meg cried. "Your aunt has been gone this month and more to Brighton. Surely had she returned we would have known about it, by the servants alone, if by no other means! It is another trick!"

"I shall wring her curst neck."

"Your aunt's?" Meg cried facetiously, unable to resist teasing him.

"Oh, do stubble it! Come! This is Hope's game and we must see the whole of it played out. I know her mind. She expects we will follow and if she is married then we shall certainly wish her joy—and then some!"

Four

The Cottage, as Lady Elizabeth's elegant manor house had been ironically named in vivid contrast to its ancient splendor, was situated slightly southwest of Matlock, but not more than five miles distant in a southeasterly line to Threshwick Hall. The only consolation Meg found in the prospect of finding Hope at The Cottage and married to Mr. Alfreton, was the fact that they were relatively close to Threshwick Hall. They could be home, therefore, before dark and sufficiently before the hour to receive those guests who had been invited to Hope's Valentine's Day birthday ball. How odd to think of so many well-wishers greeting not a young lady celebrating her birthday, but instead a newly married woman to whom they must wish joy.

Meg shuddered. How could anyone wish Hope joy upon a union with Alfreton? Impossible.

The journey from Matlock to The Cottage saw the darkly clouded sky releasing an even steadier snowfall. Soon her green bonnet, her caped shoulders, her muff and the carriage rug—which Castleton had tucked solicitously about her knees—as well as the tops of her half-boots were dusted with a pretty layer of white snow.

An easy camaraderie accompanied the several mile journey from Matlock to The Cottage. The incident last summer in both the caverns and Matlock was discussed thoroughly—Geoffrey confessed he did not know what had possessed him to so horridly importune her, but that he thought it was a mixture of his fear for her well-being and an understandable desire to punish her for so wretchedly keeping him in suspense. She in turn admitted not knowing what had possessed her to give herself so thoroughly to his embrace save that she was fond of him and perhaps had let the adventure of the moment rule her senses. But her foolishness in leaping from the carriage could in no manner be attached to his conduct even though he insisted that he was to blame for having provoked her beyond reason.

In the end, they agreed to forget all and to forgive all, especially since she was leaving for Somerset on the morrow.

Goodness! Whatever would Mrs. Macclesfield say to her when she arrived a day late with the hapless excuse that her charge of three years had eloped and she had been needed to discover the child's whereabouts? She could find no comfort in the thought of offering such a story to her new employer. But she wouldn't think of that just yet. First, they must find Hope.

For the present, therefore, when Castleton drew the curricle before the entrance to The Cottage, she turned her attention fully to the task at hand. She found her heart fluttering in her breast, her anxiety growing moment by moment. Was Hope here? Was she married? Would that she had never encouraged Alfreton to darken the portals of Threshwick Hall!

How desperately she prayed that Hope was not married!

When the curricle came to a halt, Castleton handed Meg the reins, bidding her to keep the horses in check until he could discover what was going forward. Should he learn Hope had already quit The Cottage, he meant to follow in immediate pursuit. She watched him walk briskly to the door and bang the heavy iron knocker loudly. Her gaze shifted of its own volition to the house itself, especially since she was too far from Castleton to hear the conversation which ensued when the butler opened the door.

As she regarded Lady Elizabeth's home, her anxiety for Hope began to be replaced by another, more profound sentiment—one of melancholy. Her heart grew heavy. The appearance of The Cottage, of the bare climbing-rose vines which created a weathered, Gothic appearance to the front of the mellow, gold stone manor house, drew her attention inward. In the summer, she knew the entire house would be glowing with pink roses. But for now, on St. Valentine's Day, with a light snow feathering her view of the old house, The Cottage reminded her of both the bleakness of her future away from Threshwick Hall and of a conversation she had recently shared with Lady Elizabeth.

Hope's aunt had been a regular visitor to Threshwick. Meg had come to know her as a strong, mothering figure whose sense of humor and keen wit had served to turn many a dull evening into a jovial family party. She was full-bosomed, a handsome lady of fifty, her thick black hair peppered with gray and always worn in the latest of fashions, her blue eyes never failing to sparkle with intelligence. A month earlier, during a tea which they had shared privately, Lady Elizabeth had spoken words which had overset Meg entirely.

"My dear," she had begun, her heavily jeweled fingers clasped firmly on her lap while she spoke, "you make the biggest mistake in not bringing my nephew to heel! Why do you brangle with him when you should be kissing him instead! Yes, I know it is hardly the advice to give a young lady of breeding, but in my day we were not quite so reticent to show our affection."

Meg was shocked. She had clattered her tea cup upon her saucer. Her fingers trembled as she set both items carefully upon the table which separated them. She did not know at first what to say. To dissimulate with a woman of Lady Elizabeth's perception would have been to have offered an insult. Instead, she addressed at least one part of Lady Elizabeth's concerns. "But I am his sister's governess," she had replied.

"And why should that make one whit of difference!"

"I believe it already has," she returned respectfully. "You see, Castleton has already kissed me and I fear instead of prompting his heart toward me I believe he holds me in disdain because of it."

Lady Elizabeth had tilted her head at Meg's words and narrowed her eyes. "He kissed you?" she queried.

"On several occasions. Do I shock you? And worse, I permitted him the liberty. So you see, however much I am grievously mortified to admit the whole of it to you, it would seem his heart will not be turned by a mere embrace or two. Not that that was my intention. Truly. I fear from the moment I first laid eyes on him I could not resist falling into his arms."

The older, wiser woman nodded, her gaze for the moment growing misty with her own recollections. "I know precisely what you mean," she said softly. "I felt the same way about my Edward." Her own memories kept her contentedly withdrawn and quiet for a pace. Her husband had passed away several years earlier. Meg had never known him, but by all reports he had been a good husband and father. When the reverie ended, Lady Elizabeth sighed in exasperation. "Castleton is a fool! But then I never said he wasn't! I fear there is some mischief at work here that has nothing at all to do with you. Perhaps he has never quite forgiven Isabelle for jilting him. Well, pay no heed to that! Instead, should the occasion arise, instead of permitting him to kiss you, take it upon yourself to kiss him. Yes, yes, I know it is very improper, but remember, your entire future depends upon a little courage. And mark my words, Margaret, if you leave Derbyshire without bringing Castleton up to scratch, you'll never see him again. He is not the sort of man to chase after a woman! I promise you that." Her manner softened, a smile gentling her strong features. "Will you at least consider what I have said!"

"Oh, I will. Indeed, I will," Meg assured her.

But that had been a month ago. Lady Elizabeth had left for Brighton and during that month Geoffrey had been either polite and restrained or determined to set up her back. No such occasion, as Lady Elizabeth had hoped for, had arisen upon which Meg could reasonably act upon her advice, nor had she wanted to. It would seem far too many words of irritation and annoyance had passed between Castleton and herself to allow for even a hint of passion between them—until today, that is.

Now, as she watched Geoffrey speaking to the butler, she wondered what he would have thought of his aunt's advice. She wondered what she thought of it. *Just kiss him. Just kiss him.*

In truth, she had never initiated a kiss. She had only kissed him in response to his advances. What would he think of her were *she* to accost *him?* It seemed now she would never know.

With a footman in tow, Geoffrey returned to the curricle. Her heart leapt in her breast. Then Hope must be here, she thought, only why did Castleton appear neither angry nor overjoyed, but perplexed?

The footman, wearing a long woolen coat, a scarf about his head, and top boots, clamored up beside her and politely took the reins from her. Geoffrey rounded the curricle and helped her descend.

The moment the footman set the horses in motion, Meg turned to Castleton and asked, "Tell me, are they married? Are they here? Is your aunt returned from Brighton?"

"The devil take it!" was his first response, which did not bode well. "The whole of it is the biggest piece of nonsense to which I have ever been privy! I shall wring her neck, indeed, I shall! Hope is at her tricks again! No, my aunt is not yet returned or expected, but Hope and Alfreton were here about an hour past—as they have been the entire journey—always just ahead of us! It would seem that Hope has left another charming *valentine* for us to peruse but she left strict instructions that we weren't to see it until after we had enjoyed a little refreshment! It would seem she bid my aunt's Cook to prepare my favorite macaroons, a platter of fruit, and a strong pot of tea."

Meg bit her lip. "Well, it is the proper hour, afterall!"

He shot her a biting glance. "I have no desire to hear your witticisms," he stated caustically, then held the door for her.

As she entered The Cottage, a warm rush of air flowed over her. "How very pleasant," she responded.

The butler bid her welcome and then requested they follow him. When it was clear they were not to be directed to the usual receiving room upon the first floor, Castleton queried, "We are not to be served in the drawing room?" He was clearly surprised.

The butler responded, "Miss Staveley particularly requested the orangery. But do not concern yourself. I have had the fires built up. It is sufficiently warm for you and Miss Woodville."

"The orangery?" Meg queried softly, her face paling. To herself she murmured, "I am beginning to comprehend Hope's mind, but does she know how cruel her valentine chase has been?"

Geoffrey took her arm and forced her steps to slow a trifle in order that he might place a greater distance between them and the butler. Satisfied that the servant could not hear, he whispered as they walked along. "It was thoughtless of Hope to have insisted on the orangery. Did she know of—well, of what happened that night? I don't remember seeing her."

Meg nodded, glancing up at him and feeling miserable. "She saw me in the arms of that officer—faith, I cannot even recall his name. But she never once said a word to me about it."

Castleton frowned. "I remember she came up to me and whispered that you were alone in the orangery. Meg, I came with the worst of motives! You were so beautiful that night, begowned in a deep blue silk and at my aunt's request, attending her ball as her guest instead of Hope's governess. I had had my own thoughts of kissing you. So, when I found that man—Good Lord, I behaved like a silly halfling. Have you forgiven me for planting him a facer?"

Meg smiled. "I was never more grateful for anything in my life," she admitted.

He stopped her, and turned her toward him. "You never said so! You never so much as intimated to me that you thought my interference anything less than—now what was it you said to me—boorish, ill-mannered, and entirely without right or reason!"

"How could I have told you anything else when you began to lecture me about the necessity of guarding my virtue, or some such nonsense!"

He frowned at her and shook his head. "Have I been such a sapskull, such an ogre these many years and more?"

"Not always," she answered with a half-smile. "Perhaps just two days out of three."

He grunted and continued guiding her toward the orangery. When they arrived, the butler took Meg's bonnet, cape, and muff along with Castleton's greatcoat and hat. After seeing them settled comfortably before the tea tray, he left them alone. Meg served the tea and said, "Whatever else this extremely agitating journey has been, and whatever else Hope has been desirous of achieving in her extravagant schemes, she has certainly timed our adventure to a nicety. Had I been given the opportunity of ordering anything at this particular moment in our trek through the countryside, nothing could have pleased me more than Lady Elizabeth's tea!"

"I am in complete agreement although I would not have scorned a snifter of brandy. I confess I feel as though I have been knocked sideways a dozen times since we first set out for the Two Swans Inn."

For the next few minutes, Meg fell silent to the enjoyment of sliced pears, macaroons, and tea. The fatigue of the journey was beginning to settle into her limbs.

The orangery was a warming house which housed early roses in bloom, orange trees which would produce fruit early in the season, a scattering of ferns and ivies, and several pots containing bulbs from which shoots had already broken the dark, peatish top soil. In the center of the chamber, she was seated upon a sofa of peach damask. Across from her Castleton sat on an Egyptian chair of striped green and white silk. He sat slightly forward, his forearms supported by the wooden, claw arms, a saucer in one hand, tea cup in the other. His gaze was fixed on the silver tea pot in front of him.

A frown still creased his brow. After a moment, he said, "Had you fancied yourself in love with him—the officer, I mean?" He glanced up at Meg, his expression concerned.

Meg was startled by his question. "No, of course not! I will admit I had enjoyed his compliments and his easy manners, but I promise you I was caught entirely unawares by his advances!"

Placing his cup carefully on the saucer, he said earnestly. "But he was quite eligible and would have—well, he would have made a good match for you. He would have taken you from this life of—of drudgery."

Meg considered what he said and finally responded, "I would never marry for such a reason, Geoffrey, and I don't see my life as being quite so full of drudgery as you do. My years at Threshwick with Hope have been by far the sweetest of those given to my occupation. Seeing her grow from a quite unmanageable chit with scarcely a concern for ballroom etiquette to a young lady who only last Saturday inquired as to how many sets she could accept from one gentleman during the course of a ball, has been exceedingly gratifying to me, I assure you.

But as for this nameless officer, if you want my true opinion, I shall tell you that marriage to a man who said he worshipped the high cast of my mind then proceeded to force his attentions upon me would have been a life beyond bearing."

"The high cast of your mind?" he queried, disgusted. "He said as much to you, then assaulted you?"

"Precisely."

"Good God! What a nodcock! Met him only a few times. Never could abide the fellow, really!"

"How infuriating!" Meg responded with an accusing smile. "For even though you held such an unhappy opinion of this man, still you thought he would have made a good match for me. Now how am I to interpret that, m'lord? It would seem you have a considerably low opinion of my worth."

He smiled crookedly. "On the contrary. I have an extremely high opinion of your character, of *the high cast of your mind,* of your worth. Besides, how can I blame this officer for kissing you, or accuse him of wrongdoing, when I have been many times so overtaken by your beauty that I could not resist assaulting you myself. Rather like the pot calling the kettle black!"

Meg was enjoying the conversation hugely. He was telling her things he had never told her before. Did her beauty truly prompt his reckless conduct? How intense his hazel eyes were as he regarded her. She caught her breath. How fortunate it was that the tea table separated them. She was sure if he was beside her, he would again take her in his arms and kiss her—but then what?

She remembered Lady Elizabeth's roguish advice.
Just kiss him.

Meg felt dizzy at the thought of behaving in so unmaidenly a manner, yet in spite of her fears, she found herself setting her cup and saucer on the table in front of her and rising to her feet. As though not within herself, or within her own mind, she circled the table and knelt beside him.

"What is it?" he queried, throatily, searching her eyes, her face, trying to comprehend her thoughts.

"I—" she did not know what to say. So, instead of speaking, she slipped her arm about his neck and drew him toward her.

Then she kissed him, full on the lips, without apology, her heart feeling mellow and warm in her chest, all her fears gone, her thoughts centered solely upon revealing to him that she loved him.

She loved him.

She loved him!

Even in the act of kissing, she felt odd tears burn her eyes.

She loved him.

There. Finally she had admitted the truth to herself and how liberating the truth proved afterall.

For how long had she loved him? Undoubtedly from the moment he dismounted his horse in Catmose and took her in his arms.

How long had she denied the truth to herself? From the moment he had bowed facetiously to her.

Yet she loved him.

Castleton drew back slightly from her, his hands on her arms, his mind in a torment of confusion.

Faith, but she was beautiful and the powerful feelings he was experiencing toward her told him it was not just her beauty which had enraptured him. With his hands holding her arms firmly, he lifted her to her feet and embraced her boldly as he had done so many times before. He encircled her waist and held her tightly to him. He heard her moan faintly and then utter a sound which sounded very nearly like a sob.

He kissed her harder still. Why was he doing so? Why did her nearness prompt him to kiss her? Perhaps she simply had the ability to bewitch men, to make them feel overpowered in her presence, overawed by her beauty.

His thoughts began to snake and turn. He remembered finding Isabelle in the arms of the man who later became her husband. Was Meg like Isabelle? While under his roof, had she permitted other men to take such liberties? Of course she had—the officer had been one such man! How many others? He wanted to know, he needed to know.

He released her and regarding her intently, queried, "Please tell me, Margaret, how many gentlemen have you kissed during these last three years? The truth now."

Meg felt his words touch her as though he had poured ice water on top of her head. She froze, her limbs grew rigid. At first, she couldn't even move, she couldn't even tear her gaze from his. She couldn't believe he was asking the same question yet again—and in deep seriousness, his eyes accusing.

When at last she was able to wrench her gaze from his, she also pushed at his arms, and disentangled herself—though awkwardly—from his embrace. "I can not believe after knowing me for so long, you would still find it necessary to ask? You are breaking my heart!"

She crossed the chamber and headed into the hallway which would eventually lead her back to the entrance hall.

He followed quickly in her wake, calling to her, "Don't be overset, Meg, please! I—I am not accusing you—"

"—Of course you are."

"No! No! You misunderstand me. Perhaps I ineptly phrased my question, my concern." The hallway led to an antechamber behind the stairs and here he caught her by the arm and whirled her around to face him. "What I want to know—what I must know—is—are you in the habit of kissing a great deal of men? When I first met you, a veritable stranger, I assaulted you and very improperly. But you kissed me in return as though you'd—you'd—"

"What? As though I'd kissed a thousand men?" She was angry. She could not credit it. She did not understand him or why he would believe her so unconscionable. Part of her wanted to tell him the truth—that he was the first man who had ever kissed her. But another part of her, the part that always engaged battle with him, replied instead, "What does it matter if I kissed a thousand men or only one? How many women have you kissed? Have I asked you? Would it matter?"

He seemed dumbfounded and not a little distressed. "That is another matter entirely."

"Oh, I see," she responded sardonically. "Of course it is. Well, then, I can think of no reason why I should tell you the truth about my many past adventures. Unless, of course you would choose to reveal all of yours to me as well."

She turned to go, but he caught her arm and again turned her back toward him. "That is unfair!" he cried. "You know it is! Meg, give me the answer I seek. I pray you will tell me. Before I offer for any woman I must know that she is virtuous, above reproach."

Meg wanted to strike him hard. Her anger was white hot at the accusation laden in his speech.

With several deep breaths, however, she subdued the

rage which threatened to overtake her. "Are you saying you are considering offering for me?"

He also took a series of breaths before he answered. "Yes. But I must have your answer first."

"I would rather be boiled in oil than become your wife," she responded simply. "Therefore, I see no need whatsoever to give you the answer you seek. We may both, therefore, keep our secrets and part in peace."

He released her. "It is just like you to throw a fit of hysterics, to avoid the point of the conversation, when all I require is an answer. A civil answer."

"I only give civil answers when I am posed civil questions. And let me assure you, Lord Castleton, that you have yet to see me in a *fit of hysterics*. But if you do not cease speaking to me immediately, I promise you I will throw a fit you will be recounting to your grandchildren long into your dotage!"

With that, she turned on her heel and passed into an adjoining hallway which led to the entrance hall, her half-boots resounding loudly upon the wood floors giving fair warning of the state of her temper.

When she arrived at the entrance hall, she bid a startled butler to fetch her bonnet, muff, and cape and to please see that his lordship's curricle was brought round immediately.

"It—it is frightfully cold, Miss Woodville," he offered. "The snow has begun to fall harder still. Would you prefer her ladyship's coach?"

Meg smiled with great satisfaction. "Infinitely, and I do thank you. The solitude will be as welcome as the warmth."

Since Castleton had followed on her heels and was now standing beside her, his expression thunderous, the butler lifted his brows in silent request for his approval of the scheme.

Castleton nodded curtly.

The butler seemed quite nonplussed and was about to leave the entrance hall to carry out his new orders, when he bethought himself. Crossing the chamber to a small mahogany table beside the door to the library, he picked up an ornate salver and returned to stand before Castleton. He offered the tray to his lordship.

Meg noted with an exasperated sigh that one of Hope's valentines lay upon the offending silver tray.

When the viscount picked it up, the butler quickly left the entrance hall.

Castleton sighed deeply then broke the seal and read the brief and considerably unpoetic message from his sister. *My dear goosecap of a brother, if you have not by now offered for Meg, then you are a complete idiot and beyond my poor abilities to help you. If you think for a moment I would do anything so silly as elope with Alfreton then you are an even bigger gudgeon than I had ever believed possible!*

With sincerest love and affection,

Hope

P.S. I am probably by now dressing for my birthday ball. I hope you will be able to return in time to greet our guests. If not, Mr. Alfreton has kindly offered to act in your stead.

"Vixen," he muttered, folding up the valentine and sliding it into the pocket of his coat.

"What does she say?" Meg queried. "Why won't you let me read this one?"

"It says nothing to signify, except to inform me that she is at Threshwick readying for her ball. She never had the least intention of wedding Alfreton. The whole of this adventure was meant as—as a sort of lark, to throw us together."

He glanced askance at her briefly, then let his gaze slide away from her. "There is nothing left for us but to return to Threshwick. You may take the morning mails to Somerset, if it pleases you."

"It pleases me very much, thank you," Meg responded flatly.

Five

When Meg arrived at Threshwick Hall, dusk had faded the outlines of the manor house, blending the tall, castellated rooftop into the black backdrop of stately beech trees situated behind the house. Snow-clouds overhead pressed down on the manor as well. Were it not for the rich golden light spilling from the numerous windows of the manor onto the carriages lining the snow-covered gravel drive, Threshwick would have seemed a gloomy sight indeed. But Hope's guests were arriving, enlivening the otherwise foreboding drive, and revellers were visible in the windows on the first floor receiving room. The gentlemen, young and old alike, were resplendent in formal blacks and whites. The married ladies wore regal gowns of rich amethyst, rose, and sapphire blue. Floating among the mothers and fathers and dozens of hopeful suitors, the youngest ladies danced about in fine, gauzy muslins and silks of the palest pinks, the softest blues and of course, the purest whites.

Meg watched the chamber windows for a moment, then observed the arrival of more guests. Her spirits, already at a low ebb, sank further. Here was the world denied to her because of lack of fortune and because she had wanted only to marry for love—nothing less. She remembered her own come-out ball so many years ago with a wistful longing, but when tears smarted her eyes, she blinked them back with a brisk nod of her head, refusing to dwell further on the loss of her girlhood dreams.

Instead, she bid Lady Elizabeth's coachman take her directly round to the stables that she might enter the house less conspicuously through one of the back doors. When she began mounting the servants' stairs, she heard Hope from above cry out her name. "Meg, Meg! One of the footmen told me you were come home."

Meg looked up and saw Hope's smiling face peeping down at her from over the stairwell railing. From between the rails she could see the sheer tulle covering the rose satin gown Hope had persuaded her brother to permit her to wear. She appeared very grown up and Meg could not help but smile upon her, forgetting for the present that the young lady peering intensely down at her was the reason she ached with fatigue from head to toe and could scarcely lift one leg after the other.

"Is all settled?" Hope cried in a feverish whisper. As she spoke, she moved toward the landing at the top of the stairs, the beauty of her valentine gown and the three tiers of tulle ruffles about the hem coming dramatically into view.

"Is all of what settled?" Meg responded, caught up in the lovely vision of her former student.

The expression on Hope's youthful face shifted abruptly from expectant enthusiasm to disgust. "Where is my brother?" she asked flatly. "I take it he failed to come up to scratch! And after all my efforts at forcing the pair of you together in as many oversetting predicaments I could possibly contrive. Where is he for now he must answer to me!"

"As to that!" Castleton called up to his sister from the bottom of the stairs, startling both ladies, "You have a great deal to answer for, my little vixenish sibling."

At the sight of her brother, Hope gave a shriek then disappeared toward the drawing room where laughter could be heard erupting from down the hall.

Meg would have laughed at Hope's antics had she not been both worn-out from the day's exertions and blue-devilled by her last conversation with Castleton.

Though Castleton caught up with her and made no move to pursue his sister, she ignored him. As far as she was concerned she wanted nothing to do with him.

Castleton, however, was not satisfied with their dis-cussion at The Cottage. "I have been considering what you said and I still don't understand why you can't give me an answer, why you think my questions unreasonable. At least admit to me that you have behaved oddly, if not indiscreetly, by accepting my kisses so readily. What am I supposed to think?"

By now, Meg was standing before the door of her bed-chamber. She was no longer angry, merely sad. With one hand on the doorhandle, she replied, "Suffice it to say that I think the question you have asked me would have been better posed to Isabelle."

His mouth fell open. "How do you know of her?" he asked, dumbfounded.

"Who does not know of her? Isabelle's preference for the squire's son, who perhaps does not judge quite so poorly or harshly as you, has been well-known through-out the county since I first took up my post as Hope's governess. Well, I am not Isabelle and if you cannot de-termine for yourself why I might have permitted you to accost me on the day of my arrival, at a moment when

I was sick with the loneliness of my future, then you are lacking in intelligence and I am better off with Mrs. Macclesfield and her five daughters. And when you kissed me in subsequent years, if you cannot comprehend why I would have allowed you to accost me when I had lived beneath your roof for some time, when I had come to know your gentleness to your servants, your fastidious management of your estates, your high reputation among your neighbors, then you haven't a particle of sense about you and I had best leave Threshwick before I go mad. And now I will say goodbye, Castleton, because I am fagged to death with the day's adventure and with our constant brangling."

With that, she opened the door to her bedchamber, slipped through, and quickly closed the door behind her. She found her packing where she had left it with her trunk and portmanteau gaping up at the ceiling, their lids still thrown wide.

Out of fatigue and despair, she sat down on the bed and wept.

When her tears were gone and she had steeled her heart away from thoughts of Lord Castleton, she rang for a maid. Twenty minutes later, she was seated beside Mr. Cheadle who personally drove her to Catmose where she hired a post chaise and four to take her to Somerset. She would be spending a year's savings by travelling post, but she would arrive at Mrs. Macclesfield's home— provided she travelled all night—by late the next evening. Her duty was clear and she boarded the light travelling chariot with a sense of purpose and inner peace, if not abounding happiness.

* * *

Lord Castleton dressed for the ball with as much haste as seven recalcitrant neckcloths would permit him. Afterward, he went about performing his duties at his sister's ball with meticulous attention to the ladies and a sharing of less than witty anecdotes with the gentlemen. He supposed Meg to have retired between the sheets by now and between snatches of conversations and between dances, his thoughts turned to her parting words. She had complemented him richly and he was still staggering beneath the impact of her high opinions of his character. He had also been deeply struck when she had said, *sick with the loneliness of her future.*

He suspected that was how he was feeling as he moved methodically about the ballroom, doing the pretty with the ladies and chatting with the men.

When he danced with his sister, he was still so angry with her interference in his life that he scarcely exchanged a dozen words with her. When the dance ended, she parted from him by whispering accusingly, "Dimwitted halfling. Meg is by far the finest lady of my acquaintance and always shall be. And you mean to let her go—and all because she takes pleasure in kissing you! What a nodcock!"

By ten o'clock, he knew Hope was right. He was, and had been, dimwitted from the moment he accosted Meg outside the Cat and Mouse Inn three years ago. Meg had been right as well, he *had* held Isabelle's indiscretions over her head like a whip. Having finally admitted as much to himself, he wanted nothing more than to apologize to her. In fact, he wouldn't wait until morning, he would apologize now.

He left the ballroom and headed for the servants' stairs. Once deciding to make a clean breast of it, he began to think clearly about Meg probably for the first time since he met her. What a complete idiot he was. He knew her, as well as he knew himself, and was well aware that she was virtuous, that apart from that absurd officer who took advantage of her in Lady Elizabeth's orangery, she had never permitted another man to so much as kiss her fingers, nonetheless her lips. She was a deuced fine woman, just as Hope had said, a woman of character, honor, and virtue. She was also a passionate woman and the woman he wanted to make his wife.

As these thoughts rose in his mind, as his desires for his future became intensely clear to him, so did his need to speak with Meg. He began racing up the stairs, his heart lighter than it had been in years. He knew it was improper to approach her in her bedchamber, but he didn't care. Surely she would not mind hearing his sincere apologies, his avowed belief in her character, his request that she become his wife. Surely she would be grateful to hear his speeches even with her mob cap pulled down about her ears and sleep still clinging to her eyes.

When he reached the top of the stairs, however, he nearly collided with his butler.

"Oh! I do beg your pardon, m'lord," the butler said, startled.

"All my fault," Castleton returned, smiling.

He was about to pass his butler by when his faithful retainer stayed him by saying, "M'lord, a word if it pleases you?"

Castleton did not want to stop and speak with his butler. He needed to speak with Meg, but something about the retainer's expression gave him pause. "What is it?" he queried.

"It is about Miss Woodville. I was very sorry to see her depart, m'lord. She was a fine lady and though I know it is none of my concern and that it is extremely impertinent of me to say so, I and several others on your staff had been hoping for some time that you might have found in Miss Woodville a suitable mistress for Threshwick Hall. She will be sorely missed. And now that I have said what I have said, I promise you will not hear another word pass my lips."

Castleton regarded him curiously for a moment, a feeling rather like panic rising in his chest. "What do you mean, Miss Woodville is gone? I left her in her bedchamber a few hours past."

The butler frowned, "Nay, m'lord. She left about seven. Cheadle saw her to Catmose where she hired a post chaise and four. I thought you knew she was leaving tonight."

"No, by God, I did not! Seven, you say? It is nearly ten now. That's three hours. Is the snow falling presently?"

"Nay, m'lord."

"I've got to go after her. Have Cheadle prepare my curricle again. Three hours! Good God, I shan't reach her until well into Shropshire, perhaps even Gloucestershire!"

He travelled all night. He had a scratchy stubble on his face and knew he was unpresentable when he found Meg scalding her tongue on a cup of hot tea in the parlor of the Angel Inn just past dawn. He didn't even know what county he was in, but he suspected it was Gloucestershire afterall because of the thatched roofs and golden stone walls which characterized the whole of the village.

Meg's eyes were red from lack of sleep, her green velvet cape sadly crushed, and she sported dark circles beneath her eyes. But never had a sight been created more perfectly to warm his heart.

He was certain he, too, appeared quite the worse for wear after pushing his teams hard all night. He wore his thick greatcoat over his black evening coat and white satin breeches. His stockings had been snagged on one of the curricles tall wheels during a change of horses along the way. He thought it likely he looked like the devil as he sank down into a chair opposite Meg. He watched her jump back in her seat in sheer fright at his sudden and unexpected appearance, sloshing her tea on the crisp white linen tablecloth in front of her.

"Good heavens! Whatever are you doing here!" she cried, dabbing at the spilt tea with a delicate lace kerchief, her efforts absurdly ineffective. "You look dreadful and I must—oh, dear! You must have travelled all night. Not in your curricle!" When he nodded, she again asked, "Whatever are you doing here, Geoffrey?"

"For the present, I mean to partake of a cup of the thickest coffee possible. I might even have brandy poured into it as well." He turned, and found the landlord waiting upon a family nearby. "You there," he called to the round-bellied man when he moved away from the table. "A coffee and brandy, if you please."

"Yes, sir. Very good, sir. At once." If he lifted a brow at Castleton's travel-stained appearance, a second glance at the quality of his clothes set him bustling away for brandy and coffee.

Castleton sighed and turned wearily back to Meg. "You look very tired, m'dear. Why not take a room and rest awhile. You've a long journey to go yet."

Meg watched him cautiously, unable to comprehend why he had followed after her. Did he mean to continue arguing with her? She was far too fatigued to bring order to her thoughts and finally responded, "Mrs. Macclesfield is expecting me today. I mean to get to Somerset as quickly as possible."

He reached across the table, and possessed himself of one of her hands, holding it gently. Regardless of the cacophony about him with so many travellers arriving and departing, he said, "I don't want you to go to Somerset. I want you to return to Threshwick Hall and marry me."

Meg looked at his unshaven face, at the wilt of his shirtpoints, at the crease in his black hair left by his hat. She did not know whether to laugh or to cry. Fortunately, she was too weary to do either. Instead, she gave a deep sigh. "You have travelled to no purpose at all. I am a governess by trade and probably always will be."

"Ah," he responded with a laugh. "You wish to be independent. Very admirable. But I find I can scarcely think for the present. I must have my coffee or I vow I shall fall over on this table and probably knock your tea into your lap."

At that Meg couldn't hold back a chuckle of her own.

"That's promising," he said. He continued to hold her hand, his gaze drifting out the window. "They have certainly learned to change horses in the blink of an eye, haven't they? Is that your post-chaise?"

"Yes. I asked for a ten minute respite. I ache so from travelling all night that I can hardly move."

His coffee and brandy arrived. He proceeded to pour a portion of the brandy in her tea. "Drink up," he commanded her. "You shall find your bones thanking you in a moment." He then emptied the remainder of the brandy into his coffee, all the while keeping a firm hold on her hand as though if he released it, he feared she would vanish. He began sipping the steaming black brew.

After a few minutes, when she had finished her tea, he queried, "Better?"

"Mmm," she murmured, her lids closing sleepily.

Setting his cup aside, he leaned forward and gently placed his other hand beneath the hand he was still holding. She opened her eyes and he felt her tremble. "Marry me, Meg," he said in a low, ardent voice. "I've made a mull of it, time and time again. You were right about Isabelle. Somewhere in my mind I got you confused with her, but never again. I want you to be my wife, I want to spend the next hundred years kissing you and making you forget about all the misery I've caused you over the past three years."

Meg blinked at him. "In a day or two, you will regret having asked me," she responded. "You will question my virtue again."

"Dash-it-all, Meg, I'm telling you I'm in love with you. I have been for three years, but I just didn't see it clearly until last night. Then you'd gone. So here I am. Will you do me the honor of becoming my wife?"

Meg glanced out the window and saw that her horses were fully harnessed. "I must go," she said distractedly, pulling her hand from his clasp.

She rose, feeling a little light-headed from the brandy and from fatigue. She put her bonnet back over her already sorely crushed curls.

"Here are the bricks ye ordered, miss."

Meg turned to the manservant and directed him to her coach.

Castleton pushed his chair back and stood to his feet.

"You mean to continue on to Somerset?" he queried, stunned.

She looked back at him. "I suppose you thought I would be impressed by your reckless jaunt across the midlands. Well, I am not. I have a post in Somerset. I must go. Goodbye."

She picked up her muff from the chair beside her and began walking toward the door.

"Why did you kiss me then?" he asked, sufficiently loud for everyone to hear. The parlor instantly fell silent, all ears and eyes bent their direction.

Meg turned around, dumbfounded that he would say such a thing in public.

"Why did you?" he asked again loudly. "Then I was not mistaken. You've misled a lot of men with your kissing and will continue doing so until it pleases you to do otherwise."

"How dare you!" she cried, her cheeks hot with embarrassment.

"You toy with the affections of the men you meet, you gaze at them with your emerald eyes, you permit them to kiss you, then you leave! And I thought you a lady of quality."

"You—you know I do no such thing!" she returned.

"How do I know that?" he asked. "You've kissed me half a dozen times, leading me to believe finally that your heart has been engaged, and when I ask you to marry me, you refuse me. What am I to think but that you have led me a merry chase, that you've never once held a serious intention in your heart, that your design all along has been to win my affections, then to break my heart!"

She was so astonished by his curious arguments that she did not know what to think or to say.

In two long strides, he drew quite close to her. "Leave, then!" he cried, taking yet another step forward and forcing her to back away from him. "Your carriage awaits you! Mrs. Macclesfield and her five daughters await you. A life without the arms of a man who loves you awaits you. Hurry away, Meg Woodville!" Again he stepped toward her, again she backed away, her eyes wide, her mouth agape.

"You are being absurd!" she cried at last unable to think of anything more intelligent to say to him.

"And you are being stubborn beyond permission and beyond reason. You know very well you belong with me, in my home, in my bed."

She heard several gasps go up about her. She knew her cheeks were turning darker still from her acute mortification.

Again he stepped toward her. She stepped backward, only this time, she felt the wall against her back. She lifted her chin and finally responded coldly, "I have kissed a score of men! There! You now have the answer you have sought for the past several years. Now you may be content and despise me as much as you wish."

"You are lying," he countered, a faint smiling on his lips. "You've not kissed twenty men."

"A dozen, then," she responded, lifting an imperious brow.

"I don't believe you," he stated firmly, smiling a little more.

"No fewer than six," she countered, her heart beginning to melt in her breast as an answering smile suffused her lips.

"You were an innocent when I kissed you in Catmose," he said quietly, his hands on her arms, squeezing her gently.

"Yes I was," she whispered.

"I was a fool," he responded tenderly. "I was a fool to have believed anything else of you all this time."

"You were."

"I am no longer a fool, my darling Meg. Will you not accept of my hand in marriage and become my wife?"

She heard several strange sniffling sounds from the ladies present in the room.

Just kiss him.

Lady Elizabeth's advice floated up through her bewilderment and her fatigue. His lips were but a breath away. She felt her muff drift away from her hand. She felt the soft fur plop against her boots. She encircled his neck with her arms. "I will marry you," she said at last. "Though I promise you I shall make you regret it every day of your life."

"I hope for nothing less," he responded, smiling lovingly down into her face.

She placed her lips against his. She tasted coffee and brandy. She tasted a future without Mrs. Macclesfield's five daughters. She tasted children running through the receiving rooms of Threshwick Hall, Hope dandling her nieces and nephews upon her knee. She tasted love, just as she had the first time he had ever kissed her.

When at last he released her, it was to the general applause of the bustling chamber.

The following day, when Meg stood beside Castleton in the entrance hall of Threshwick Hall, Hope's voice rang down to them from the landing on the first floor. "It is all settled, then!" she fairly squealed.

"Yes," they responded in unison as Castleton slipped an arm about Meg's waist.

"Excellent!" Hope returned as she began tripping down the stairs. Once at the bottom, she hugged Meg quite thoroughly and afterward her brother. But the moment she completed her congratulations and well-wishes on their forthcoming marriage, she cried, "I have the most famous news, you will not credit it! Alfreton has decided to accompany us to London! For the Season!"

Meg exchanged a glance with Castleton. His complexion was suddenly high as it always was when Alfreton's name was mentioned. She caught his gaze and gave him a small shake of her head. He glared at her, then suddenly broke into a smile and laughed. Turning to his sister, he placed a kiss on her cheek. "How delightful," he murmured.

Hope received his kiss by winking at Meg. When he drew back from her, Hope addressed her brother lovingly. "Gudgeon," she said with a soft smile.

"Ninnyhammer," Castleton responded in kind.

Meg looked from one to the other and marvelled at the changes three years had wrought. Hope was a lady fully grown and Castleton—here, she glanced up at her husband-to-be—well, Castleton would always be Castleton, a bit of a gudgeon, quick to rise to the fly, and forever the man she loved.

Lovers' Vows

by
Meg-Lynn Roberts

Mirabell: A fellow that lives in a windmill has not a more whimsical dwelling than the heart of a man that is lodged in a woman.

Millamant: . . . Well, I won't have you, Mirabell—I'm resolved—I think—you may go—ha, ha, ha! What would you give, that you could help loving me?

Mirabell: I would give something that you did not know I could not help it.

—*The Way of the World,* Act II, William Congreve

"For the last time, I will not do it, Clementina!"

"But Ned, I'm counting on you to take the male lead in my Valentine's Day play. It's a family tradition and you have never refused before—when you've been in England, anyway, and not off with the army fighting the French. You can't let me down this year!" Lady Clementina Sutcliffe pleaded with her brother, Edward Hadleigh, the Marquess of Wexford.

"For the Lord's sake, Clementina, you have cast Vicky Colefax as the female lead. You can't expect me to play Romeo to her Juliet. Don't you remember, it was immediately after your Valentine's Day play last year that she threw my engagement ring back in my face, saying she wanted none of me."

"Yes, I know, Ned, and I felt she was wrong to do so, though neither of you would ever tell me the real reason for the breakup of your engagement." She looked at him hopefully, waiting for the long overdue explanation.

He ran a long-fingered hand along his jaw and looked away from her too observant eyes. "Never understood it myself, if you must know. Thought all was well in train for the wedding. The two families had planned it forever. Thought she was looking forward to our marriage."

"What did you *do,* Ned?"

"Nothing, Clem. Nothing. Treated her with the greatest courtesy and deference. Never made any demands on her. Told her I knew it was an arranged match when we got engaged, but planned to give her all due consideration as my wife. Told her she would make an excellent marchioness and that I couldn't have done better, if I had chosen myself."

"Oh, I *see*. Is that all?" Clementina replied, rolling her eyes at the thickheadedness of her handsome brother. "Well, no wonder she threw you over, Ned. I daresay it was no more than you deserved."

"What is that supposed to mean?" her brother asked with a menacing gleam in his dark eyes.

She turned away from him. "Don't know if I can still feel as sorry for you as I have done for this past twelve-month. And I do not blame Vicki in the least, now I've heard how you've treated her. Would have expected better from you. My own baby brother, after all."

"How I've treated her? What do you mean, Clem? I was the soul of courtesy and consideration."

"That's what I mean, Ned. I ask you, what can you do with such a sapskull?" Clementina threw her hands wide in supplication, appealing to some invisible audience for understanding. "If Vicki is half the woman I take her for, she doesn't want courtesy and consideration from you."

"Not want courtesy and consideration? Well, what the deuce does she want, then?"

"How about a declaration of love, a vow of undying passion, a few stolen, slightly improper kisses, a little romantic excitement . . ."

"You're mad, Clem! Those are not things a well-brought up young lady from a good family wants. Those are things to be saved for one's mis—er, for another class of woman."

"Ned, Ned," she said, shaking her head in disbelief at his density. "I despair of you. Really I do. That's what all women want, my dear."

"Surely the proper Victoria Colefax doesn't want that."

"Oh, yes, even the proper Victoria Colefax. Trust me, Ned. I am a woman—a happily married woman. And I know what women want."

He digested this, but still looked disbelieving. "I had no mind to be married so soon anyway, you know. Was just that blasted codicil in Papa's will begging me to secure the succession with all possible speed."

"Ah, hah! Now we come to it! If you didn't want to be married, you must have communicated your attitude to Vicki somehow."

"No, I did not. 'Sides, I've changed my mind. I think Papa was right. Been looking around me. When I left here and went to town last spring, I cast my eyes over the new crop of eligibles at Almack's. Didn't see any who took my fancy. Even went up to town in the autumn for the Little Season, and emerged heart whole."

"Well, it's a whole year later and you are still unattached. And so is Vicki."

"Can't say I am surprised that no one else has come up to scratch," he said, concealing the fact that he had been worried sick. "Vic's got a bit of a temper and she isn't exactly the most beautiful girl on the marriage mart. 'Sides, she's what—three, four-and-twenty now? Getting on."

"Plain? Vicki Colefax? How absurd! One might say she is refreshingly pretty rather than beautiful, but I think she is even lovelier this year than she was last. Why, when she arrived yesterday, I hardly recognized her at first, she has grown so smart. You have not seen her yet?"

"No. I've scarcely been here two hours. I haven't even seen Sutcliffe yet," he said, referring to Clementina's husband Charles, the Earl Sutcliffe, "nor Mama or the girls, either. I'm glad Mama decided to come on ahead last week. Spared me having to deal with Delia and Cynthia for three days on the road," he said with a shudder, thinking of the hair-raising schemes their seventeen-year-old twin sisters could have devised and the numerous scrapes they could have become involved in on a long carriage journey.

"Well, I daresay you'll be in for a surprise when you do see Vicki, my lord of Wexford. Will you even know her, I wonder? She has cropped her hair most charmingly and she has a new style of dressing. More stylish, I would say. . . . And you are a fine one to talk of getting on, Ned. You will be thirty in March. *Tempus fugit,* you know."

He waved away her comments. "This play we're to do, Clem, what is it this time?"

"Oh, something new I've commissioned from a friend."

"Your Valentine's plays are always rather—well, exceedingly romantic, and sometimes they even border on the overly sentimental, Clem."

"Yes, they do, don't they? And of course they're romantic. We're celebrating Valentine's Day—a day to express feelings of love and romance, remember? Why, I recall when you were at university, you could hardly wait for our Valentine's plays. You used to plead and beg on your knees for the lead male role."

"Yes, so I did," he agreed with a reminiscent smile.

"I must admit, I always greatly enjoyed winning the heroine at the end. Sometimes I even got to kiss her. Chastely, though, Clem. Chastely."

"*I* remember you liked to flirt with *all* the girls. You made a most convincing romantic hero, too, dying of love for the heroine, even if it was only playacting. We all missed you dreadfully while you were away fighting the French, you know, my dear, and I don't just mean when we needed you to play our hero."

"Yes, well, there was no help for it, Clem."

"I know, Ned. We are all so grateful that you are here now."

He looked away from her for a moment and asked, "Just what am I letting myself in for this year?"

"Oh, Ned, dear, you'll just have to trust me," Clementina purred sweetly.

"Never, little vixen. I know you of old, sister mine . . . Clem?" he called to her back, as she prepared to quit the conservatory where they had been talking.

She looked back inquiringly over her shoulder. He joined her and they walked some way out of the room into the vestibule beyond.

"I'll think on what you've said."

"You want her back, Ned?"

"I don't know." They walked a little further along. "I suppose I do," he admitted rather grudgingly.

She put her hand on his arm and gave him a straight look from under her finely drawn, dark-winged brows.

"Yes, I would like a chance to see if you are right, Clem."

"I know I am. If you do my play for me, you will have your chance, Ned."

"What if she won't take me back?"

"Nothing ventured, nothing gained, you know, Neddy," she reminded him, affectionately using her old pet name for him. "I find some significance in the fact that you are both still unattached. And great encouragement in the fact that she has accepted my invitation this year."

"Well, mayhap you're right, Clem. The next days will tell."

Vicki Colefax dared to peep from behind the leaves of a large banana tree where she had hidden herself when Lady Clementina Sutcliffe and her brother, the Marquess of Wexford, had suddenly come into the conservatory and taken her by surprise. Their voices had preceded their persons into the glass-paned room, and she had had time to jump up from her seat and conceal herself behind one of the lush tropical plants that thrived there. But now they were gone.

She had retired to the conservatory in the first place because she wanted privacy to study the copy of the play Lady Sutcliffe had given her. And there was something decidedly strange about her copy of the play, she had noticed at once. The last scene was missing. She had enjoyed the sparring between the strong male and female leads during the first four scenes, but she wondered who got the better of whom at the end. The heroine certainly had enough cutting things to say to her suitor. Surely she got the better of him in the end. But why was that last scene missing? Had it accidentally been left out, or had Lady Sutcliffe deliberately omitted it? And if so, for what reason?

How utterly chagrined she had been when her hostess

and Wexford began discussing her broken engagement to the marquess. And how embarrassed she had been to learn that Lady Sutcliffe had guessed her secret.

Vicki had not been able to hear what they said, once the marquess and his sister left the conservatory, but what she had overheard when they were in the room was enough to leave her boiling with anger. He had not wanted to be married at all, had he not? He had looked over the new crop of eligible young girls at Almack's a few weeks, perhaps only days, after she had broken off their engagement, had he? And he thought her a termagant. And plain! Oh! how right she had been to call off the wedding, she thought now, beating her fists against her sides. And what a fool she had been to have broken her heart over her hasty decision to end the engagement and to have agonized over it for the past year.

There had been an understanding between their two families, since Vicki was a young girl, that she and Ned Hadleigh would wed one day. There was already one alliance between the families. Her mother's cousin, Charles, Earl Sutcliffe, had married Lady Clementina Hadleigh some fifteen years ago, and that union had turned out so satisfactorily that everyone was certain a match between Vicki and Ned would turn out just as well.

The unfortunate war with France had kept Ned away from her side when Vicki made her come out and had kept him away from England for several years after that. He had held a vital position on the staff of General Sir Arthur Wellesley, now the Duke of Wellington, during the latter half of the war. Then, when his father died and Ned became the new Marquess of Wexford and was all set to resign his commission and return to England, Na-

poleon escaped from Elba and Ned had had to resume
his duties on Wellington's staff until after the grim Battle
of Waterloo. The duke had insisted that Ned was indis-
pensable to the English war effort.

Vicki had treasured in her heart the memory of Ned
as a mere boy of three-and-twenty, proudly clad in his
regimental scarlet, who had paid a courtesy call on her
one gloriously sunny day in the spring of 1811. He had
said he felt it only right to bid her farewell before he
left for the Peninsula, even though they were not offi-
cially engaged. She had been only eighteen at the time.
He had explained that, while he would not be leading
troops into battle, his would nevertheless be a dangerous
mission. He had said that she should not feel obliged to
wait for him, that he would understand perfectly if she
wished to be released from the understanding between
their families.

Fighting tears and determined to enact him no scenes,
she had said softly that she would wait. He had taken
her hand, pressed it and given her that devastating smile
of his that never failed to cause her stomach to do a
flip-flop. And then, his dark eyes flashing, he had given
her a half salute, turned and walked out of her life for
four years.

And she had waited. Waited patiently for those four
years. She had not seen him again until he returned to
England late in the autumn of 1815. He had become the
Marquess of Wexford by then. His father had died the
previous year, but he had not been able to come home
and take up his new duties until after Waterloo.

They had met formally and briefly that autumn, and
after Ned's *pro forma* proposal, they had agreed to announce their engagement at a family Christmas party

held here at Sutcliffe Manor little more than a year ago. The new marquess had been all that was correct and proper toward her. The only kiss they had exchanged had been last Christmas when they found themselves being teased by one of Ned's mischievous younger sisters because they were standing right under a mistletoe bough. He had barely pecked at her lips. Other than that, he had contented himself with kissing her hand occasionally, in the most cold and formal of ways, of course.

There had been only that single kiss for her to treasure until they appeared together in Lady Sutcliffe's Valentine's play last year. In the last scene, the hero and heroine had come together and acknowledged their love for one another, and Ned, improvising outrageously, had taken her in his arms and sworn his undying love. She had flubbed her lines and told him that she loved him, too. He had wrapped her in a warm embrace and kissed her for what had seemed like an eternity, but must have been less than a minute, to the delighted applause from the audience of their friends and relations.

She had felt something in that embrace and that kiss that she had been longing for ever since she was sixteen and had decided that tall, dark Ned Hadleigh with his flashing black eyes and heartstopping smile, was the most handsome, the most dashing man in all of England. When he had kissed her, Vicki thought she might die of pure happiness. Though only playacting, it had warmed her and thrilled her and left her tingling all the way down to her toes. She had gone weak at the knees and afterward was thankful Ned had kept his arm about her waist. It was all that had kept her upright.

But when they had taken their bows and walked off

the stage arm in arm, to disappear behind the makeshift curtain, Ned had been greeted by several of the other girls who had had minor parts in the play. He had removed his arm from hers and begun congratulating and chatting to the other girls. One of them was Arabella Rutledge, a beautiful black-haired, sloe-eyed young widow who had been giving Vicki sly, jealous looks for several days and who, it was whispered, had wanted her part. Arabella had flung her arms up about Ned's neck and invited his kiss.

Ned certainly had not been slow to respond. And only moments after the kiss he had shared with her!

Vicki had thought she would die of embarrassment . . . and fury . . . and a broken heart.

She had looked on the proceedings white-faced and shaking. When he straightened up, grinning like a monkey, she had asked if she might have a private word with him. He had winked at her and said certainly.

He had followed her to the library where he had tried to put his arm about her waist once more and draw her to him. She had jerked away, removed her engagement ring from her finger and handed it to him, saying that she found they wouldn't suit after all. He had been stunned, but she hadn't waited for his reaction. She had turned and run from the library. She hadn't stopped running until she reached her bedroom. She and her mother had left Sutcliffe Manor the next day at dawn.

And all these past months, she had been wondering if she hadn't been wrong to end their engagement.

Well, now she knew how right she had been to break off with him! And all her regrets, her broken heart, all those scalding tears that had soaked into her pillow over the months had been wasted on this unfeeling monster who thought her a vixen and a plain old maid. The cad! What if she had overlooked his behavior with Arabella Rutledge and married him anyway? Would she be terribly unhappy with a philandering husband now and regretting that she had given in to her lovesick longings? That question had vexed her for a twelvemonth.

If only she hadn't let Lady Sutcliffe extract that promise from her to come this year! But she had not really wanted to refuse, had she? She had been so unsure that she had done the right thing last year. She had thought that perhaps his behavior after the play had just been playful high spirits and that she had been too quick and too jealous in her reaction. Perhaps, after all, they could have had a good marriage and he could have come to love her as much as she loved him.

Oh dear Lord, whatever had possessed her to accept Lady Clementina's invitation? If only she hadn't given in to all those romantic yearnings in her soul and come! But now here she was among the large gathering at the lovely manor of the Earl Sutcliffe and his countess, all set to accept a role in the Valentine's play and try to satisfy her unresolved feelings toward Ned Hadleigh.

And she had just learned exactly what he thought of her.

Whatever was she to do now? Vicki moaned. Turn again, and run? No! That would be too cowardly.

She must face him. Face him and show him how little she cared for his good opinion. Yes. She would do everything in her power to show that conceited oaf of a Ned Hadleigh that she couldn't care less if he were the last man on earth.

* * *

"Good Lord! Is that you, Vic?" Ned asked as he backed away from his chattering young cousin, Elizabeth Hadleigh, and literally bumped into Vicki, treading on her toes.

"Er, I mean, I hardly recognized you, Vic, ah, Miss Colefax. How well you look!" he exclaimed, feeling his face grow warm as he desperately tried to cover up his *faux pas*. He remembered that Clem had warned him that he would not know her when he saw her. And Clem had been right, devil take her. He cast an uneasy eye at his sister across the drawing room over the heads of her other guests who had gathered there for dinner. She beamed back at him, nodding her encouragement.

"Good evening, Lord Wexford," Vicki replied with chilly haughter. Not recognize her, did he? Well! It was all of a piece with his earlier words. He had never really known her at all.

"This, um, new way you have adopted of doing your hair is what threw me," he said, trying to excuse himself. He looked approvingly at the way her wary dark blond hair had been cut and shaped around her pretty head, with short curls in front and longer tendrils caressing her cheeks and neck at the sides and back.

"I am so glad you approve, my lord," Vicki said, summoning up a saccharine smile that was almost a grimace. She almost had to crane her neck to look up at him. Could he really have grown in the past year? Or had she just forgotten how tall and imposing he really was with his broad shoulders, slim waist, and long, muscular legs?

"Yes, yes, I do," he replied, regarding her uneasily. He wished he dared run a finger round his suddenly too-

tight neckcloth. Blast that new valet of his! He would
have to tell the man not to tie the deuced thing so tightly
next time.

"And that is a most fetching gown you're wearing tonight," he added approvingly. And by Jove, it was, too!
A clinging, pale green silk with cream lace trimming,
the gown brought out the green lights in her eyes and
outlined her tall, well-shaped form most admirably.

He looked more closely at the lowcut gown. Since
when had Victoria Colefax acquired such a womanly figure? he wondered in some surprise. She used to be a
very tall, narrow girl. And last year when they were engaged he had hardly noticed her figure, clothed as she
always had been in rather nondescript, colorless, high-cut
gowns.

"I had you in mind when I chose it," she said sweetly,
with a glint of fire in her eyes.

"You did!" His brows shot up in surprise. Maybe it
would be easier to win her back than he had thought. A
slow, appreciative smile spread across his face. That self-
same smile had made him famous among the ladies on
the continent and won him many a female heart.

"Yes, and I am most humbly grateful to have the approval of such a noted connoisseur of ladies' fashions as
yourself, my lord."

"Connoisseur?" His smile faded and he lowered his
brows in bewilderment at her tone. "I wouldn't have said
I'm a connoisseur of ladies' fashions exactly," he replied
uncertainly, feeling the ground shift beneath his feet. He
looked more closely into her eyes to see if he could divine her meaning. Good Lord! He hadn't realized Vic
had such large, crystal clear green eyes. The irises, outlined by a sooty black ring, contrasted most startlingly

with the emerald interior. They were beautiful. Now why had he never noticed *that* before?

"Oh? Then your flattering words were only so much empty air?"

Those beautiful eyes were sparking green fire at him now, he saw.

He rocked back on his heels, at a loss at how best to make amends for whatever he had said to antagonize her. "Er, no, indeed. Was only my humble opinion, my dear, for you do look most enticing tonight," he said, his eyes on the entrancing swell of her bosom where it rose above the creamy lace at the neckline of the gown.

"Humble? You, Wexford?" she said with the lift of one well-shaped brow. "I have always taken you for a proud man." She gave an artificial laugh.

Now he was certain that she was deliberately baiting him. What the devil ailed her? he wondered. This was not the Vicki Colefax he remembered. He had been used to thinking of her as a sweet, shy girl who never put herself forward. Now he knew better. Well, if she wanted to fight, she would get as good as she gave, he thought angrily, clenching his teeth.

"Yes, I'm a proud man. Too proud to offer you Spanish coin, and so you should know very well. I see you've turned into a spitfire since I knew you last, Miss Colefax, ready to quarrel over such a trifle." He bared his teeth at her in what might have passed for a smile under other circumstances.

Vicki felt herself go pink at his words. "A spitfire, am I?" she hissed at him. "Well, you, my Lord Wexford, are a toplofty, cold-hearted cad!"

"Cold-hearted?" he uttered furiously, in a low voice. "I'll have you know, Victoria Colefax, that I'm the most

warm-blooded man in all England!" By God, but he
wanted to lay his hands on her and show her how warm-
blooded he was!

They felt rather than saw that someone had joined
them, interrupting their wrangling. Vicki turned grate-
fully to see Wexford's cousin, Richard Hadleigh.

"Good evening, Miss Colefax. I trust I see you well?"
Richard said, giving Vicki a slight bow and a broad smile
as he looked at her through his gold-rimmed quizzing
glass.

"Very well, Mr. Hadleigh. It is good to see you here
this year," Vicki replied with a smile of relief, glad to
have the uncomfortable tension of the past few minutes
broken. "I don't believe we've met since we were children when my family used to be invited to Hadleigh family house parties at Wexford Hall."

"Has it been so long? Tsk. I see I have been depriving
myself of the great pleasure of your charming company.
We'll have a comfortable coze after dinner and catch up
on the intervening years," he promised with a meaningful
smile, half closing his eyes and giving her a long seduc-
tive look before he turned to his cousin.

"Hello, Ned. Haven't seen you since you returned all
in one piece from the wars," Richard said, extending his
hand to his older cousin. "And I see you're up to your
old tricks, capturing the most beautiful girl in the room
all to yourself without giving the rest of us a chance."
He pushed playfully against his cousin's shoulder, and
winked at Vicki.

"Since when did you become such a dandified fop,
Richard? When I left you were a budding Corinthian,
interested in nothing but horses and driving and sport,"
Ned said, shaking the hand of his darkly good-looking

young cousin while he eyed the young man's modish, extremely colorful, turn out.

"Appreciate my duds, do you, coz?" Richard asked, striking a pose and showing off his fashionable outfit of cut-away coat of blue superfine worn over canary-colored inexpressibles that fit his form with not an inch of material to spare. The waistcoat that covered his white shirt was fashioned of multicolored silk, with a brilliant peacock blue color predominating. It brought out the color of his eyes and had been chosen for just that reason. His shirt points were so high they nearly swallowed up the lower half of his face.

"Look like you're ready for a funeral, all rigged out in black like that, coz," he quizzed the marquess with his glass, looking over his cousin's severe black silk evening jacket and pantaloons, that were relieved only by a pristine white shirt and modestly tied white linen neckcloth. "We who once basked in your shadow are used to seeing you rigged out in all the glory of your scarlet regimentals. This is a sad come down from your former gorgeous plummage."

"Ah, are you suggesting I follow your lead in sartorial matters?" Ned bantered with his cousin.

"You could do worse, Ned. You could certainly do worse."

"Well, if I should ever feel the need to strut about like a peacock, perhaps I shall take you for my model, Dick."

The cousins grinned at one another, each taking the other's raillery in good part.

"And to whom would you award the palm tonight, Miss Colefax?" Richard asked.

"Oh, I couldn't possibly choose between you. You, Mr.

Hadleigh are quite handsome, while Lord Wexford shows his true character in the color he's chosen."

Ned's lips tightened at her disparaging remark and Richard threw Vicki a startled look, then laughed.

"Taken my cousin in dislike, have you, Miss Colefax? Don't blame you. Never see him in town anymore and, from what I hear, he's grown monstrous staid and dull since he's become a country rustic."

"Hear, I say, Dick, that's coming it a bit strong. I've been up to town several times in the past twelfthmonth."

"What, for a sennight at a time? Didn't even take the time to call on me."

"Well, my business took up much of my time," Ned muttered, thinking that he really did not enjoy giddy town life. His duties at Wexford Hall were many and arduous, keeping him tied by the leg to the estate. Not that he minded, of course. He felt it was time to settle down after the harrowing years of warfare far from England's glorious green countryside.

Vicki, remembering that Ned's "business" had been to look over the crop of eligible young ladies in order to choose a wife, lifted her chin and stared at him coldly.

"You look quite lovely tonight, Miss Colefax. Might I hope that my slow-top of a cousin has been so busy admiring you that he has forgotten to engage your company for dinner?" Richard asked.

"You might be correct, Mr. Hadleigh," Vicki told him flirtatiously.

Richard laughed with delight. "Then you will allow me?" he said, extending his arm. Vicki smiled dazzlingly and placed her hand on his sleeve.

"Here, I say, Vic, I hoped you would allow me—" Ned began, but the couple had already stepped away from him to follow the other guests who were proceeding in to dinner.

His vivacious cousin Elizabeth, Richard's younger sister, bounced up to him just then and demanded his arm. He did not doubt that she had been egged on to do so by his mischievous twin sisters, who were even now grinning in his direction.

It was left to him to lead the giggling girl in to dinner and seat himself beside her. She was in tearing spirits. She had recently graduated from the schoolroom and this was the first year she had been allowed to join the adults. She seemed determined to enjoy every minute of it.

Dinner was a frustrating affair for Ned. He had to suffer the sight of Richard flirting with Vicki to the top of his bent across the table and a little way down from him. And Vicki looked damned enticing, too, as she chatted and laughed with Dick. She never once glanced in his direction, he noticed, whereas his eyes were trained on her throughout the meal. The only bright spot was that Jane Fenners, the Earl's sister, was seated to Richard's other side and claimed almost as much of his attention as Vicki did.

He was brought up short once or twice when he felt Clementina's eyes on him, reminding him of his duty to entertain his dinner partners. But with the laughing, chattering Elizabeth to one side of him, and his largely deaf great-aunt Henrietta, who was happy to address her meal, to the other, he did not have to strain himself unduly.

Clementina had gathered the usual large party of family and friends for her Valentine's entertainment. His sister loved to surround herself with congenial company and her doting husband gave her full reign to organize and hold several house parties throughout the year.

His mother, Barbara, the Marchioness of Wexford was there, of course, with the twins, the Ladies Delia and Cynthia Hadleigh. It was hard to believe the girls were seventeen now and would be presented next year. They had always plagued the life out of him when he had been younger, and now he was their guardian, they *still* plagued the life out of him, but for very different reasons. Now they were always clamoring for yet more fashionable new gowns and other feminine fripperies, begging to leave off their studies in the schoolroom a year early so that they might enjoy themselves at some fashionable Devonshire seaside spa before they went up to London for their season, and myriad other favors they never ceased pestering him for.

He was sure his hair would turn from coal black to gray next spring when it would be his responsibility to shepherd those two hoydens safely through a London season, with his mother's supervision, of course. That they could be fired off without any missteps would be a minor miracle, he felt sure. Another reason to persuade Vic to become his wife soon—she could take some of the burden of the twins' presentation from his shoulders.

Richard and Elizabeth's parents, Uncle Henry, his father's brother, and his wife, Aunt Joan, were here this year with two of their three children. Their studious middle child, twenty-year-old John, was still up at Cambridge. And Great Aunt Henrietta, Lady Martindale, was present as usual. Clem's husband, Charles Fenners, Earl Sutcliffe, had invited his mother, Alice, the Dowager Countess, and his younger sister, Lady Jane. And, of course, Charles's widowed cousin, Margaret Colefax, was here to chaperone her daughter Vicki.

Two of Clementina's children were in the house, but were not yet old enough to join the adults at table. Ten-year-old Sarah and eight-year-old Mary Jane were still in the schoolroom. Their brothers, Thomas, fourteen, and Andrew, twelve, were away at their boarding school, as Easter term was already underway.

Various friends and neighbors who lived nearby would be invited to the play on Valentine's evening, too, and to the entertainment afterward. Ned knew from past experience that it was Clementina's practice to give a few of the young ladies and gentlemen from the neighborhood parts in the play. Customarily, they would drive over during the day to rehearse, although he wouldn't be surprised if they were invited to stay at the house for a day or two both before and after the play. It would be more convenient for all that way.

His thoughts swiftly drifted back to Vicki. He could not get over the change in her. He had never seen her looking so well, or behaving so coldly to him before. It was almost as though she were acting a part. Of course, he had to admit, he had been very little in her company since she had grown into a woman.

He thought back over their acquaintance, remembering that they had spent one month in the summer together when she was a coltish sixteen and he a gangly, still wet-behind-the-ears, one and twenty. He had very much liked the sixteen-year-old Vicki and had done everything he could think of to impress her. He remembered with chagrin how, with all the greenness and boastfulness of untried youth upon him, he had tried to overwhelm the young Vicki with feats of reckless daring do, like foolhardily jumping a five-barred gate on an untried horse, risking certain death with one misstep when he had climbed to the top of the tower of a crumbling, ruined abbey in the vicinity, and daring her to meet him at midnight down at the lake one stormy night.

It was only later he realized that he had been using her as practice for his dealings with females when he went up to town the following autumn. What a clothhead he had been! The amazing thing was that Vic had always been game to follow him, whether it was on the wildest rides cross country, or meeting him clandestinely at that lake. And, gratifyingly, she had always seemed to be suitably impressed with his foolish, reckless feats, unlike the females he met later in town. He had swiftly learned that young, high-society ladies were more impressed with polite drawing room behavior, than with imprudent, athletic stunts.

He had not thought of Vicki often when he had been abroad. There was too much danger and hard work in the immediate present of wartime Portugal and Spain and later Belgium and France, and too much depended on his clear, incisive thinking, to dwell on thoughts of home. But when his father died and he inherited the title and the family solicitor made him aware of the codicil in his father's will, he had thought of her. He knew then that, when he went home, they must wed with all possible speed.

When he had returned to England, he had gone to see Vicki after only a week with his mother and his younger sisters at the family estate. Of course, he took the family engagement ring along on the visit and presented it to her in a rather offhand fashion, saying casually he guessed she had been expecting it.

After their engagement, she had seemed very delicate and fragile, like a sweet, pale flower, and he had fallen completely in love with her. He realized he was ready for commitment and marriage. But he had been afraid of alarming her with any attempts at lovemaking before they were wed. It had been a severe strain, but he had limited himself to simple kisses on her hand.

Until last year's Valentine's play.

Lord, but he had made a fool of himself when he had declared his passion for her right there on stage in front of an audience of their friends and family for all to see. And then that kiss! It made him go all hot to just think of it.

It had started as an excess of high spirits, exuberance at the end of an enjoyable, but tense two hours of stage play. He had decided to improvise a few lines and some of the action. He had taken a surprised, but not unwilling, Vicki into his arms and held her in a close embrace and kissed her for several minutes. His own mouth had been open over her lips and he had pressed her to him so tightly that he was aware of every inch of her body through her flimsy costume. Finally the clapping and whistling and laughter and cheers from the audience had penetrated his consciousness and he had released her. He had felt his knees go weak, and he had had to keep an arm about her waist to keep them from buckling under him.

Just one year ago.

Richard and Ned reached Vicki's side virtually at the same time when the men joined the ladies in the drawing room after the meal.

"Time for our comfortable coze, Miss Colefax," Richard said, bowing over her hand.

"Why, I have been looking forward to it all evening, Mr. Ha—" Vicki began.

"You monopolized her all through dinner, Dick. It's my turn now," Ned interjected before Vicki could finish her sentence. Damned, if he would let Dick walk off with her under his very nose *again!* he thought. "I must speak to Vicki about this play we are to do." He took her hand and placed it on his sleeve before she knew what he was about and could mount an objection. "Why don't you go speak to Jane, Dickon? She's smiling at you even now."

Richard turned his head to smile at Lady Jane, the earl's quiet, pretty sister. "Ah, so she is. Until later, then, Miss Colefax," he said smoothly, giving her a look full of secret promise.

"Deserter," Vicki muttered under her breath as Richard walked away. "Why do you think I would want to spend time in your company, Lord Wexford?" she said aloud to the marquess. "I thought I made it clear last year that I wanted nothing more to do with you. I cannot think what we possibly have to discuss now." She desperately hoped he could not see through the blatant untruth of her declaration.

"Well, my dear Miss Colefax, if you wanted nothing more to do with me, then why are you here at my sister's house party where you knew you were bound to encounter me?"

To answer him was unthinkable, so Vicki colored up prettily as she raised her chin and looked away, saying nothing.

Ned recollected himself. He had set out to charm her,

not to give her any more reason to be angry with him. "Ah, forgive me. I will not tease you about the past. Clem asked me to entertain you after dinner. And one always likes to please one's hostess," he answered, giving her a brilliant smile that set her pulses racing.

"Oh? It was not your inclination to do so, then?"

"Er, I didn't say that. Why would I not be inclined to talk to a pretty young woman and seat her beside me so that I could enjoy her company and the pleasure of gazing at her countenance." He had himself well in hand now, and refused to be goaded into bandying words with her.

"Ah. It is not *my* company specifically you wish for. I suppose any woman would do who met a certain minimum standard of attractiveness."

"No. Only you, Vic," he whispered, leaning nearer so that his breath brushed her cheek. He seated her gracefully on a small sofa apart from the company, lifted the tails of his jacket and sat down closely beside her, crossing one long, muscular leg over the other.

"I see. Now that we are no longer betrothed, you feel it safe to flirt with me."

"Safe? With those eyes of yours flashing sparks of green fire at me, piercing me most cruelly at every turn? I assure you, I tremble for my very life when I come near you."

She turned her head away from him, disturbed and excited by this new manner of speaking to her he had adopted.

"Did I not flirt with you when we were engaged?" he continued, speaking in a low, caressing voice for her ears only. "How remiss of me. Now that you have pointed out my mistake, I will make haste to correct it."

Her head whipped back round in his direction. "Mistake? I never said I wanted such empty dalliance and ridiculous behavior from you, Ned Hadleigh!"

"Has anyone ever told you how pretty you are when you're in a passion, Vic?"

"I am not in a passion!" Vicki insisted from between clenched teeth, enunciating each word distinctly.

"Then Lord help me when you are!" Ned responded, rolling his own eyes teasingly. A lock of his dark hair fell over his forehead as he looked down at her. "I am looking forward to the coming days when you *will* be in a passion. And with me as your beloved object, too."

"Whatever do you mean, my lord?" Vicki asked, looking up at him in bewilderment.

"I refer to this play of Clem's where we are to act opposite one another. From past performances, I would say that Clem has chosen something that will bring out the 'passion' in both of us. After all, we are doing this to commemorate Valentine's Day. And Valentine's Day is a time for lovers, you know. A time to celebrate love and passion."

Vicki colored up prettily. "You are wasting your attentions on me, Wexford. We are nothing to one another now. Why do you not wait until some of the neighboring ladies arrive? Perhaps they will appreciate your flagrant attempts at gallantry and enjoy your improper insinuations."

"With the emphasis on 'sin,' eh?"

"Oh!" Vicki cried, jumping up from her seat. "I will not stay to listen to any more of this indelicate talk."

She walked away, holding herself regally erect, as she went to speak to some other members of the party.

Ned watched her go with a speculative gleam in his eyes. He was not displeased with their little sparring match. Vicki was not as delicate a creature as he had thought. Winning her back would be challenging and exciting. A soft smile curved his lips as he formed his strategy and anticipated the spoils of victory.

"This will be the first time I've acted in one of my sister-in-law's plays," Lady Jane Fenners said to Richard Hadleigh the next morning as those who had been assigned parts in the Valentine's play gathered in the music room for their first rehearsal.

"How have you managed to escape Clem thus far?" Richard asked with a smile. "She's always been a tyrant at forcing her nearest and dearest into participating in her little dramatic productions."

"Oh, Clementina has been very understanding about my stage fright. But she's talked me into doing two very small parts this year."

"You're not nervous about doing this little amateur performance, are you, Jane?"

"I must admit, it scares me silly. I'm not used to standing up before people and speaking. It is a good thing I have very few lines. I could not trust myself to remember much. It will be a miracle if I don't trip over my own feet," she said with a self-deprecating laugh.

"Relax, Jane. You have nothing to worry about. . . . May I call you Jane, by the way? As we are connections of a sort I don't feel we need to stand on ceremony with one another, do you?"

"Oh! Oh, yes. Of course you may call me Jane, Mr. Hadleigh."

"Please, Jane, call me Richard, or Dick, if you prefer. And, remember, the audience will only be our family and friends—not one London critic among them, I promise.

The idea is to have a bit of fun. Cousin Clem has been keen on acting since we were children, you know. As the oldest Hadleigh cousin, she was always the bossy one. She used to assign us all parts at Christmas time, so that some of us were shepherds and some angels and so on. Those who were in special favor, or judged to have been specially good during the previous year, were asked to play the Holy Family. I believe the only time I earned that honor was when I was pressed into service as the baby Jesus when I was a toddler."

Jane laughed outright. The very idea of the handsome and extremely modish Richard Hadleigh as a baby wrapped in swaddling clothes for Clementina's Christmas play was utterly incongruous.

He reached out and flicked her cheek, causing her face to flame brightly at his touch. Before either could speak further, their attention was distracted by a stir at the door to the music room. A few of the young people from neighboring families were just arriving to make up the numbers needed for all the parts in the play.

Vicki was sitting on a piano stool in a far corner of the music room, trying to concentrate on learning her lines and trying not to think of Ned and the way he had spoken to her last evening. Trying not to read too much into his rather brazen flirtation, or to dwell on the way his dark eyes had seemed to light up with interest as he looked at her, or the way his lips has curved up into that beguiling smile of his, or how he had lowered his voice seductively when he spoke into her ear. Trying not to get her hopes up.

He could not possibly want to resume their engagement, could he? She had overheard how little he thought of her when she was concealed in the conservatory yesterday afternoon. Yet last night he had looked at her the way a man looks at a woman he desires. She could only fear that he had decided to flirt with her and peak her interest as a way of punishing her for subjecting him to embarrassment when she had broken off their engagement last year.

At the sudden sound of laughter, Vicki looked up from her study of her lines to see that a few of the Sutcliffes' neighbors had arrived. The Laponte brothers, George and Nigel, had come in along with Arabella Rutledge and her brother, John Lindley. Her spirits fell. She had wondered if Arabella would be here this year, hoping against hope that the beautiful young widow would not be invited. But it seemed that Arabella and her brother were both to have parts in the play. She could not forget Arabella's part in her impulsive decision to break off her engagement with Ned last year.

Vicki saw that the marquess as well as Clementina had gone up to greet the newcomers and that Arabella was looking up and laughing into Ned's face as she reached out to lay her hand on his arm. She was saying something to him that made him smile. Oh fie upon it! Vicki thought in flustered annoyance, trying to damp down her anger. She refused to let jealousy eat at her. After all, Ned was nothing to her now. Nothing at all.

Lady Clementina handed Arabella a script and pointed out her part and then Arabella walked with Ned over to one side of the room while Clementina turned to John Lindley to explain his part. This was the first time the rather bashful twenty-one year old John had participated in one of her plays.

"Oh, bother, I hoped I would get to play the heroine this year, my lord. It would have been such fun to play

opposite *you* as we did before you took up your commission six years ago, remember?" Arabella said to Ned.

"Indeed, how could I forget! But recollect, we shall
be on stage together again this year, so what odds what
parts we play," he said flirtatiously, not immune to her
beauty and not about to waste an open invitation. She
had cast out lures to him last year. Perhaps if things did
not work out with Vicki, he would take her up on her
invitation and indulge in an affair.

This lively, and quite breathtakingly lovely, neighbor
of Clem's had married George Rutledge, a dashing cavalry officer, when she was eighteen, the year after Ned
himself had left England to take up his military duties.
Arabella had been widowed three years later and had
come back to live with her parents. The Lindleys were
the Sutcliffes' nearest neighbors.

Ned remembered that they had had a lively time when
Clem had cast Bella as the heroine in the Valentine's play
the year before he left for the continent. Bella had seemed
to invite his addresses off stage as well as on, and he had
been attracted by her dark beauty and lively manner. But
he had known that he was about to embark on a dangerous
mission, with who-new-what results. Besides there was
Vicki, his unofficial betrothed to consider. He had managed to fend off Arabella six years ago.

But now here she was looking more fetching than ever
with a more mature, curvaceous figure and her midnight
black hair dressed high on her head with one alluring
curl falling over her left shoulder, and her large brown
eyes looking warm and inviting and sultry.

"Who is to play the heroine then? Not Lady Jane Fenners?" Arabella asked, looking over at the girl who stood

quietly talking to Richard Hadleigh. "She's so quiet, she'll never carry it off."

"No. I believe Jane has a very minor part, and as for shy, I believe she's less so each year. As you see, Clem has invited Miss Colefax again this year," he said, gesturing toward Vicki who was glowering at them from her corner, despite her best intentions to pay them no mind. "She is to play the heroine."

"What! But, how awkward for you, my lord!—I mean, your engagement to Miss Colefax was broken off last year, wasn't it?"

"Yes, it was. I suppose the whole world recollects the event."

"And you, you haven't made it up with her?"

"Er, no."

"Well, I must say, what an irksome situation this must be for you, my lord! How could your sister be so insensitive as to invite her? And to cast her opposite you, too?"

"Oh, you make too much of it, Mrs. Rutledge. Vicki and I have known each other forever. Our past engagement was an arranged affair, you know. We are just friends now," he heard himself say with some annoyance. The last thing he wanted to do was to discuss his campaign to resume his engagement to Vicki with Arabella Rutledge.

"Ah, then you are back to the footing of friends with no thought of an alliance," she remarked with a relieved smile.

Ned looked uncomfortable. "Er, yes. I believe that is the case."

She smiled a satisfied smile, looking like a cat who had just got at the cream. "And you must not stand on ceremony with me you know, *Ned,*" she said leaning to-

ward him and resting her hand on his arm. "Call me
Bella as you were always used to do. When anyone addresses me as 'Mrs. Rutledge,' I feel a hundred years
old!" She gave her tinkling laugh.

Clementina called the group to order and they all gathered round in a circle to go through their first reading,
scripts in hand.

As Vicki read her lines and Ned responded, she noticed that her strong character consistently got the better
of this flawed rake, and with each speech her confidence
grew. She began to feel that she could throw herself into
this part with a vengeance.

When they reached the end of scene four, Clementina
explained that last scene was very short and that she was
saving it until she was satisfied that everyone knew their
parts for the first four scenes.

"Neddy, dear, I think you could use some extra practice. You were uncharacteristically wooden in your reading of the male lead, Lacklove. You need to put more
fire into your interpretation of him to carry him off, don't
you think? Why don't you and Vicki read your parts
through together and see if you can put a little more
liveliness into your voices?" she asked with seeming
guilelessness.

"It's a warm day for February. I think the both of you
should walk outside and practice your parts. It will be
sheltered in the Bestiary Garden. You can practice there,"
she concluded, arranging matters to her satisfaction without consulting the wishes of either party. "You will have
about an hour until luncheon is ready. I will continue to
work with the others in here."

Vicki blushed. "Please excuse me, Clementina, but I
must speak with Mama. I have not seen her all day,"

she said the first thing that came into her head, trying to create a plausible excuse to avoid this *tête-à-tête* with the marquess.

"Well, you will just have to wait until later this afternoon to do that, my dear. Your mother drove into the village with Aunt Joan and my mother about an hour ago. I believe they were planning to have luncheon there. You are free as a bird," Clementina told her.

"Yes, Vic. I could use your help. I can't seem to get the measure of this Lacklove fellow at all. Perhaps you can give me some clues," Ned spoke up after receiving a significant look from his sister. If Clem had been standing nearer to him, he knew she would have trod on his toes.

"Oh, I really don't think it's a good idea—," Vicki began in embarrassment.

"I would be more than happy to read Miss Colefax's part for her," Arabella purred sweetly, "and give Lord Wexford some practice."

"How kind of you to offer, Bella, but you have a large part of your own to learn. I think it would be better for you to work on Mistress Dazzle's lines," Clementina intervened quickly. No, it would never do for her plans to bring Vicki and Ned back together to throw him into company with that minx, Arabella Rutledge. She wished she could have avoided inviting the girl this year without offending the Lindleys, but she could not.

Arabella pouted.

"Oh, Clemmy, *I* don't have a speaking part. I'll read Vicki's part for her and work with Neddy," Delia spoke up, seeing Vicki's reluctance. She could not wait to be old enough to play the heroine in one of her elder sister's plays. She and Cynthia were to play servants this year, but they had only one speaking part between them. She would have to satisfy her histrionic talents by prancing about on stage and mugging for the audience.

"No, I want to do it. You can read Mistress Dazzle's part," Cynthia said and the twins began to bicker between themselves.

"Girls, girls, I really don't think either of you has enough experience at this sort of thing," Ned said, trying to quell them. "Besides, if I'm to play opposite Vic, I think I can better understand the proper nuances of my character if I work with her."

"Yes, you are very right, Neddy," Clementina seconded him and gave Vicki a little, unobtrusive push in his direction. "Ring the bell, my dear, and one of the maids will fetch your outdoor things."

Ned picked up their scripts and took Vicki by the elbow, assisting her out into the hallway where they could await their outdoor wraps. They would have to bundle up warmly before going outside, for, despite Clementina's optimistic words, it was still quite cold at this time of year.

Arabella was not at all happy to see that Ned was going off with his former fiancée, but rather than let her ill-humor show, she turned immediately to the personable Richard Hadleigh and soon engaged him in a light flirtation. He was ready and willing to oblige her.

Lady Jane turned away and quietly settled herself next to John Lindley, not looking back at the laughing couple as she spoke in a low voice with her brother's young neighbor.

It was a fine, sunny day for early February, but there was a distinct chill in the air when the marquess and

Vicki made their way along a gravel path that ran through the extensive sloping, green lawns behind the large, red-brick manor house. There were several fine gardens arranged on either side of the pathway, but the couple didn't stop to admire the handiwork of the estate's gardeners. They had a specific destination in mind. The gravel crunched under their feet as they made their way to the topiary garden where they would be more sheltered among the boxwood hedges that the estate's army of gardeners had cut into various fantastic shapes.

The Sutcliffe Manor Bestiary was the pride and joy of the earl and countess and was famous throughout the county. The dark green box, one of the most suitable of all hedges for topiary, had been pruned and shaped to represent various animals and toys by the estate's skilled gardeners to amuse the children when they were younger. The earl had designed hedges that were cut to look like a child's top, spinning on its side, a hoop, a cricket bat and stumps, among other things. Green lions, elephants, bears, wolves, horses, deer, and foxes chasing hens, loomed on either side of them as Vicki and Ned turned down one of the mazelike paths that ran between the hedges.

"I think I'll ask Clem to have one of her box hedges cut into a heart with an arrow piercing it specially to commemorate this occasion," Ned remarked humorously. "Or perhaps I should plant such a topiary garden at Wexford Hall and have one of my gardeners cut and prune one of the hedges into such a shape for me. What do you think, Vic?" he asked.

"Why would you want to do such a nonsensical thing? And don't call me 'Vic.' We are no longer on intimate terms, my lord."

"Ohh, you have me trembling and shaking in my shoes when you address me in that fierce voice, *Miss* Colefax."

"You are being ridiculous, my lord, as I told you last night."

"Oh, Vic, must you keep on addressing me in that formal fashion?" He linked his arm through hers and drew her close to his side. "Call me Ned. Makes me feel I'm some sort of ancient grandfather if you keep on 'my lording' me to death every time you open your mouth."

She did not answer his teasing. In her heart, he would always be 'Ned,' but if she allowed herself to assume their old informality, she feared she would be leaving herself open to hurt again. Besides, it irritated him for her to call him "my lord." And for some reason she wanted to irritate him. Perhaps she wanted to pay him back in some small measure for the heartbreak he had caused her over the past six years.

"Besides, it puts me at a distinct advantage over you, you know, if you refer to me by my title." He bent his dark head and peered into her face beneath her fashionable winter bonnet.

"Indeed? How so, *my lord?*" Vicki asked perversely. She felt a distinct quickening of her pulses at his nearness.

"Why, if I'm your 'lord,' you are my subject and must obey my every wish," he teased, smiling at her suggestively and gazing quite blatantly at her lips that were parted in surprise. He was tempted to pull her into his arms and steal one of those "romantic" kisses Clem had mentioned as part of his campaign right now.

"Oh, you are just being ridiculous. I agreed to come out here with you to work on this play. If you're deter-

mined to utter silly nonsense, I have better things to do."
Vicki dropped his arm and turned about on the path.

"Wait! Come, Vic, don't let us quarrel," he called.

She turned back to look at him.

"I'll behave. I promise." He smiled disarmingly and
pressed one hand to his breast where it was covered by
his dark woolen cape.

She was skeptical of his pledge, but turned back to
rejoin him, reluctantly admitting to herself that she did
not really want to leave his company just yet.

When she returned to walk at his side once more,
pointedly not taking his arm, Ned returned the conversation to safer ground and asked, "What do you make
of this play of Clem's so far?"

"Well, I can see why an audience would enjoy the
sharp sparring between the various characters, but I fail
to see how my character, Mistress Proudheart, can ever
overcome her revulsion for such a posturing, self-satis-
fied rake like Lacklove. I don't know how she could ever
be attracted to such a vain creature or believe that he
could ever reform his fickle ways for her sake. She is
wise not to believe a word he says."

"Oh, nonsense. She is too harsh in her judgment. Her
ears have been poisoned by her friend, Mistress Dazzle.
I think Lacklove is a fine figure of a man. He is just
wary of being trapped by a woman who does not truly
care for him."

"Dazzle seems to think differently."

"But, Vic, don't you see. Mistress Dazzle is jealous.
She likes Lacklove and wants him for herself. They've
been, er, close friends in the past and if she can't have
him back, she's determined that this new rival won't have

him either, so she discredits his character, slandering him to Mistress Proudheart."

"Oh? How can you tell that? I don't see anything specific in what Dazzle says that would indicate so."

"Oh, yes, there are plenty of hints. Look." He thumbed through his script and showed her two passages where Mistress Dazzle speaks in an aside to the audience. "Here. And here, again."

"Hmm. I suppose you may be right."

His finger brushed her cheek as she leaned over his script to see the lines he was pointing out, and Vicki felt sensation sizzle through her breast and tingle all the way down to her toes.

"Thank you." He grinned at her, pleased to see that she could agree with him about something. "I really don't see why Mistress Proudheart should reject Lacklove's protestations of love," Ned continued his argument.

"Oh, but he is not seriously courting her. He is just trying to make a conquest of her, and win his wager with his friend, of course. My character sees through him."

"Really? I don't see it that way, Vic. It seems to me, once he's met the lady, he tries his hardest to lay his heart at her feet, but she won't believe him. She humiliates him over and over again. Poor fellow. I certainly would not continue courting a woman who rejected me time after time, and in such a cutting fashion, too."

"Would you not, my lord?"

"Never! And Proudheart is too cold and hard-hearted. I like my women to be soft and sweet and feminine," he said, glancing at her meaningfully.

Vicki met his eyes and stared stonily back, moving slightly away from him. Was he telling her she was none of those things he admired? she wondered, hurt.

Ned could not imagine what he had said to earn such a frown from Vicki when he had only been trying to compliment her. "I wonder how they come together in the end? Clem is teasing us by not letting us see the final scene yet. What surprises does she have in store, I wonder?"

"Oh, I think Proudheart will humble her arrogant, care-for-nothing suitor. He will come to *truly* value and love her. When he's proved himself, she will condescend to forgive him and a mutual love and trust will ensue that will make a marriage between them possible," Vicki asserted with conviction.

"Forgive him? Forgive him for what?"

"Oh, for being so careless, and taking her love for granted. For thinking that all he had to do was offer for her and she would jump at the chance. The conceited oaf! Such a proud, intelligent lady is not to be won so easily."

"Oh, you think that will be the way of it?"

"If I were to write the final scene, it would."

"Well, *I* think Mistress Proudheart's hard heart will be softened when she sees how she's made her suitor suffer, and how truly he loves her. She will search her heart and, realizing how unfairly she has treated him, she will throw off that proud, cold, unfeminine manner of hers. Finding that she truly *does* love him, she will agree to marry him. *And,* to make up for all her past cruelty, she will allow him to kiss her at the play's end. . . . Yes— the play will definitely end with a kiss. I think we should rehearse that part right now, don't you? It's sure to be the crowning touch in Clem's Valentine's play and we wouldn't want to let her down, now would we?"

"Oh! Will you be serious?"

"But I am being serious. Completely serious."

"I see you are determined to treat this in a light-hearted, careless fashion!"

"But, my dearest girl, why shouldn't l? *Lovers' Vows* is not some solemn, stiff Puritan production, with an improving moral text to bore us all witless. It's a light-hearted play, when all's said and done. We're meant to have fun doing it, you know. And I can't think of anything more enjoyable than kissing a pretty woman."

Ned stopped on the path, let his script drop to the ground and put his hands on Vicki's arms. He smiled down at her roguishly and began to lean his head toward hers.

"Oh! I suppose you think I will stand still for your mauling me right here in the middle of the garden where anyone might come along and see," she said in a temper, half-heartedly trying to shake off his strong hold on her arms.

"Ah, if that's all that worries you," he said, leering down at her, and gaining encouragement from the way she had phrased her protest. "I think we might be quite private if we move around this corner here."

He pulled her forward several steps around a bend in the path behind a large topiary elephant, and before she realized that he wasn't just teasing her, he pulled her into his arms, holding her against him so that they touched at all points from chest to knees.

"Let me go, Ned," she protested feebly, pressing back weakly with her hands against his chest. Her heart was hammering against her ribs and she felt the blood surge through her veins in an alarming rush.

"Just a brief rehearsal of our kiss, first. We want to work on the chemistry between our characters so that they'll be believable, don't we?" he asked, putting up one hand to push her bonnet off her head and holding her about her waist with the other. "I think it should be something like this," he whispered as he touched her lips in a soft butterfly of a kiss.

Vicki made a little sound in her throat, whether of protest or desire, she was incapable of knowing. The brief touch was not enough for her. She pressed her lips to his, involuntarily lifting her hand to caress the fine hairs at the nape of his neck.

Ned's whole body strained toward hers when he sensed her response. He had intended to tease her gently this time, but he quickly forgot his original intention and was soon lost to anything but the feel of her lips under his, her body leaning warmly against his. His lips opened over hers and he teased her closed mouth with his. My God, but she was sweet! he thought.

"Mmm. There, that wasn't so bad, was it?" he asked when he let her go at last, feeling distinctly bereft when she was no longer there against his body. "But I think it will need a little more work."

Lord, but he hoped Vicki wasn't aware of how much trouble he was having trying to catch his breath after that simple kiss. It had taken a superhuman effort to stop at a mere kiss, he thought, congratulating himself that he hadn't let his passion get the better of him under almost irresistible inducement. Kissing Vicki Colefax was all that he had been remembering for the past year, and more. She was all sweet, feminine curves and warm, desirable woman.

And eager and willing woman, too, kissing him back like that! He knew he wasn't mistaken. She had been warmly compliant in his arms, enjoying that kiss, he could swear it!

Was this the time and place to propose to her a second

time? he asked himself in some confusion. Should he go down on his knees now? he wondered, or would he just make a prize fool of himself if she rejected him again, and make the next few days when they would be doing this play together excruciatingly painful and embarrassing? He stood undecided.

Vicki was looking away from him, straightening her bonnet and tying it under her chin with shaking fingers. The glimpse he had of one of her cheeks showed him that it was glowing a bright red.

"I supposed you are satisfied with that performance, Lord Wexford?" she spat at him, "forcing yourself on me like that!"

"But I didn't! You know I didn't, Vic. You were enjoying it as much as I was," he protested, hurt.

"Oh, my acting was that good, was it? Well, in that case, you can see that we have that scene down to perfection. There is no need for any more 'rehearsals.'" With that she sailed off down the path, sending up little sprays of gravel under her shoes as she marched away, leaving him standing alone.

Ned scowled in frustration and addressed one of the mythical beasts towering over him. "What would you do to win fair lady, my fine fire-breathing friend?" he asked facetiously. "Would that slaying *you* would accomplish the task!" he exclaimed, swiping at the mute green dragon with his fisted hand.

"Oh, Margaret, I am so hoping that this year something will come of our children's proximity. My son is such a dolt! To let a prize like your Victoria slip through his fingers last year. Tsk. What's a mother to do with such a slowtop of a son?"

"Well, Lady Wexford, I do not think your son was entirely to blame for the engagement's being called off. It seems that much of the fault lies at the door of my foolish daughter. Though, in my opinion, she has regretted her hasty decision all year."

The marchioness reached over and patted Margaret Colefax's arm. "I think Ned has regretted it, too. And, Margaret, dear, do call me Barbara. We are such old friends that you mustn't stand on ceremony with me. And, who knows, if we get our heart's desire, we shall be joint grandmothers one of these days." Barbara Hadleigh, Marchioness of Wexford, laughed gently and looked around her daughter's fashionable drawing room where everyone was gathered for conversation and coffee after dinner.

A group of young people, including Richard and Elizabeth Hadleigh, Lady Jane, John Lindley, and George and Nigel Laponte, were standing in a cluster near the door, laughing and talking together. Lady Jane and Lindley stood somewhat apart, talking quietly to one another. The marchioness noticed how frequently Richard turned his eyes toward them.

"My niece, Elizabeth, seems to be in her element talking with those two handsome Laponte boys. She is to go up to London for her season soon, you know. I believe she is as excited and anxious as my twins are about being presented to the *ton*. However, they will have to wait for a year. . . . It looks to me as though young Lindley has taken a fancy to Jane," the marchioness pointed out to Margaret.

"Yes, it looks that way, doesn't it?" Margaret agreed. "He quite doted on her at dinner, I noticed."

"My nephew Richard looks somewhat irritated by that state of affairs," Barbara mentioned.

"Do you think so?" Margaret asked, not at all sure she could read as much into the situation as the marchioness seemed inclined to do.

"Perhaps I'm wrong. I *do* like to watch people and wonder what they are thinking, though. My children are always chiding me for it. . . ." The marchioness gazed hopefully across the room to where her son was approaching Vicki Colefax. However, Vicki turned her shoulder on Ned and walked away to speak to Nigel Laponte. Ned looked after her with a frown on his face. He was immediately joined by a smiling, simpering Arabella Rutledge. The young widow swiftly coaxed a smile to his face his mother saw with vexation, and soon they appeared to be deep in a flirtation, if the amount of light laughter and eye play on Arabella's part was anything to go by. The marchioness's lips tightened with annoyance.

"Mama, just look at that shrewish Arabella playing up to Neddy like that!" Delia exclaimed in an undertone as she came up to her mother. Her twin, Cynthia, stood right behind her. "This will never do. It upsets all our plans."

The marchioness listened in astonishment to her daughter's bold declaration.

"Don't worry, Mama. Cyn and I will soon put a stop to it," Delia declared, marching off to her brother's side, Cynthia going with her.

"No, Delia dear, I don't think—," the marchioness began, putting out her hand to stop her impetuous daughter, but both twins were quickly out of her reach.

"You know the plan, Del. You talk to Arabella, while

I distract Neddy," Cynthia whispered to her sister as they approached the pair.

"Right," Delia answered, a determined glint showing in her eyes.

"Why, Mrs. Rutledge, is that a wine stain upon your beautiful silk gown?" Delia asked sweetly, ruthlessly interrupting the conversation between Arabella and her brother.

"Oh, no! A stain on my best silk gown?" Arabella exclaimed, turning to look down at her gown. "Where?"

"There. Down near the hem. You had better go to your room and have your maid work on it right away. You know that the stain will set, if you don't deal with it straightaway."

"I don't see anything, Delia." Arabella, still looking down, sounded puzzled.

"Why, I didn't know you were shortsighted," Delia said cunningly, hiding her smile behind her hand. "I'll go with you and point out the mark to your maid." She grasped the other woman by the elbow and began to lead her from the room.

"Neddy, Delia and I need new gowns for the spring," Cynthia said, taking hold of her brother's arm and pulling him away from where Arabella stood speaking with Delia.

"What! You've only just had several new gowns for Christmas. Surely they will last through the spring."

"Oh, Neddy, what a typical man you are!" Cynthia put her hands on her hips and almost stamped her foot.

"Why, I should hope so," he replied humorously.

"Those were winter gowns. They were lovely, especially the red velvet for me and the green velvet for Delia at Christmas. But we need something light and bright for spring, sprigged muslins and such. Besides, we've grown since Mama called in the dressmaker last autumn."

"Grown? I don't notice that you and Delia are any taller, Cyn. You two have come up to my shoulder for the past two years and you still do," he said, measuring her head against his shoulder.

"Not taller, Ned," she said in exasperation. "Fuller. You know," she said, looking down at her chest. "Our winter things are too tight."

"Oh," he said, reddening. "Well, perhaps you're right," he admitted in a distracted way. "I will discuss it with Mama."

Blast the twins! he thought. They were always putting him in uncomfortable situations. And speaking of uncomfortable situations, the last thing he had wanted to do that evening was to engage in a flirtatious *tête-à-tête* with Arabella. He wanted to get on with his romantic courtship of Vicki.

He felt he had made a good start that afternoon in the garden, despite the way she had run away in embarrassment leaving him frustrated. Now he needed to insinuate himself in her good graces so that he could persuade her to resume their engagement. But where had Arabella disappeared to, anyway? he wondered, looking all around.

Seeing Vicki speaking with a group of young people, he quickly took the opportunity to step to Vicki's side.

As Ned reached the group, Richard was just moving away with Jane, to look at some music books that lay on the pianoforte. The instrument sat in a darkened corner of the large room, with only a single candlestick on a nearby table for illumination.

"Well, Jane, you seem to have made a conquest in

young Lindley," Richard said in a tight voice as Jane leaned over the piano to glance through some music.

She straightened up with a start. "Who? I? No, no, you are mistaken, Mr. Hadleigh. Why, Mr. Lindley and I have only become reacquainted today in a friendly way."

"I believe he's smitten with you already though, and who could blame him?" Richard sighed dramatically and raised Jane's hand to his lips for a quick, clandestine kiss. "And you are to call me, Richard, remember?"

"Oh!" She pulled her hand away and hid it behind her back. "Why did you do that?"

He gave her a crooked grin. "Temptation. You present an insurmountable temptation to me, you know, looking all flushed and lovely over here out of sight of the rest of the room."

To his surprise, Jane laughed. "Oh, you are teasing me, aren't you?"

His blue eyes crinkled at the corners. "Yes, my dear child, I am teasing you—in a way. But, believe me, when I tell you that you are truly lovely. Many men will tell you so, I'm sure, when you go to town for your presentation. So, be on your guard, my dear, against hardened flirts and fortune hunters."

"Oh, Richard. It—, it's kind of you to say these things to me, but I must tell you that I'm past the age when I would make a come-out."

At his disbelieving look, she smiled and continued, "I am one-and-twenty now. Though Charles and Clementina were all set to take their family to London and oversee my presentation two or three years ago, I finally persuaded them that I could not go through with it. It would have been exquisite torture for me to put myself on the

Marriage Market. I—, I am too shy, you see, and am happy to go on just as I am."

"You astound me, Jane. Not to enjoy a come-out? Why, I thought it was the ultimate dream of every young female. I know my sister has spoken of nothing else for the past twelvemonth and my cousins cannot wait until they are presented next year."

"Yes. I know. They are all three quite high-spirited girls, and not at all shy like me, you see."

"Yes . . . but I would have thought you would want your own home, a family," he continued quietly, surprised by the girl's words. She was so purely innocent and completely lovely, she took his breath away.

"Well, but by not going to town, I don't think I've precluded that, have I?" she asked, looking up at him with her heavily fringed hazel eyes opened wide.

Richard, a careless, play-happy, man-about-town, was lost.

"How goes it, my dear?" the earl asked Clementina when she joined him in his library where he had gone for a brief nightcap after all their guests had retired to bed.

"Oh, Chas, I don't know what to make of the situation," Clementina confessed, casting herself against her husband's chest and looking up into his very blue eyes. "Neddy is trying his hardest, I can see, to make it up with Vicki, but she is not cooperating. She turned her back on him three times tonight. I counted. And then finding himself at loose ends, Ned allows himself to be distracted by Arabella Rutledge. Oh dear! Why ever did I invite her?"

"Because you have *always* invited the young people

in the neighborhood to your productions, my dearest Tina. And because you don't want to offend the Lindleys, of course. They have always been good neighbors."

"Oh, you are right, as usual," she complained, beating him lightly on the chest with her fisted hand. Then she smiled up at him and planted a light kiss at the corner of his well-shaped mouth.

"Shall I pour you a drop of brandy, my love?"

"Yes, please do, dearest. I shall never get to sleep else, thinking of all I have to accomplish in the next few days."

He quirked a brow at her and gave her a lopsided smile as he handed her a crystal snifter with an inch of brandy shifting like molten gold in the bottom. "Oh? I think I might be able to help you there, Tina, my love. I have an idea of how to distract you from your problems for an hour or so. And afterward perhaps you might feel a bit more relaxed and sleepy."

Clementina flushed and turned her beautiful profile away from her husband. "You have always delighted in teasing me most shamelessly, my Lord Sutcliffe. I refuse to let you put me out of countenance after all these years."

He laughed and she turned to glare at him. "If only you could see your own face right now, my love, you would know that your beautiful countenance is most certainly, er, 'out.' "

"Oh, you can do nothing but joke when I want to be serious. Ned's future happiness depends on what happens in the next few days," she said just as a strong hand removed the glass from her fingers, and Charles pulled her into a firm embrace.

"If it's serious you want, my love—," the earl whispered just before his lips came down to capture hers.

After a satisfying interval, Clem raised her head and

said, "Mmm. Your kisses always were able to turn me
inside out." She sighed. "You still have that same magic
touch after all these years."

He laughed softly. "You gratify me exceedingly, my
love." He kissed her briefly once more. "And how is the
play coming along? What plans have you made for the
rest of your cast of characters, I wonder?" Charles asked,
moving with her to one of the deep, soft chairs that faced
his desk, where he sat down and settled her on his lap.

"Well . . . you know that we've worried and worried
about Jane," she began. When his only answer was a
grunt, she continued, "Richard seems most interested.
Although his parents and sister have come to us in the
past few years, Richard has always made some excuse
to avoid my house parties. I suppose he felt they would
be too dull for a top-of-the-trees young man like him."

"That, or he's heard of your fearsome reputation as a
matchmaker and has taken good care to stay out of your
reach."

"Oh, Chas! You know I only try to pair people off for
their own good."

She could feel his chest shaking with laughter where
she lay against him but his lips only twitched as he replied, "Precisely, my love."

"Humph! Perhaps I should just keep you in the dark
about this, then."

He tweaked one of her ebony curls. "Not if it concerns
my only sister."

Clementina kissed him on one cheek and confided
her suspicions about how there was an attraction between his sister and her cousin. A mild argument ensued over whether Clementina should take any hand in
the affair.

* * *

Ned went to bed frustrated. He had looked forward to the evening with enthusiastic high spirits, determined to get on with his wooing. But he had not sat with Vicki at dinner. She had wedged herself between his Uncle Henry and Richard, and he had found himself seated next to Arabella, who, along with her brother and the Lapontes, was to stay over for the next few days until after the play.

When he had tried to draw Vicki apart from the others in Clem's drawing room after Arabella had disappeared, she had resisted his efforts and stayed firmly planted, chatting to several of the other young people in the room.

He was especially annoyed that she seemed to spend a lot of time with, and use up a lot of smiles on, Nigel Laponte. Nigel was a big, handsome neighbor of Clem's who, with his brother George, lived on a bordering estate where they were putting into action all sorts of modern agricultural ideas. Actually, Ned had wanted to sound out the Lapontes about the success of their methods, thinking that he might try some of their more effective innovations at Wexford Hall, but he didn't have the chance that night. He had spent his time glowering at Laponte, jealously standing guard over Vicki.

She was not indifferent to his person, he knew from their interlude in the garden. But *something* made her resist him. Why was she trying to avoid him at every turn? If she truly wanted nothing further to do with him, she would not have come here, would she? He decided he would just have to redouble his efforts to overcome her mysterious resistance.

Vicki, too, had a restless night. She had been feeling too flustered after the marquess's behavior in the topiary

garden to encourage him when he first came downstairs
before dinner. Then once the meal was ended and they
were all gathered in the Sutcliffes' large, formal drawing
room, she had felt too unsettled, too unsure of his intentions, to stay alone in his company. She had sought safety
in numbers.

However, out of the corner of her eye, she had taken
note of how he laughed and flirted with the widow. The
way the two dark heads had leaned toward one another,
the way Ned had responded to Arabella coquetting, the
way he had smiled at the beautiful widow—smiling that
special smile that was enough to melt Vicki's bones.

Yes, she thought jealously, despite their interlude in
the garden—even after that heartstopping kiss—he was
still susceptible to other attractive women. He must have
been toying with her that afternoon. Oh, she was furious
with him for eliciting that response from her when she
was trying so hard to fall out of love with him! And her
very enthusiastic participation in that kiss must have
done wonders to soothe his wounded masculine pride at
her rejection last year.

She beat one fist against her pillow in frustration at
her inability to resist him. If only he had felt some measure of what she had when he kissed her, then she would
have some hope that he would one day come to care for
her, that a marriage between them would be possible. *If*
he planned to renew his addresses. But she would not
allow herself to hope. That way lay the possibility of too
much pain.

She didn't trust him. Or, more to the point, she didn't
trust herself. If she allowed him to flirt with her and kiss
her and lead her on, she was afraid she would be as
deeply in love with him as ever. He might hurt her even

more than she was already hurt. She dared not give him a chance to do that. No. She must protect herself and continue to reject his efforts at friendship or flirtation or revenge . . . or whatever it was he was trying to achieve.

"Well! You two have certainly put something fiery into your characters," Clementina exclaimed to Vicki and Ned as she drew them apart from her other players. They had just reached the end of scene four on their second day of rehearsals. She looked displeased. "However I question whether it's the 'fire' that's needed to make them come alive," she chided them.

"I seem to recall that that's just what you ordered us to do, Clem. Why are you angry that we've obeyed you?" Ned asked in a puzzled voice.

"I want plausible renditions, yes, but I don't want you to sneer at one another, as though you hate each other. Your characters are attracted to one another. They try to hide that fact in witty banter, but some of the attraction must show through. You are both intelligent adults. Surely, you two can bring that off . . . It's some consolation, at least, that you both seem to have memorized your lines in such a short time," she added, looking at them expectantly.

Vicki felt like a schoolgirl again, being taken to task for her faults by her governess, then offered a crumb of praise. She knew that she had behaved badly, but she still hadn't forgiven Ned for his behavior in the garden the day before, for making her lose control, and more importantly, for his blatant flirtation with Arabella last evening. Despite her resolutions of the previous night not to let him affect her, when he was there before her, looking so darkly hand-

some and solidly *real*—and so utterly beyond her reach—
she couldn't *help* but be affected.

"I—, I'm sorry, Clementina," she faltered, with a
quick apologetic glance at Ned. "I shall try to do better."

Ned was smiling at Vicki encouragingly. "Me, too,
Clem. Come, let us cry friends again, Vic." He held out
his hand to her and she put hers in it.

Clementina gave them an approving smile. "Good. I
trust I can count on you to do better next time. Remember, you have the leads—the success of my play depends
on your performances. Now we must all adjourn upstairs
where I have the costumes laid out. Wait until you see
yours, Vicki. I think it will suit you admirably." She
turned quickly, clapped her hands and asked the others
to follow her.

Ned detained Vicki for a moment. "I'm sorry for
whatever I've done to upset you, Vic. Believe me, I had
no such intention." He continued to hold her hand with
one of his while he ran his other impatiently through his
hair, then he grinned at her engagingly.

"Yes, well, I'm sure we can bring off this play of your
sister's without being at one another's throats the whole
time," she allowed grudgingly, not daring to meet his eyes.

"Being at your throat is the last thing I want, Vic,"
he said with an appealing look. He was still holding her
hand, rubbing his thumb back and forth across her
knuckles, his dark eyes gazing intently into hers. Vicki
was growing more uncomfortable by the second as he
stood there looking at her while the others were filing
out of the room.

"Are you coming, my lord?" Arabella called over her
shoulder from the doorway.

"You go with the others, Bella," he answered. "Vicki and I will be along in a minute."

Arabella swished out of the room, clearly displeased.

"Friends?" Ned asked, his dark eyes holding a question Vicki couldn't read.

"Yes, friends," she agreed, smiling at him naturally for the first time since she'd arrived at Sutcliffe Manor.

He smiled back, causing her heart to do a somersault, then dropped her hand and turned to formally offer his arm. "Miss Colefax, allow me."

Vicki accepted his offer of escort and they followed the others upstairs, each in better humor with the other, each a little more hopeful that things could be worked out between them.

When they reached the second floor, they found that Clementina had the gentlemen's costumes laid out in one room and the ladies' garments in another. The costumes had been made up in gorgeous silks and satins, embellished with colorful silk embroidery, rows of satin ribbons and bows, lace frills, flounces, pleats, and other fine decorative trim. To make up all the costumes for her play, the countess had employed a talented dressmaker who had copied patterns from designs that had been popular some century or more ago.

For the gentlemen, there were knee-length, collarless coats (collarless to accommodate their full wigs) in rich jewel tones of red and blue and green and gold satin with flared skirts that were to be buttoned only at the waist. Some of the coats were decorated with gold frogging, some with passementerie along the cuffs, the pocket flaps and the front buttoned edges.

The deep cuffs that turned up and buttoned back through intricately worked buttonholes were to be worn over rather full white lawn shirts topped by brocaded waistcoats that were elaborately patterned all over with light-catching gold and silver threads or colorful silk embroidery. The gentlemen were to wear narrow satin knee breeches and white silk cravats tied round their necks. On their feet, they were to wear white silk stockings and heeled leather shoes with turned-down tongues and small buckles.

Slim walking canes or swordsticks and long lace-edged handkerchiefs worn halfway up one's sleeve were provided as props for the men. Clementina had omitted the gold braid-trimmed black felt tricorne hats that had been popular at the time because she didn't want her actors' faces obscured from the audience.

But the gentlemen *were* to wear full wigs over their hair. Several of the men groaned in protest when they saw the long, curled hairpieces that would surely make their heads overly warm. The countess was deaf to their complaints. She assured them that they could suffer the discomfort for a brief hour in the name of artistic accuracy.

George Laponte's costume was the most elaborate of all. The easy-going, no-nonsense George was to play Sir Foppishly Nethersby, an overdressed and painted fop. His costume was to reflect his character, and Clementina had had great fun consulting with the dressmaker about designing something excessively over-decorated. They had decided on pale blue satin for his coat and breeches, with falls of white lace that dangled from his coat sleeves to the ground and large pink and white bows to tie his breeches at the knee. Then they had proceeded to ice him like a cake, with piping, rosettes, leaves, and bows in various colors distributed over his costume.

Poor George closed his eyes in disbelief when he saw

the outrageous outfit. And he protested in vain about the pair of bright red, bejeweled high-heeled shoes he was to wear, and about the pale blue and pink bows attached to his wig. Clementina had had to take him aside and assure him that it was all in the name of good fun, reminding him that he would be on stage for but a brief ten minutes.

Clementina did not mention to him that she had definite ideas about how his face was to be painted, as well. She would save that surprise for the evening of the play when she planned to apply his make-up herself.

The ladies "ohhed" and "ahhed" with delight when they saw their elaborately detailed gowns made up in pastel shades of satin with low, square necklines, edged with lace frills. The moderately full skirts of the gowns were looped up at the sides to show the elegant underskirt, while the bodice that laced down the back, over which was fitted a separate panel, richly decorated with graduated rows of ribbons. The bodice itself fitted quite tightly down to the waist, and its three-quarter length sleeves ended in long falls of lace. A profusion of lace, bows, ribbons, flowers, pleats, and flounces served as decorative trim on the gowns. Collarettes of ribbons and lace had been provided for the women to wear around their necks.

On their feet they were to wear embroidered velvet shoes with high, curving heels, jeweled buckles, and pointed toes. The ladies were luckier than the men with their headpieces. Only those who were to play highborn ladies were to wear tall headdresses of looped ribbon and lace.

The essential props for the ladies were richly constructed and decorated folding fans.

The fan Vicki was to use was made of delicate ivory sticks with richly painted vellum stretched over them. Before Vicki could even try on her costume, Clementina came up to her and had great fun giving her a lesson in the art of using the fan. The countess demonstrated just a few of the bewildering variety of positions in which the fan could be held. Vicki was not sure if she would remember all the things her hostess had tried to teach her.

While Clementina explained the art of the fan to Vicki, there was much delighted laughter all round them as the other girls tried on their beautiful costumes. When Vicki was finally free to try on her gown of shimmering pale green satin that opened over an underskirt of palest yellow, she found that the low, square-cut neckline of the bodice was even more daring than the current fashion for plunging necklines. The tips of her breasts were barely covered by the lace frill edging the neck. She tried to protest to Clementina, but the countess only laughed and assured her that lace edging would hide everything and that there was no time in the play when she had to stoop down so that her décolletage would be exposed.

"Well, but, when I look down at myself I am quite embarrassed."

"Oh, but no one else has your vantage point, my dear Vicki. You look quite, quite perfect," Clementina said with her typical insouciance before she laughed gaily and sailed away to inspect the gentlemen, leaving one of her abigails to assist the girls.

All those playing servants were to wear simple costumes of cream-colored homespun, tied with brown sashes. But when Delia and Cynthia had tried on the costumes Clementina had provided for them, they were not satisfied. After a whispered conversation, they de-

cided it would be simple to introduce some subtle altera-
tions that would make their waiting women's costumes
more alluring. They giggled together, knowing that their
mother and Clem would stare when they realized what
they had done.

Cynthia and Delia had another plan to put into opera-
tion that morning. Seeing that Arabella had monopolized
the attention of the abigail and that she was already
dressed in her costume of pale lavender over a darker
purple underskirt and was preparing to leave the room,
the twins had no doubt of her destination. She was determined to find their brother. Delia was delegated to
stop her.

Meanwhile, Cynthia noted that the abigail was helping
Jane adjust her gown and that Vicki was standing at one
side of the small room, frowning and pulling at the material of her bodice. Cynthia went up to her and offered to
help her adjust the various bits and pieces of her costume.

"Here, Vicki, it's too cramped in here to fit your costume just right. I can't think why Clem chose this room.
Why don't you come across to my room? There's a full-
length pier glass between the windows where you can
see yourself to better advantage," Cynthia told her.

"Well, I suppose that would be a help," Vicki admitted.
She had already begun to take off the costume, even
before she had tried it on properly. The low bodice worried her. She felt too exposed. But she supposed that she
should make sure it fit properly now, if she were to wear
it for the play. "Thank you, Cynthia."

Perhaps she would strategically add a bit more lace,
Vicki thought on a relieved note as she followed Cynthia
from the room, clutching the partially unlaced bodice to

herself with one hand and carrying other bits and pieces of her costume in the other.

"Oh, I thought your room was just across the hall," Vicki exclaimed as Cynthia began to lead her down the long passageway. "I can't go out like this," she added in a whisper, referring to her state of dishabille. "One of the gentlemen might see."

"No, no. They are all quite safely engaged in fitting their own costumes. You know how vain men are. They will primp and preen for an hour. Come on, Vicki. Hurry. My room is just around this corner," Cynthia said, smothering her laughter as she hurried along, leading to a room quite some distance from where they had been trying on costumes.

"Oh, we've forgotten your headpiece," Cynthia cried when they reached her room. "I'll just go back and fetch it," the girl said, whisking herself out the door.

"What? No, I don't think I need my headpiece now, Cynth—," Vicki began, but the girl was gone.

Meanwhile Delia had followed Arabella and intercepted her as she prepared to knock on the door to the gentlemen's dressing room.

"Oh, Arabella, that costume certainly compliments your figure. And the lavender brings out the color of your eyes and hair. I wish Cyn and I could wear gowns like that instead of these horrible servants' smocks."

"Why, thank you, Delia," Arabella said, preening herself. "But these gowns are not for children, you know. I'm sure when you've grown up, you will be allowed to wear such things, if you appear in one of your elder sister's plays."

Delia considered herself quite grown up already, but bit back a sharp retort to ask innocently, "What in heaven's name is that black smudge on your cheek? It quite mars your complexion, you know."

Arabella's hand flew to her cheek. "Oh, dear," she cried, picking up the heavy skirt of her costume with one hand and rushing back to the ladies' changing room.

Delia snickered into her hand as Arabella rushed away, then knocked on the door where the gentlemen were donning their costumes.

Her cousin Richard stuck his head out the door, "Hello, Del. Come to ogle the men, have you?"

"Certainly not! I wish to speak to Ned, if he's decent yet."

Richard laughed at her and went to check. Soon Ned's head appeared around the door. When he saw his sister, he frowned and walked out into the hallway, shutting the door firmly behind himself.

"I see I'm going to have to speak to you about modest behavior, Delia," he began to ring a peal over her head. "What do you think you're doing, coming along to the gentlemen's dressing room?"

"Oh, not now, Ned. No need to cut up stiff over such a trifle. I wanted to see how you looked in your costume. I wasn't going to come *in* to ogle the gentlemen, you know. There's no one in there I fanc—, er, I must say, you *do* look magnificent."

"Delia—" he began.

His sister walked all around him, observing him from every angle as he stood there in his red satin coat and breeches with the gold and black braid trim. "You look magnificent, Neddy. It suits you even better than your officer's uniform, I believe. But I don't think you've got that coat on properly. Surely it buttons one buttonhole lower. And, tsk, your cravat is askew. It seems to be tied

under your left ear." She giggled. "Come along to my
room. There's a looking glass there tall enough to en-
compass all of you." Delia gestured at his height and
giggled again. "There's such a lot of you to see. You can
make the adjustments to your costume more easily if you
can view yourself from head to toe."

"I daresay you're right, for once, little sister. Lead on,
Delia," Ned said, with no suspicion of her suddenly so-
licitous concern as he followed her down the long, winding hallway. "But I want you to behave yourself in
future."

"Oh, I've forgotten something, Ned. I'll be right back
to help you," Delia said as Ned stepped through into the
room. She closed the door behind him with a snap.

"Ned! What are you doing here?" Vicki turned around
at the sound of the door closing and clutched her open
bodice more tightly to her chest.

"I didn't know you were in here, Vic. Delia brought
me here. It's her room and I was just going to make a
few adjustments to, er, ahem, as I see you're dressing in
here, I'll just go back—"

"Delia's room? But I thought it was Cynthia's room?"
Vicki said in puzzlement as Ned tried the doorhandle to
find it wouldn't budge. He yanked harder.

"Locked! Bloody hell! Just wait until I get my hands
on those blasted twins!"

"What's the matter? Won't the door open?"

"No, it won't. It seems my devious little sisters have
decided to play a plaguey trick on us, my dear. They've
hoaxed us and locked us in here together for some mad
reason or other. I swear, there must be a hidden streak
of insanity in our family that Papa never told me about!"
Ned cursed under his breath. "Just wait until I get out

of here," he expostulated, yanking harder on the door handle. "I'll put those two mad-brained chits on gruel and water! They'll wear sackcloth for the next year! I'll cancel their seasons!"

"Well, you don't have to behave as though you fear being *compromised*, Lord Wexford, if we spend a few moments alone together in this room until someone comes along and lets us out," Vicki said, thrusting her chin up challengingly.

"Wha—?" Ned turned to look at her as she stood clutching the unlaced satin bodice to her chest. Then he grinned.

"Why, my dear Victoria, I've never seen you looking so, so, delectable," he said, with a wicked gleam in his eye. "That pale green is just your color. It brings out the lights in those magnificent eyes of yours. Umm, perhaps I should reward Delia and Cynthia for this mad stunt, rather than punish them."

Seeing the dangerous glint in his dark eyes, Vicki swallowed awkwardly and wished she could call back her hasty words.

"I see you need some assistance in getting into your gown," he said, advancing on her purposefully.

"No! Don't you come near me, Ned Hadleigh," Vicki said, backing up until she hit the large oak wardrobe.

Ned put his head on one side and regarded her with laughter in his eyes. "You know whoever comes to let us out is going to assume the worst unless you let me help you lace up that gown, Vic."

Her eyes were huge in her pale face. She licked her dry lips, seeing the logic of his words. "I suppose you will be highly gratified to know that I agree with you."

"No. I will just think what I've always thought. You're

an intelligent woman, one of the most intelligent I've ever known. Of course you can see the logic when it's pointed out to you."

"When it's pointed out to me!" she repeated on a spurt of anger. "Ned Hadleigh you are the most arrogant, the most conceited—"

"I know, I know, the most oafish, top-lofty non-gentleman you've ever known. Turn around, Vic, and present me with your back." His hands were on her shoulders and he was turning her around before she could protest further.

"Oh!" she said, stamping her foot as she felt his fingers at her nape, gently lifting her hair so that he could begin tying the laces that fastened the bodice of her gown. "This is intolerable!" she uttered from between clenched teeth as she held the skirt in place while he worked.

"I agree." He had worked quickly and was halfway down her back.

"What!"

"Intolerable that I should be fastening you up. It goes sorely against the grain to be acting as your ladies' maid. I would much rather be unfastening these ties, you know. . . . There! The last one. You look wonderful, by the way, but what a nuisance ladies' garments are with all these infernal bows and ties and strings!"

Vicki was so upset, she was on the point of tears. The situation was entirely beyond her control. She stifled a sob.

"What's this, my sweet?" Ned asked, feeling her shoulders trembling. He put his long, slim hands up to her neck and began to gently stroke her neck and shoulders, trying to soothe her agitation. "Do not upset yourself, my dear. Nothing will come of this, if you don't want it to," he said quietly, bending to kiss the top of her head.

She leaned back against his comfortable warmth and sighed imperceptibly. "No. I didn't really suppose it would."

Ned continued to hold her and soothe her, running his hands over her neck and arms and cradling her back against himself. "You are so very lovely," he whispered. And he buried his mouth in her hair when Vicki sagged back against him and allowed his hands to encircle her waist. "I can't resist you." Then he began a slow circling movement up her sides and down again. He moved his hands to her neck once more, allowing his fingertips to trail gently down the front of her neck to feather along the lace edging at the top of her bodice, while his mouth moved from her hair to the back of her neck, his heated breath brushing the fine hairs at her nape as he nuzzled her there. "So lovely, so sweet," he murmured huskily against her skin.

Vicki turned suddenly and was in his arms. His mouth came down to cover hers in a hungry kiss and they were lost to the world.

"You know Clem and Mama, too, want Vicki and Ned to get back together," Cynthia said in an undertone to her twin as they stood whispering together outside Delia's bedroom door. "We're just helping along Clem's scheme, you know, Del."

"Well, I must admit, it is a masterful plan, Cyn," Delia confirmed in a low voice. "We shall leave them locked in together for an hour and see what happens."

"I shall peek in the keyhole and tell you what's going

on," Cynthia said, silently removing the key and gluing her eye to the small keyhole.

"No, you won't. I want to see," Delia insisted, pulling on her twin's shoulder.

"Shh. They're kissing," Cynthia giggled.

Ned lifted his head when he heard the suppressed giggle at the door. "Blast it all to hell," he muttered under his breath, not wanting to release his hold on Vicki, but realizing that they were under observation. "I'm sorry, Vic," he whispered, lifting his hands from her waist to rest them along her jaw while he caressed her face with his thumbs, "but, if I'm not mistaken, my blasted little sisters are watching us through the keyhole in that door."

"Oh," she murmured, looking up at him out of passion-glazed eyes, not comprehending what he was saying. "Oh!" she exclaimed more strongly as the meaning of his words penetrated her dazed brain. Her hands came up to grasp his wrists and push him away.

Ned gave her a quick kiss on the lips, then turned and strode to the door. "Girls," he commanded in a low, ominous voice, "open this door at once! If you do so immediately, your punishment will be light. If you delay, I will speak to Mama about postponing your season next year. You two will most definitely *not* be going to London until you can show more modesty and mature judgment. Do you hear me?" His voice rose to a roar. "I know you're out there!"

He trod on something sharp, looked down at his feet, and saw that the key had been slipped under the door. He picked it up, fitted it in the lock and turned it in one smooth movement, but when he wrenched open the door, there was no one in sight.

* * *

As he put the finishing touches to his costume, Richard heard gales of laughter coming from the hallway. That peculiar sound could only come from his madcap sister, he knew. He stepped out into the hallway to see what had amused Elizabeth so violently, and saw that she was laughing at George Laponte. George had drawn the short straw when the minor parts were assigned and was to play Sir Foppishly Nethersby.

"Oh, Dickon, come and look at George!" she cried when she spotted him.

"I've seen him already, Lily," he said, but she was already pointing out the absurdities of George's costume to him.

"Just look at the blue and pink bows in his wig, Dick! Oh, I've never seen anything so funny!" She laughed again, until the tears were streaming down her cheeks.

"I'm glad I'm providing you with so much amusement, Miss Hadleigh. If I had known what Lady Clementina had in mind when I agreed to do her play, I believe I would have suddenly recollected that I had business in London," George said good-humoredly.

"And those sh—shoes," Elizabeth said on a laugh, pointing to the high-heeled red shoes on his feet.

"Yes, you may well laugh. They are absurd. I only hope I don't break my leg, tottering along on these heels."

Richard patted him on the shoulder. "Never fear, old fellow. You will earn Clem's undying gratitude for allowing yourself to be made a fool of. She's had me dressed as a clown, a jester, a village idiot, and a madman in her little theatrical productions 'ere now. Beware what she tries to make you do next time!"

"You've given me fair warning, Hadleigh. I *know* I shall have business in London next year," he said, looking pointedly at Elizabeth.

Elizabeth was looking quite pleased with herself, dressed as she was as the naughty Mistress Hornsby in a scarlet and green costume that contrasted strongly with the other ladies' pale satins. She hooked her arm through George's and said, "Come on, Sir Foppishly, I shall support you so that you won't fall. Clem wants to see you."

Elizabeth carried him off to the room assigned to the dressmaker where the countess was working with the seamstress on some last minute adjustments to the various costumes.

"Where are you two off to in such a hurry?" Richard called to his young cousins, Delia and Cynthia, as they sped past him. One dark brow arched in amusement. "They've been up to mischief, without a doubt," he murmured. Seeing that Jane was standing a few feet away down the hall talking with Lindley, he strolled over to join them.

"Ah, Jane. How well you look as Mistress Pontefract! Do you not agree, Lindley?" Richard asked.

"Yes, indeed. She looks wonderful, as I've been telling her. And you, Mr. Hadleigh, look right in your element as an eighteenth-century rake," John answered. He was dressed in simple livery for he was to play Waitley, Lacklove's servant.

"Ah, I don't believe my character, Tender, is meant to be such a care-for-nothing gentleman as his friend Lacklove. But, be that as it may, I'm sure Tender is rewarded beyond his just deserts when Mistress Pontefract agrees to walk with him," Richard said, bowing formally in Jane's direction.

Jane blushed and thanked the gentlemen for their compliments. She was feeling quite pleased with the appearance she made. The peach-colored satin gown opened over a pale cream satin underskirt that was tied back with blue ribbons. The gown was edged with blue piping and there were horizontal rows of blue ribbon attached to the stomacher over the bodice from its low, square neckline to its tight waist. A lace frill edged the top of her bodice and there was a long fall of lace at her sleeves.

"I believe this vivid blue suits you, Richard," she said, admiring how handsome he looked in his bright blue satin coat and breeches, with the silver embroidery along the sleeves and frogged buttonholes. Then, remembering her other companion, she turned to John Lindley. "Perhaps next year you will play one of the heroes and wear an elaborate outfit, Mr. Lindley. I'm sure you would look well in such a costume."

"Thank you. You are most kind, Lady Jane," John said. "You must not think I am dissatisfied with this servant's livery, though. I am quite content to play a small part."

"Yes. So am I," Jane said, smiling warmly at the young man. "I should die, if I had to play the heroine and remember all those lines!"

Richard's lips tightened at the confidentiality that seemed to exist between the pair.

"Where are you off to, Ned?" Richard asked as the marquess strode past with a murderous look on his face.

Ned stopped briefly. "The twins?"

"Making for the stairs, two minutes ago," Richard answered with a grin as his cousin dashed off, taking the stairs two at a time.

"Oh, my! I'm afraid Delia and Cynthia have done something to put the marquess in a miff," Jane said, rais-

TAKE ADVANTAGE OF THIS SPECIAL OFFER,
AVAILABLE *ONLY* TO
ZEBRA REGENCY ROMANCE READERS.

You are a reader who enjoys the very special kind of love story that can only be found in Zebra Regency Romances. You adore the fashionable English settings, the sparkling wit, the captivating intrigue, and the heart-stirring romance that are the hallmarks of each Zebra Regency Romance novel.

Now, you can have these delightful novels delivered right to your door each month and never have to worry about missing a new book. Zebra has made arrangements through its Home Subscription Service for you to preview the three latest Zebra Regency Romances as soon as they are published.

3 **FREE** REGENCIES TO GET STARTED!

To get your subscription started, we will send your first 3 books ABSOLUTELY FREE, as our introductory gift to you. NO OBLIGATION. We're sure that you will enjoy these books so much that you will want to read more of the very best romantic fiction published today.

SUBSCRIBERS SAVE EACH MONTH

Zebra Regency Home Subscribers will save money each month as they enjoy their latest Regencies. As a subscriber you will receive the 3 newest titles to preview FREE for ten days. Each shipment will be at least a $11.97 value (publisher's price). But home subscribers will be billed only $9.90 for all three books. You'll save over $2.00 each month. Of course, if you're not satisfied with any book, just return it for full credit.

CONVENIENT HOME DELIVERY

Zebra Home Subscribers get the convenience of home delivery, with only $1.50 shipping and handling charge added to each shipment. What's more, there is no minimum number to buy and you can cancel your subscription at any time. No obligation and no questions asked.

TO GET YOUR 3 FREE BOOKS
FILL OUT AND MAIL THE COUPON BELOW

3 FREE BOOKS

Mail to: Zebra Regency Home Subscription Service
120 Brighton Road
P.O. Box 5214
Clifton, New Jersey 07015-5214

YES! Start my Regency Romance Home Subscription and send me my 3 FREE BOOKS as my introductory gift. Then each month, I'll receive the 3 newest Zebra Regency Romances to preview FREE for ten days. I understand that if I'm not satisfied, I may return them and owe nothing. Otherwise, I'll pay the low members' price of just $9.90 for all 3 books and save over $2.00 off the publisher's price (a $11.97 value). A $1.50 postage and handling charge is added to each shipment. I may cancel my subscription at any time and there is no minimum number to buy. In any case, the 3 FREE books are mine to keep regardless of what I decide.

NAME _____

ADDRESS _____ APT NO. _____

CITY _____ STATE _____ ZIP _____

TELEPHONE (____) _____

SIGNATURE _____
(if under 18 parent or guardian must sign)

RG1694

Terms and prices subject to change. Orders subject to acceptance by Zebra Home Subscription Service, Inc.

GET
3 FREE
REGENCY
ROMANCE
NOVELS—
A $11.97
VALUE!

ing one delicate hand to her cheek. "I should be in a quake if he approached me with such a look on his face."

"I'm sure you would never do anything to earn such a look, Jane," Richard said with a smile, thinking that she did not have a mischievous bone in her whole angelic body.

She smiled back at him, a bright, sunny smile that lit up her whole face and turned her hazel eyes to shimmering gold. Richard's breath caught in his throat at the sight.

Vicki tiptoed through the door of the music room, holding her candlestick high. The flickering light cast eerie shadows over the darkened room as she walked forward. She saw that the stage had been set up at one end of the room on an elevated platform much as it had been the previous year. There were makeshift curtains open to each side to reveal a painted background scene of a flower garden. A few tasteful props were placed here and there along the sides and back of the platform where they would not get in the actors' way as they walked back and forth across the stage. Rows of chairs and benches had been set up before the stage for the audience.

Vicki walked further into the chamber and turned in a slow circle to see that the room was swathed everywhere in red and white fabric. That was a new touch.

And over there was another. A little stone statue of a Cupid with an unholy look of gleeful mischief carved on his smiling face had been brought in from the garden and set up on a pedestal to one side of the stage. The Cupid stood in an archer's stance with his bow drawn, facing the audience. Someone had woven a wreath of laurel leaves and placed it on his chubby stone head. The iron arrow notched in the bow had been gilded with gold paint, Vicki saw, so that it glimmered in the flickering light of her candle.

Trust Clementina to think of such a thing, Vicki thought with a low-throated laugh. Yes, indeed, her hostess had done an excellent job in seeing that all was set to rights for the performance tomorrow night. Or rather, later today, for it was already past midnight. Valentine's Day had dawned. Well, not quite dawned, she amended with a small smile, as she gazed out into the darkened room.

She had been too keyed up to sleep, thinking about her upcoming performance . . . and all her confrontations with Ned over the past few days. Was all his making up to her, those two sizzling kisses, leading up to a second proposal of marriage or not? At times she thought he was on the verge of such a proposal, but at other times he simply seemed to be amusing himself. He enjoyed teasing her and leading her on, inducing her to respond to his expert lovemaking. Vicki blushed hotly as she recalled their several heated embraces—surely not seemly behavior for a man and a woman who were not yet promised to one another.

And then there was today. Ned had not approached her since he had charged out of his sister's room yesterday, no doubt in search of the mischievous twins so that he could give them a thundering scold for their harebrained prank. Imagine his sisters locking them in like that? The twins had approached her and apologized last evening, but she thought they had not looked overly sorry about the incident. But she had had no private conversation with Wexford since then, other than at their double rehearsal this morning and this afternoon when they had perforce to interact with one another.

Vicki had to admit that she had been so discomposed by what had happened, by how she had allowed herself to be seduced into kissing him again in his sister's room and allowing him to touch her so intimately, that she had repulsed all his efforts to converse with her last evening and today. At least he had shown no sign of trying to engage Arabella's interest, Vicki remembered with some consolation. Out of the corner of her eye, she had seen the widow approach him several times today, but the marquess had soon walked away from her, and Arabella had eventually allowed herself to be drawn into conversation with George Laponte. Clementina had confided to Vicki that George had a tendré for the beautiful widow.

After she had retired to bed that evening, Vicki had paced about in her bedchamber for an hour, trying to decide if Wexford would offer for her again, or not. Becoming annoyed with herself for dwelling on nothing but *his* unknown intentions and *her* confused feelings for her former fiancé, she decided to go downstairs to the music room and run over her lines.

"Oh, the devil fly away with him, I'll tease myself about the matter no longer," she had exclaimed crossly to herself. She was determined to put the maddening man from her mind and concentrate on her upcoming performance.

Now, seeing the makeshift stage set up before her, she lit a brace of candles sitting to one side of the platform with her taper, set her candlestick down, and mounted the steps to the front of the stage.

"You, Mr. Geoffrey Lacklove, are a cynic and a rogue!" she proclaimed with great energy to the empty room, pretending to hold her fan up to her face as she swept around in her dressing gown, turning a cold shoulder on her invisible antagonist.

"And you, Mistress Proudheart, are a heartless tease!" a deep masculine voice proclaimed from out of the shadows of the room.

"Ned!" Vicki exclaimed, whirling about at the sound of his voice and clutching her dressing gown tightly to her chest.

"Ah ha! Caught you. Couldn't you sleep, either, Vic?"

He walked forward to the stage so that he was gazing up at her. He was clad only in his shirtsleeves and a pair of dark pantaloons, she noticed, and his shirt was open at the neck where quite a bit of the darkly haired bare flesh of his upper chest was revealed. And his hair looked decidedly tousled, too, with a long, dark lock falling negligently across his forehead that made him appear as if he'd just risen from his bed.

Vicki had never seen him looking more devastatingly handsome.

She could only gape at him in confusion, acutely aware of her own dishabille and the lateness of the hour.

"What brought you down here at this ungodly hour? You're not nervous about your performance tomorrow, are you?" he asked.

"Well, no, not exactly." She took a deep breath, sighed and pushed her loose hair back behind her ears. "I guess I'm just too keyed up to sleep."

"Yes, I can understand the feeling. Would you be game to help me go through our lines one more time? I confess, I've been so distracted in the past few days, that I'm not sure I have my part down pat. And I don't want to let Clem down tomorrow."

His dark eyes were half closed, shadowed by his lashes. He looked half asleep, Vicki thought, and far less dangerous than the last time she had encountered him alone. Perhaps there would be no harm in obliging him. She didn't want to let Clementina down either. And, although she was loathe to admit it, there was something deliciously thrilling in being alone with him in the middle of the night.

Half wary, half eager, she gazed back into his dark orbs. "Well, I—I suppose I could do that. Just let me go upstairs and dress first," she said, knowing that it was highly improper to be standing there talking to him clad as she was in her thin cotton nightrail, covered only by her warm, but very plain, white wool dressing gown.

"No, no need to do that. You're fine as you are. You are covered more modestly than you will be tonight in your costume. Though perhaps you fear the sight of your naked toes will enflame me," he said with a mocking grin, looking down at her pink toes where they peeked from under the hem of her dressing gown. He reached forward and covered them with his warm hand and chafed her cold feet for a moment.

"What are you doing?" she whispered, not really wanting to disturb the lovely feeling of his large, comforting hand massaging her feet.

"Warming your feet for you. They're like ice, Vic. We wouldn't want our heroine to come down with the sniffles because her feet were too cold, would we?"

She smiled back at him. The lateness of the hour, the darkness surrounding them, their low-voiced conversation, all added to the unreality of the scene. It seemed quite dreamlike to Vicki, and made her forget how improper it was.

"Look! What's this?" Ned asked, abruptly moving his hand from her toes to pick up a few pages from where they lay to one side of the stage. He began to thumb through the sheets and moved over near the lighted candles so that he could read them more easily.

"What is it?" Vicki asked.

"Why, I do believe it's the last scene of our play. Hmm. Let's see what that dear, devious sister of mine was hiding from us by not letting us see these lines earlier."

He held a copy up to the light and began to read through the short scene. "Hah!" he exclaimed at one point, and muttered something under his breath that sounded to Vicki like "Oh, the devil fly away with her!" Whether he was referring to Mistress Proudheart, or his sister, Vicki didn't know.

"Oh, do let me see, too, Ned," Vicki said, kneeling at the edge of the stage beside him and putting her hand on his arm that held the precious script.

He pulled the papers out of her reach, grinning. "Ah, ah. What will you give me for a peek?"

She looked back at him, seeing the teasing, devilish lights in his dark eyes, and decided that he had the Hadleigh streak for mischief in full measure. "You are no gentleman, my lord." She sat back on her heels, determined somehow to see the pages he held so tantalizingly near.

"Now, Vic. I have something you are eager to have. Surely a small trade can be arranged to our mutual satisfaction."

"Do you mean to imply that *I* have something you are eager to have, my lord?"

"Indeed, ma'am," he drawled, "so I've been trying my best to hint to you these past several days."

"Oh, you are a wretch, Ned Hadleigh. I have said that I will go through the play with you here and now. Surely that is payment enough." She was blushing furiously as she spoke. She could only hope the darkness hid her flaming cheeks from his interested view.

"Hmm." He looked at her consideringly, his dark brows arched, then grinned and thrust the papers into her eager hands.

As Vicki read, a smile lit her features, then a slight frown.

"I assume Clem meant to give this to us in the morning and have us work all day on memorizing the words," Ned remarked casually, but Vicki didn't look up from her reading. "Of course, it won't be difficult to do that. The action and words *do* seem to follow naturally from what has gone before."

Ned rested his elbows on the stage floor and leaned forward to watch Vicki as she read. A little smile played about his mouth and his eyes softened as he watched her, looking so soft and virginal in her white night clothes. He lifted one hand and smoothed back the lock of hair that had fallen forward over her face.

Vicki looked up, her face only inches from his. Her face tingled where his fingers had touched her. She studied his intent expression for a moment, then rose to her feet and said, "Come on. If you want to go through the play, we had better get started. And now we can go through that last scene, as well."

He vaulted up onto the stage and they ran through the play with more verve and high spirits than they had done before, each concentrating on bringing out the best in their characters. They even managed to put some emotion into their first read-through of the last pages of the play as they shared the precious script. When they reached the end of the scene, Ned took Vicki in his arms.

"There is nothing about a kiss being exchanged in the script, Ned," she protested weakly.

"It is clearly implied, though. You can't deny that it is, Vic. . . . Besides, the audience will be expecting one. You know Clem's Valentine's plays *always* end with a kiss."

Indeed, Vicki did know, but she didn't wish to seem forward, however much she was longing for Ned to kiss her at that moment.

"So Mistress Proudheart, accept your fate and submit to your virile lover," Ned said in a mock fierce voice.

Vicki giggled, but she didn't resist him. "Those aren't the right lines, Ned."

"I know. I'm just improving the text," he murmured outrageously as he lowered his mouth to hers in a warm, seeking kiss.

"Umm," Vicki said, still laughing but beginning to wind her arms about his neck as she gave herself up to his kiss. Just as she did so, one of her feet tangled in the trailing hem of her dressing gown, causing her to trip, and pull them both down so that they were sprawled on the stage.

Vicki found herself sitting in Ned's lap, her arms still twined about his neck and her head resting against his bare chest. Umm, he smelled good, she thought closing her eyes and snuggling closer, glorying in the slightly musky smell emanating from his warm flesh, not wanting to move her head.

"Omph! Are you hurt, my dear?" Ned asked.

"No. You cushioned my fall quite gallantly, *Mr. Lacklove.* Are you alright?" She tried to rise from his lap, but he held her in place.

"Hmm. I am not at all sure that I am. I feel distinctly winded. I think I'll just rest here a moment and try to catch my breath." He bent forward and rubbed his nose against hers, then kissed her cheek softly. "I think you should offer me some comfort for acting so quickly. After all, my quick action prevented me from falling on top of you and squashing you to a pulp."

"Fie on you, sir. I think you are trying to turn this accident to your advantage."

Her words were scolding, but he noticed that one of her arms was still tightly wound round his neck and that, after one brief attempt, she hadn't made another move to get up or pull away from him. He took that as distinct encouragement to continue what they had started.

"Damn right, er, that is, dashed right I am." He began to press little kisses all over her face and neck while one hand moved along her back, playing under her curls then stroking down her spine in a warm, sensuous movement that had Vicki tingling all over.

He took her lips in an open-mouthed kiss, then increased the pressure until she opened her lips for him. He slipped his tongue inside and began to fence with hers.

Vicki's breathing accelerated and she strained toward Ned, giving herself up to the wondrous pleasure of his kiss.

Ned felt Vicki moving closer to him on his lap with delightful, but certain rather uncomfortable, consequences. He shifted her to one side and slipped a warm hand inside her dressing gown. When she made no move to push him away, he began to run his hand tantalizingly up and down her side, then he dared to run his fingertips over the fullness of her breasts, back and forth, back and forth until he heard a little moan rise from her throat.

That small sound almost broke the last vestiges of his control. He kissed her more insistently, provoking a more passionate response from her.

Vicki couldn't suppress her reaction to the marvelous things Ned was doing to her, the new sensations he was arousing. She was floating on a warm cloud of sensual feeling in this unknown place he had taken her to, where her senses were acutely alive to his every touch, every shift in the pressure of his mouth, the feel of his breath against her skin, the touch of his hands as they moved on her body, every move of his body against hers.

Ned tipped them sideways so that they were lying rather than sitting on the stage. He clamped one long, muscular leg over Vicki's thighs and pulled her dressing gown open. He was frustrated to find that her thin nightrail was fastened at the neck with a satin ribbon that was tied in a series of tiny bows under a delicate fall of worked lace at her neck. He fumbled at the slippery strings, almost yanking them open.

"Oh! What are you doing, Ned?" she protested huskily, coming to her senses out of the sweet, misty land where he had transported her.

"Oh, darling, please, just let me . . ." He was reaching down and pulling up the hem of her nightrail.

"Oh, Ned, no! Please stop!" Vicki cried, alarmed. She pushed at his hand and tried to slide out from under him.

"I want to love you. Please, Vic. I want you so much."

"Oh, Ned. My dear, we can't. We're not—ah, that is . . . this is something for married couples, is it not?" Vicki asked, coming more fully to herself and pushing him away with deep regret. She saw that his breathing was light and rapid and his eyes were glazed with passion.

"You're right," he rasped out. "We must wait. But it will be soon. Yes?"

Vicki was too astonished by his words to respond. Did he mean what she hoped he meant?

When Vicki said nothing, Ned laughed shortly and continued somewhat breathlessly, "You shouldn't have broken off with me last year, you know. Then we could be enjoying ourselves right now. . . . Why did you do it, Vic? I never understood your reasons. You certainly seem to like me well enough now." He sat up, his knees bent and his head resting in his hands while he tried to reclaim his breath.

"I . . . I—," she began.

Ned tensed at her words, closing his eyes tightly, afraid that it would hurt to learn the truth at long last.

She licked her dry lips, trying to settle her whirling thoughts—trying to find the courage to confess that she had been so foolishly jealous of his attentions to Arabella last year, that she had wanted to pay him back for the hurt he caused her. "I'm as sorry as I can be that I ever did such a foolish thing. Forgive me, my dear." With those words, her courage completely deserted her and she fell silent.

"Oh, then—Vicki! My dearest love, come here!" At her words, Ned opened his eyes and stretched out an arm to her.

Vicki longed to put her arms about him again, but she didn't trust herself. It was too dangerous to stay with him a moment longer. She scrambled to her feet, grabbed up her candlestick and fled out the door, calling, "Oh, no. I mustn't. Not tonight. Goodnight, dearest Ned."

Fleeing from desire and temptation, she ran up to her bedchamber, afraid that if she had allowed herself to stay for another minute, she would have permitted him the ultimate intimacy. She was afraid not so much of him, as of herself. She had never dreamed that she could desire something like that, something so purely physical. And she loved him so very much.

She ran up to her room on bare feet. Were they engaged again or weren't they? Vicki wondered after she was safely behind the door of her bedchamber once more. If they weren't, they soon would be, she was sure now. Early dawn's rosy light was just breaking through her windows. She bit her lip, noticing for the first time how tender it was, then collapsed on her bed with a blissful smile on her face.

The following morning, Valentine's Day, the day of the performance, an excited, refreshed Clementina called her players together and distributed copies of the final scene.

"Here, you see, the scene starts with an exchange between Proudheart and Dazzle. Vicki, would you and Bella be so good as to go over your parts together first? Then I have another plan," she told them coyly. "I would like for Richard to read Lacklove's part to help Vicki rehearse her last lines. And Jane, could you read Mistress Proudheart's part so that Ned can learn Lacklove's lines?"

At a nod from Jane and an agreement from Richard, Clementina turned with a radiant smile to see her brother bearing down on her with a frown on his face.

"What? I'm not to rehearse with Vic?" the marquess asked, coming into the music room just in time to hear his sister's words.

"No, Ned. I want the pair of you to confront each

other freshly tonight, knowing your lines, but not having spoken them to one another before."

"Sounds deuced odd to me, Clem," Ned said, looking at his sister with a puzzled frown on his face. Neither he nor Vicki had admitted to Clementina that they had found the script last night and gone over their parts already. "I would have thought Vic and I should work together on the final scene."

"Yes, but Ned, don't you see? If you've not played the scene with one another before, the action and your words will take on added meaning. It will give more poignancy, more emotion to the ending, I think."

"Well, have it your way, Lady Director. I suppose you *think* you know what you are doing."

"I *do* know what I'm doing. You'll see, Neddy," she said, coming up to him and resting an arm affectionately on his shoulder. "You will both know your parts beforehand, but there will be more sparks between you during the actual play, if we do this my way."

He tried to conceal his grin, thinking that there had certainly been plenty of sparks already in the early hours of that morning. He put an arm about his sister's waist and gave her a hug, then went off to rehearse with Jane, giving Vicki a broad wink and his warmest smile before he went.

Vicki watched Ned leave the room with mixed feelings. She had been all a tingle with excitement ever since she arose that morning, remembering what they had shared the evening before. But she still puzzled over his words. Were they engaged or weren't they?

And she knew it was all her own fault that she was in such a state of uncertainty. If she hadn't been so much of a coward and run away, everything would be settled. She had hoped to have a private moment or two with him that morning to sort things out, but he had not been at breakfast when she came down, and when Clementina called them all to the music room soon after, he was nowhere in sight. She had been afraid to approach him when he finally did come into the room, looking so strikingly tall and imposing . . . and so breathtakingly handsome.

When he was holding her in his arms and kissing her, she could believe that he loved her as much as she loved him. But when he was not with her, all her doubts came rushing back and she could not believe that the very wealthy, very virile Marquess of Wexford would chose *her* as his marchioness, despite the long-standing friendship between their families. How could a man like Wexford really desire her as his wife? Vicki wondered, thinking of herself as a plain, insignificant sort of a girl compared to the women of beauty and wealth he could have courted.

So she sighed when he left the room and resolved to concentrate on learning the remainder of her lines. Learning how Ned truly felt about her would have to wait until later.

The morning seemed interminable to the twins. They could not wait to don their costumes and tread the boards that evening. After luncheon, instead of resting as their mother and elder sister recommended, and as the other ladies had done, they went outside for a trudge round the grounds. Over an hour later, when they were making their way back to the house, they overheard voices in the Bestiary.

Delia put her finger to her lips, cautioning her twin

to say nothing. Cynthia motioned to Delia, indicating that they should conceal themselves and listen to the conversation.

"But I assure you, Mr. Hadleigh," Lady Jane was saying to their cousin, Richard, "there is nothing between Mr. Lindley and me."

"Richard, Richard, Richard. Please Jane, can you not bring yourself to call me Richard?"

She nodded and turned away from him. He sighed audibly, then ran one hand through his hair. "I'm sorry, my dear. 'Tis just that you seem to spend much time talking with him, and I'm sure he admires you."

"No. We are just friends. Please believe me, Mr.—, Richard."

"Yes, I am just . . . never mind. Are you all set for tonight?" he asked.

"I'm not certain, Richard. I know my lines now, but will I remember them when I'm up on that stage?" Jane replied in a strained voice.

The twins peeked through the hedges and saw Dickon take Jane's hand.

"You're trembling, my dear. Come, come. It won't be so bad. How many lines do you have anyway?" He was teasing her, rubbing her cold hand with his warm one and gazing right down into her beautiful hazel eyes.

"Only three, thank the Lord!" Jane replied sincerely. "Two as a serving maid and one as a fashionable lady."

Richard laughed. "Say them aloud for me. If your voice deserts you completely, I will imitate your voice and say them for you."

Jane giggled at the thought. "Well, that would get a laugh from the audience. And though you are funning, if I opened my mouth and could force out no sound, I do believe you would do it."

Richard's grin faded and he said seriously. "I would do anything for you, my dear."

"Oh, you are kind." Jane pulled her hand from his and turned away to pull some of the leaves off a twig that served as one of the whiskers of a topiary cat.

"It's not kindness exactly, Jane—though I hope I am a kind person. But my dearest Jane, I can no longer keep silent. This—this thing that's between us. I'm sure you feel it, too. Help me, Jane. Look at me."

At the sound of distress in his voice, Jane turned back to see Richard gazing at her with worried eyes. She reached a hand toward him. He reached out both arms and pulled her up against him for a tight hug.

Cynthia tapped Delia on the shoulder and motioned that they should leave. Delia shook her head, but Cynthia took her by the arm and led her away.

Richard rocked Jane back and forth in his arms for several moments, then whispered tightly, "I love you, Jane. My dearest girl, will you marry me?"

"Oh, Richard. How can I answer you? We've only known one another for three days."

"We've known one another for years, my dear," he whispered with the trace of a laugh against her ear. "It's just that we've been aware of one another *romantically* for just three days. But if you need more time, I will wait. But not forever, my dear. Would you be able to answer me in, say, a month?"

"Oh, I don't know what to say!" Jane cried, tears beginning to form in her eyes.

"My dear love, don't distress yourself. Please! If you cannot love me, I will leave you in peace. Believe me, the last thing I would ever want to do is cause you any hurt."

"Richard! Richard!" Jane was openly weeping now. She reached up and wound her arms tightly about his neck and kissed him chastely on the lips.

"I hope that means yes, my love," Richard whispered shakily.

"Oh, yes! I love you," Jane managed to gulp. "And I will marry you tomorrow, if you wish it."

Her answer rendered Richard so happy that he responded not in words but with a heartstopping kiss that left them both breathless and trembling.

"Oh, I am so silly, I do not know how you can bear with me," Jane said with a laugh, wiping her eyes on the handkerchief Richard had handed her. He kept a comforting arm about her as she composed herself.

"You are not so much silly as incredibly sweet. I cannot help loving you, you know, Janey." He planted little kisses over the side of her face that was nearest him.

"And I cannot help loving you, Richard. You are so incredibly handsome and kind," she said, lifting her mouth for his kiss once more.

The twins reached the house and grinned at one another while they stood in the hallway removing their outdoor things. "Well, there's one couple down. Just one to go. Come on, Del, let's tell Clem," Cynthia said and the girls rushed upstairs to their elder sister's dressing room.

Arabella overheard Cynthia's words and wondered to whom the girl referred. Surely she was not speaking of her brother and Miss Colefax! Bella had watched carefully since she had been staying at the house. To her great annoyance, Wexford still seemed to have his eye on that overly tall gawk of a woman. Yet, while the marquess and his former fiancée seemed to be on friendlier terms than she could like, she was sure they were not lovers. Why, they hadn't exchanged even a single word today! And the silly Colefax woman turned her back on him at every opportunity, except when they were rehearsing the play.

Bella still had not forgiven those hell-born twins for playing such a vexatious trick on her the other night when she had finally seemed to be making some headway with Wexford. Telling her that clanker about her gown being stained, indeed. And then Delia had told her that she had a smudge on her face just when she was all set to show the marquess her costume. Oh! And she had fallen for their hoaxing tricks like a green girl! They had deliberately kept her away from their brother for some reason.

She had been trying her hardest to attract the marquess's interest these past few days, but to no avail. What he could see in such a plain, old maid as Victoria Colefax was beyond her ken. For heaven's sake, why the silly woman had called off her engagement to such a matrimonial prize as the Marquess of Wexford was beyond her.

Well, if Victoria Colefax didn't want the marquess, Bella certainly did. She resolved to make one last attempt to pique his interest. Perhaps even more than pique his interest, she smiled smugly to herself. She had a provoking feeling that Wexford was more interested in an affair with her than marriage, but she would settle for nothing less than wedlock. If he were found in a compromising situation with her, would he not feel obliged to offer marriage? She hoped so. It was a gamble, but certainly worth a try.

Bella picked up her skirts and quietly made her way up the stairs to the marquess's room. He must be in there, she thought. She had hunted for him all over the house with no luck and had even sent a servant down to the stables to learn if he had gone for a ride. But no one had seen him at the stables and his mount was still in its stall.

She tapped quietly at the door.

"Who is it?" Ned asked. He was standing near the window, looking over his lines for the last scene one more time.

Instead of answering, Bella pushed the door open and boldly stepped into his room.

"Bella! My, my, what a surprise. What brings you here?"

"Hello, Ned." Bella closed the door softly behind her and stepped forward. "We've all been so busy rehearsing the play every day that there's been little time for you and me to renew our acquaintance."

"Yes," he drawled, folding his arms over his chest and quirking a brow.

"Well," she smiled and licked her dry lips. "This seemed like a good opportunity."

"Did it? Er, a good opportunity for what exactly, Mrs. Rutledge?"

"Well, I—, ah," she opened her big brown eyes wide and gazed at him innocently. Then she flew across the room and cast herself against his chest. "Oh, dear Ned, I have fallen in love with you, and I don't know what to do about it."

"Have you, now? I'm sorry, Bella, but I don't believe a word of it!"

"Oh, but Ned, I have!" She stamped her dainty foot for emphasis and tried to squeeze some tears from her eyes, but failed, settling for a little dry sob instead.

He grasped both her wrists and put her firmly from him. "Now see here, Bella. You know perfectly well you should not come to my room. If anyone has seen you, you will be compromised. You must leave immediately."

"If I scream, someone will come and think you have lured me in here," she threatened.

"Ah, so much for true love and devotion," he said with a grimace. "You are well cast indeed as Mistress Dazzle."

"I beg your pardon," she said sarcastically. "What are you talking ab—"

"You may beg my pardon some other time. Now, out." He took her by the elbow, opened the door, and shoved her out into the hallway.

Bella was furious. How dare he treat her like that! As though she were some child who had misbehaved. She stood absolutely still for a moment, then put her hand up to straighten her hair. She ran her hands down her gown to smooth it, before she walked away angrily, thinking she would redouble her efforts toward Richard Hadleigh. Now there was a gentleman she was sure she could wind round her finger in a trice. Though he was not so big a prize as his cousin, the marquess, he was handsome enough to make the effort worthwhile.

Vicki had just come in from a walk and was making her way upstairs to her bedroom when she turned the corner and saw Ned's door open and Arabella come out. She backed up quickly and peered round the corner, watching as Arabella straightened her hair and garments. Vicki's heart felt as though it had cracked in two.

It seemed Ned was secretly meeting with Arabella in his room, after he had all but proposed to *her* last night! Oh, marriage with him would be hopeless! He would always be a womanizer and would never reform, she thought angrily, stalking to her room. But halfway there, she turned back, determined to give that rakehell of a Ned Hadleigh a piece of her mind.

She approached Ned's room and rapped firmly on the door.

"I thought I made it clear to you, Bella, that you are to go away and not bother me. It is no good, your coming to my room," Ned hissed angrily through the locked door. "I am not interested in an affair with you. And you should be seeking a good second marriage, not an affair with me. Heed my counsel, girl, and behave yourself. Go away now, Bella, for I have no intention of opening this door."

Vicki was astounded by his words and she scurried away with a lighter heart, wondering what would happen next.

"The music room is full, Clem," Ned said to his sister as he took a quick glance into the room. He was nervously waiting for the play to begin. "I've never seen so many people at one of your little productions. What did you do, invite the whole county?"

"Just our neighbors and the townfolk, and some of the people we know from church who live farther away. Oh, and I believe Chas asked Squire Boothby, the local Master of Foxhounds, along and he's brought a large contingent of his hunting friends."

"Well, I hope none of the girls is put off by such a large audience. It's a bit intimidating, even I must admit." After a largely sleepless night, he had decided not to ask Vicki if he might have a few words with her in private as soon as she arose that morning. They had been busy with the final preparations for the play all day, and he had hardly seen her. Which was all for the best, he supposed. But now he was feeling somewhat on edge. On edge and full of anticipation about the performance—and about the surprise he had planned for Vicki during the final moments of the play.

"Don't worry, you will all do well, Neddy. You were all superb in your last rehearsal. And, I must say, everyone looks the part in their costumes. Vicki has just the height and figure to carry off the look of a grand lady at the turn of the eighteenth century. She looks quite delectable, don't you think?"

At his grunt of assent, she continued, "You look quite wonderful in this costume, my dear," she said, running her hand down the satin of his long coat. "I knew red and gold would suit you, Ned, for you used to look so imposing in your regimentals. And this wig gives you a certain rakish appearance I've never noticed before. You'll bring my play off to perfection, I make no doubt."

"Easy for you to say. You won't be on stage."

"Yes, I will. I plan to read an epilogue. Why do you think I've donned tights and a mannish wig?"

"Well, Clem I've known you all my life and you've always been full of mad starts. I just thought you enjoyed making yourself look foolish."

"Oh, you," she said, buffetting him on the shoulder. They both laughed.

She thought he looked a bit more relaxed. "How is

your courtship of Vicki coming along, my dear?" she asked with a sidelong look.

He tried to conceal his quick grin, but Clementina noted it. "I *think* I may have an interesting announcement to make after the play tonight."

"Oh, I knew you would not fail to persuade her," she crowed, giving him a hug, then straightening his costume and wig where she had disarranged them. "I hope you've put my advice to good use."

"And what advice was that, Clem?" he asked innocently.

"Why, to court Vicki *romantically,* with declarations of undying love and devotion, some passionate poetry, a few stolen kisses," she said, looking closely at his face to see if he had followed her instructions.

"Is that what Charles did to win you?"

When he saw his sister flush, he knew he had scored a hit. Ned grinned hugely.

"It was all a long time ago," she answered vaguely, wishing she did not have such a tendency to color up so readily. "And we are speaking of your courtship, Ned."

"But you remember every moment of your own." He laughed at her, then forebore to tease her further. "This play we're to do, you say a friend of yours wrote it, Clem? Who is she?" he asked, fiddling with his costume, checking that his cravat and cuffs were in order.

"Oh, she's too shy to give me permission to reveal her name, but as you can tell, she's written a kind of pastiche of the comedies that were popular on the London stage at the beginning of the last century. *I* find it highly entertaining. And it will serve us well, you'll see, Neddy."

"Here we go. Best of luck to all of us, my dear," Ned

said, planting a quick kiss on his sister's cheek as he prepared to take his place for the opening scene.

Lovers' Vows
(Set in London, 1700; players are garbed
in costumes of the time.)
Dramatis Personae

Mr. Geoffrey Lacklove, a fashionable man about town—Edward Hadleigh, Marquess of Wexford

Mr. Francis Tender, his friend—Richard Hadleigh

Waitley, Lacklove's servant—John Lindley

Mr. Truly Constant, a suitor to Mistress Proudheart—Nigel Laponte

Sir Foppishly Nethersby, an overdressed and painted, lisping gallant, follower of Mistress Proudheart—George Laponte

Mistress Phoebe Proudheart, a fashionable beauty, new come to town—Victoria Colefax

Faithful, Proudheart's waiting woman—Cynthia Hadleigh

Mistress Margery Dazzle, London beauty, formerly friend to Lacklove—Arabella Rutledge

Sharpish, Dazzle's waiting woman—Delia Hadleigh

Mistress Hornsby, fashionable lady—Elizabeth Hadleigh

Mistress Pontefract, fashionable lady—Jane Fenners

Polly Teazle, serving wench at the Cock of the Walk Tavern—Jane Fenners

Various fashionable townspeople, servants, etc. milling about

The epilogue read by Countess Sutcliffe

(*Scene one: The Cock of the Walk Tavern where Lacklove and Tender are casting dice against one another in desultory fashion; Waitley stands behind his master.*)

Lacklove: "You talk of love and marriage and everlasting devotion in one breath. No, no, Tender. I'll none of it. Give me a lively tumble with a new lightskirt any day."

Tender: "Ah, but Lacklove, just wait until you cast your eyes over Mistress Phoebe Proudheart. I defy you to remain unmoved by her beauty. She's a very Calliope, lovely enough to inspire one to take up pen and write an epic poem to her glorious attributes, a new Helen, beautiful enough to induce princes to give up kingdoms to vie for her hand."

Lacklove: "My dear Tender, can this paragon you speak of be living flesh? Or is she some picture of a woman, some richly adorned cold marble statue of the love goddess, and you her Pygmalion, with your warm words of praise breathing life into her?"

Tender: "No, no, my friend. As I live, she's a living, breathing woman—all lovely, warm flesh and blood. Ah, such a face, such a figure defies my poor attempts at description—men have died for less, ere now, I promise you. And her wit is said to be matchless. I vow, there will be no help for it, Geoff, you will fall in love with her straightaway and swear your undying devotion the minute you glimpse her and hear her melodious voice."

Lacklove: "Sing me no raptures on the glories of a beautiful face and everlasting love, Frank. You'll waste your breath, my friend. True love? Pshaw. I protest, there's no such a thing."

Tender: "Ho, Geoff! You choose to doubt me, do you?

I hazard, you will lose your heart entirely and sing the lady's praises night and day."

Lacklove: "Ha! And I say I shall *not.* Come, a wager on it! Two-hundred guineas says I will remain heartwhole after a week of quite constantly casting myself in her way, pretending to throw myself at her feet. And, as for the lady, I shall leave her languishing after *my* addresses after such a time, too. Come, come, a wager, what say you?"

Tender: "Done! (*They shake hands on it.*) Ah, Lacklove, never was there such a sure thing as your falling victim to the manifold charms of Mistress Proudheart. I am quite content. I feel two-hundred guineas the richer for this rash wager of yours." (*Pats his pocket.*)

(*Enter Polly Teazle, serving wench, with two tankards of ale.*)

Polly: "Your ale, sirs." (*Serves them.*)

Lacklove: "Ah, Polly, come and sit upon my lap and while away an hour or two."

Polly: "La, sir, what a teasing gentleman you are. As though I had nothing better to do with my time." (*Exits with a flirtatious look over her shoulder at Lacklove.*)

Tender: "You're losing your touch, my dear Lacklove."

Lacklove: "What! With a mere serving wench. Ha, ha. That one is holding out for a ring from the ostler, I believe. Come, let us waste no more time here. I am of a humor to see this paragon of yours. Lead on, Frank." (*Exeunt omnes.*)

(*Scene two: A sunny garden where two fashionable ladies are walking, followed by their waiting women.*)

Dazzle: "You have scored a triumph since you have come up to town, my dear Phoebe. I swear, you have more followers in a week than Miss Platterface, the great heiress, had in a year! How gratified you must be."

Proudheart: "Heigho, it is all so tedious to me to be petitioned by fools and fops all the live-long day."

Dazzle: "But you have secured the devotion of Mr. Truly Constant. There is not a more steady man in all of London, I believe."

Proudheart: "Perhaps, you speak true. But Constant is quite dull and lacking in conversation. Are there no men of sense in London, dearest Margery?"

Dazzle: "Aye, there are a few gentlemen of marked wit. And men of handsome parts, too. Here comes one of them, now, if I mistake not."

Proudheart: "Ah, yes. It is the gentleman who was so importunate at the opera last evening and his friend, Mr. Tender."

(*Enter Lacklove accompanied by Tender and Waitley.*)

Lacklove: "I bid you good day, ladies. The sun shines not brighter than your fair countenances. (*Aside to audience: "Ah, her eyes do strike a spark in my breast!"*) "May we walk with you awhile here in this Eden, oh fair Eve?"

Proudheart: "Good day, Mr. Lacklove. I see you are a gentleman of flowery and fulsome address. You think to exercise your wit upon us. Will you banter words at our expense, or for our entertainment, I wonder?"

Lacklove: "Madam, since first I saw you, it has become my primary business to 'entertain' you. To please you will ever be my most sincere endeavor."

Proudheart: "Prettily said, sir. But I believe it is rather an amusing *game* to you, than a sincere endeavor."

Lacklove: "You wrong me, madam. Assuredly, you do. When you come to know me better, you will see how your words have wounded me."

Proudheart: "Pshaw, sir! This is too heavy. You go too fast for me."

Lacklove: "Do I weigh so heavy upon you already? I shall lighten the burden and go more slowly."

Tender: "Mistress Proudheart, Mistress Dazzle. You are like two new open'd flowers, one not outbidding the other in the brilliant beauty of your colorful spreading petals."

Proudheart: "You are *très gallant,* Monsieur Tender. We thank the gentleman for his flowery compliment, do we not, Margery?"

Dazzle: "Assuredly we do. Mr. Tender is ever courteous and effusive in his attentions to us of the frailer sex."

Lacklove: "I see you wear my nosegay, my dear Mistress Proudheart."

Proudheart: "Were these *your* offerings, sir? Ha, ha, ha. What a lucky chance then that we should meet this morning—I chose at random among several nosegays, liking the color of these roses with my gown."

Lacklove: "How honored I am to have won such high favor! (*He strikes a pose with his hand over his heart.*) That I should lie upon your breast after but one evening's acquaintance!"

Proudheart: "Fie, sir! Were you to lie so closely upon these thorns, you would prick yourself most sharply. I had a fancy for roses today. The delicate velvety sweetness of such flowers all circled round by fierce, thorny guardians quite suits my mood."

Lacklove: "To be so pierced by you, madam, I would consider pleasure rather than pain. To lie amidst the velvety sweetness of such . . . petals . . . of yours and risk the thorns 'tis the whole of my ambition."

Proudheart: "You would risk being wounded among the thorns?"

Lacklove: "Aye. My resolve to do so is stiffened by the twin sirens of your beauty and wit." (*He reaches out and touches one of the roses pinned to her corsage and pricks his finger then sucks the blood away.*) "And once pricked, like a withered flower, my life blood ebbs away and I slowly die"

Proudheart: "When these *flowers* of yours wither and die, I shall not lack for others to choose from."

Lacklove: "Fear not that you shall have to choose from *inferior* offerings, not so much to your taste. I have another rose that blooms just for you."

Proudheart: "Fie, sirrah, you touch upon country matters."

Lacklove: "I confess, I like to spend a fond hour or two in the country." (*Lifts his hand to show her where he's hurt it.*) "I had best 'ware the sting of these sharp shafts dipped in the sweet dew of your flowers."

Proudheart: "You had best 'ware, sir, lest by the sharp point of Cupid's dart, you be pricked more fiercely in another organ."

Lacklove: "And you, madam? Have you been pierced by love's sharp arrow ere now?"

Proudheart: "La, sir, you have a lewd tongue to speak so broadly." (*Turns her back on him and speaks to her friend.*) "Do you hear the creature, good Margery? If he thinks by these artful conceits to find favor with me, tell him 'tis folly, his efforts are wasted. His gilded tongue spews forth so much impudence and false flattery. I do not seek his approbation or his favor."

Dazzle: "My friend says your wanton words are wasted on her, Mr. Lacklove. Take yourself off and try your rogery on some other, more gullible vessel. Be gone with you, sir."

Lacklove: "Mistress Proudheart knows I do but bandy words with her. I mean her no harm. She has bewitched me with her charms. I cannot rest without a sight of her to enliven my lonely day and banish the dullness that besets me."

Dazzle: (*Whispers to Proudheart*) "He is a handsome rogue and has a very flattering tongue, my dear. I have known him ere now make such seeming honest protestations of devotion to other ladies in the town. Laying siege to unwary hearts 'tis almost his profession."

Proudheart: (*Confers with Dazzle*) "Ah. Say you so, indeed? I thought his face, his figure, too fine, his air too experienced, to mark him an honest man. He has about him the look of a London rogue, full of trickery and treacherous deceit toward us poor creatures. Shall I lead him on and teach him a lesson, then, and be revenged in some measure for all our sex? What advise you?"

Dazzle: "Do not seem to favor him, my dear. Spurn the creature, turn aside his flattery with jests and disinterest."

Proudheart: (*Still whispering*) "Yes, I shall do so. Yet, it amuses me to see what absurdities the creature speaks."

Dazzle: (*Aside to audience: "She heeds me not. He has beguiled her despite her denials. What shall I do to part them?"*)

Lacklove: (*Aside to Tender: "Draw off Mistress Dazzle that I might have private speech with my proud lady."*) "Madam, turn not your glorious countenance from me and direct your silver-voiced comments to another. If you would address me, though you do but chide, I would consider myself favored beyond my desserts to have gained some measure of your notice."

(*Tender pays his compliments to Mistress Dazzle and they walk apart followed by her maid, Sharpish.*)

Proudheart: "I protest, sir. You have a flattering tongue by which you seek to insinuate yourself into my good graces with these comely airs and graces. In one so facile of speech and easy in manners, I detect a man who has much experience in the game of dalliance. Think you to overcome my virtue by such artifice? You will not succeed, sirrah. Nothing is more likely to prove false than an excess of gallantry."

Lacklove: "I protest, madam, you do wrong me and wrong yourself. The edifice of your virtue is too strong to be overcome by any poor artifice on my part. I vow, I speak true when I say that you have beguiled me."

Proudheart: (*Unfurls her fan and holds it up below her eyes.*) "Then what do you wish to gain by your marked attentions, sir?"

Lacklove: (*Aside: "Egad. She has me there. How shall I answer without revealing my true purpose?"*) "Why, to pay my suit to your charms, oh lovely goddess. I beseech you to look upon me favorably and beg you to give me some little of your time so that we may enjoy a delightful hour or two together each day."

Proudheart: "To court me? 'Tis not in my mind to marry, sir. No, no. 'Tis an estate I dream not of. I fear a man would be forever hanging round my skirts, too importuning of my attention. Too eager, demanding, persistent, urgent, troublesome in his attentions. In short, I wish to remain my own woman. To belong to myself. Not to be at the beck and call of some tedious creature forever begging one thing or another of me, expecting me to behave according to his ideas of wifely propriety, as if I were his property. To be some man's toy, formed for his pleasure. Faugh! I thank you, sir, you may keep your suit. I'll none of it!"

Lacklove: (*Aside: "Ha! She speaks of matrimony, which I have no thought of. But I must seem to argue for that tack."*) "But what think you of the power of love, madam? Do you not admit the power of passion to transform that cold, stony heart of yours into a flaming ember? Were your breast to be pierced by one of Cupid's keen arrows and that delicious ecstasy of passion were to steal over you, would not you consent to ascend to the marital state?"

Proudheart: (*Making play with her fan*) "And have you, sir, been felled by one of those sweet shafts from the quiver of Aphrodite's son that you are now ready to descend from gallant to husband?"

Lacklove: (*Going down on one knee before her*) "You have my heart, madam. You stole it away at first sight. Your lily-white neck, damask cheeks, rosebud lips, those emerald eyes—all your charms have slayed me. I never dreamed such beauty, such wit, could exist in one exquisite creature. 'Tis all of my ambition in this world to call you mine own."

Proudheart: "Ha, ha, ha! How little you know me, sir. You think to play on my vanity. You cannot love me on such slight acquaintance."

Lacklove: "I vow, my pretty one, your charms have overcome my heart. I have never loved till now." (*Aside: " 'Od's truth, but she has wounded me!"*)

Proudheart: "Oh? And is it ecstasy you feel, sir? Pray, tell me, what is it like?"

Lacklove: "Do you mock my vows of devotion, madam?" (*He rises and resumes a proud stance, his hands on the lapels of his jacket.*)

Proudheart: "Your false words I do." (*Energetically plies fan.*)

Tender and Dazzle return.

Dazzle: (*Aside to audience:* "*See how she blushes! In faith, my arrogant gallant has conjured her. I shall disenchant her.*" *Draws Proudheart apart and whispers:*) "You have made a conquest, I see. And of one who is known throughout the *beau monde* for his flowery courtesies. He has made such lover's vows of undying affection to me, ere now, and to a dozen others."

Proudheart: (*Whispers*) "He did not prove constant in his devotion, I see."

Dazzle: "Ha! His impassioned words are as fleeting as the clouds drifting on the breeze through a summer sky. His conquests are legion, his amours a byword in the *ton*. I have suffered through his faithless attentions to me."

Proudheart: "I thank you for your timely counsel, my dear Margery." (*Aloud*) "Adieu, sirs. I must tarry here no longer."

Lacklove: (*Calling after her*) "You take my heart with you, divine lady!"

Proudheart: "Ha, ha, ha. 'Tis no such thing, you foolish creature!"

Exeunt Proudheart, Dazzle, and their waiting women.

Tender: "What progress have you made? Does she favor your suit?"

Lacklove: "It progresses apace. I think she begins to favor me. She gave me her company until, I make no doubt, Dazzle polluted her ear with some tale against me."

Tender: "Then why look you so dissatisfied? Confess, you have felt the pangs of passion in her presence."

Lacklove. "I have felt the pangs of . . . frustration. She does not incline to my suit as I would like. 'Tis early days yet, though. I fear not I shall win our wager yet."

* * *

(*Scene three: Evening promenade in St. James's Park, many groups going back and forth across the stage. Lacklove and Tender standing at downstage right, Proudheart, her waiting woman, and two or three gallants at upstage left.*)

Lacklove: "Is it not pleasant to quiz all our acquaintances who are walking here amongst the greenery of the park this sultry evening? By my oath, 'tis as good as a play to see each night's new pairing of couples. They are as changeable as the moon in its monthly course!"

Tender: "You do not accost Mistress Proudheart, Lacklove? She stands there yonder with a group of gallants paying her their compliments."

Lacklove: "I see her. But 'tis better to let her wonder why I do not approach and converse with her as I have done these three evenings past. I will walk with some comely damsel tonight and see if the green-eyed monster does not invade my lady's breast and make her jealous." (*Aside to audience: "Ha! Would such a thing were possible, but my Mistress Disdain cuts me at every turn. 'Tis I who suffer the monster's fierce fangs in my breast!"*)

Tender: "Oho! The lady inclines not to your suit, then? She is as virtuous as she is witty. Come, confess, my dear Geoff. Her beauty, her goodness, has touched you. You have conceived some tender feelings for her. You turn away and look sneering at such a thing, but I will persist in believing that you do love her most truly."

Lacklove: "You are ever a tender soul, my dear Frank, to believe such an impossibility. This so-called love you speak of is a thing entirely outside my experience. To my mind, constancy to one woman 'twould soon grow dull and stale."

Tender: "In faith, but you protest too much, my friend. . . . Look. Here is Mistress Hornsby coming along without her husband again. She is a loose creature, looking for a new frend. Will you walk with her?"

Lacklove: "Assuredly. 'Twill be a pleasant way to while away half an hour. The lady has some little of wit and a modicum of beauty. Besides, she cannot put horns on my head as she has done for poor Hornsby. Will you walk with me, good Mistress Hornsby, and enjoy the salubrious air on this fine evening?"

Hornsby: "La, is that you, Lacklove?" (*Makes play with her eyes and fan*) "You are quite the stranger of late, having deserted all the fashionable haunts where you were used to seek pleasure, to put yourself at the feet of that cold Proudheart creature. Has she released you from the spell that has held you captive at her side this past week and more?"

Lacklove: "Ah, by your words, I see that you have missed my company, my dear lady. Come, let us talk not of others, but compliment one another, instead. Then you may tell me all the latest gossip." (*Inclining his head to hers and talking and laughing together he walks with her back and forth in front of Proudheart and her friends.*)

Tender: (*Hails a fashionable lady walking alone*) "Good evening, Mistress Pontefract. It is my good fortune that I see you unaccompanied. Will you walk with me?"

Mrs. Pontefract: "Oh, Mr. Tender, how kind of you to offer to escort a poor creature such as myself."

Tender: "Poor creature? You? You are a lady of great beauty and charm. I will slay anyone who says differently, my dear Mistress Pontefract!" (*They walk about arm in arm at back of stage.*)

Proudheart: "Oh, you make me laugh with your foolishness, Sir Foppishly. You cannot possibly take two hours to dress!"

Sir Foppishly: "By my troth, madam, I thwear I would die of thame before I would be theen without an hour'th worth of painting and patching and bewigging. Then it taketh another two to make my thuit prethentable. Everything must be just tho, you know. Might ath well be dead, ath be out of fathion."

Faithful: (*Aside to audience:* "But the fool *is out of fashion. He's out of his suit—his suit to my lady! Ergo, he's a dead thing. If he be dead, why does he prattle so?"*)

Proudheart: "And is that why you pay court to me? Has it become the fashion? And you would as soon be out of your suit, as out of the fashion, would you not, Sir Foppishly?"

Foppishly: "By gad, madam, in truth, it *ith* the fathion! But that ith not to thay that my pathion is feigned only to follow the fathion. I trutht I thall not be out of my thuit to you! Thou art perfection itthelf, not more gloriouth than your fathe ith that wit by which you are known to betht even the nimbletht of clever fellowth, the motht needle-witted of humorithts."

Proudheart: "What! When I am peevish with you, you fawn and smile and call me the most amiable of creatures. When I laugh at your protestations of everlasting devotion, you take it for favor, and plague the life out of me with your rhymes and posies. No, no. Do you think that I wish to make cruelty to one's suitors the newest fashion?"

Foppishly: "Faith, my dear, I've no notion of what you like to do. You are a woman and full of odd humorth."

Proudheart: "Believe me, Sir Foppishly, when I say that I *do* not, *will* not, *cannot* favor you. A word to the wise, sir. Take your courtesies elsewhere."

(*He looks poutingly at her as he leans one hand on his ostentatious gold encrusted and beribboned walking stick and lifts a delicate lace handkerchief to his nose with the other.*)

Constant: "You do believe me when I say I am your devoted slave, do you not, oh most amiable Mistress Proudheart? I beseech you, good lady, allow me to be your faithful gallant."

Proudheart: "You, Mr. Constant, are a man with all the virtues. But, I will be plain with you, sir. I value your friendship, but no more."

Constant: (*sighing*) "Ah, me. Then I shall be content to be your friend."

Lacklove: (*Aside with a grimace: "By heaven, she marks me not! but banters with these fools."*)

Foppishly: "Monthieur Lacklove, what thay you to this lady'th contention that it ith only the fathion that cauthes one to fall into a pathion for her?"

Lacklove: "Why, one who is a gentleman hesitates to contradict a lady, Sir Foppishly. It may be the fashion to pay court to Mistress Proudheart, but the fashion changes as one changes one suit of clothes for another. The lady should beware that the fashion does not change before she bestows her favor on some one or other of her worthy suitors, 'fore she finds herself *out* of fashion. If the lady spurns all suitors, she will soon fall from fashion and the gentlemen will lay siege to some other, less cruel, vessel of pulchritude."

Proudheart: (*Plying her fan energetically*) " 'Twas never my desire to be *in* the fashion, sir."

(*Sir Foppishly salutes Mrs. Hornsby and they walk apart. Constant takes his leave sadly.*)

Lacklove: (*Draws Proudheart apart from the others milling about*) "You are discomposed. Can it be that I have put you in a passion at last?"

Proudheart: "Pshaw! You have no such effect upon me, sir! You think yourself irresistible to women. Well, I resist you, sir."

Lacklove: "How can you tolerate these fools about you? Admit it. You have missed my company."

Proudheart: "Ha! You flatter yourself, sir."

(*He draws her arm through his and walks downstage with her, leaning close and speaking intimately.*)

Lacklove: "My heart, admit that you love me." (*He takes up her hand and presses his lips to it.*) "Say that you long to press your lips to mine. Say that you *will* be mine! Meet me tonight at my lodgings, or where you will."

Proudheart: "You ask such a wicked thing? Never, sir!" (*Turns her head away but leaves her hand in his.*)

Lacklove: "What! So shy! Why, you are the strangest creature in the world. Your eyes tell me you will submit, yet your words are contradictory."

Proudheart: "Let my words, and my eyes, tell you that I love you not, sir. This is a sport with you and I will not be your pawn. You shall not boast to all the *ton* that you have added me to your list of conquests. Let me go. You will not, you *shall not,* have me. I like you not, sir."

Lacklove: "You will not, you shall not? Does it humor you to torture me? If so, then you will be gratified to know, madam, that you have succeeded. I cannot eat. I cannot sleep. I cannot tell what day it is. I no longer know what I say. I mean to have you, my lady, will you or nil you! Else I shall expire in the trying."

She breaks away and runs offstage. Lacklove follows her purposefully.

•

(*Scene four: Lacklove's lodging rooms. He sits in a dressing gown at a table.*)

Waitley: "Mistress Proudheart bade me tell you that this is her answer to your letter, master." (*Pours the fragments of a letter torn into tiny pieces onto the table in front of Lacklove.*)

Lacklove: "What! Torn? Did she not even read it first?"

Waitley: "Alas, no, master. Seemed to put her in a passion when she recognized me as your servant after I had begged private speech with her. When I said the letter was from you with your compliments, she ripped it from my hand and tore it to shreds and bid me return it to you and not to show my face at her house again, nor you either, master."

Lacklove: (*Groans*) "She's not to be won, then. She won't see me. Won't read my letters. Sends my posies back. I've failed. Go you, Waitley, buy me three bottles of the best claret. Here's a coin." (*Exit Waitley, flipping the coin in the air. Lacklove sits with his head in his hands. Enter Tender.*)

Tender: "You look haggard, my friend." (*Aside to audience:* " 'Tis but one day more and my wager's won.*"*) "How lies your disposition toward the lady, and what says she to your suit now?"

Lacklove: "The lady is not won, but, forsooth, your wager is, I fear. Ah, me. She is *that she* above all others

I would take to wife. But, alas, she will none of me. She cannot like me. She cannot love me. She cannot endure me. I am a lost thing." (*He drinks from a wine bottle.*)

Tender: "She heeds her friend's warning that you toy with her. My lady Dazzle has poisoned her ears against you, for I swear, I have seen Mistress Proudheart casting fond looks your way when your eyes were turned from her, Geoff."

Lacklove: (*Laughs bitterly*) "Oh, give me not false hope, Frank, my friend. She disdained my suit. She will not have me. I am to cease and desist from pestering her with my vile attentions."

Tender: "She thinks you mean not well by her. Dazzle has told her of your previous conquests."

Lacklove: (*Jumps up from the table*) "Oh, my lady Dazzle is a spiteful rogue! So my proud lady believes I mean unlawful congress. No. Never. I shall disabuse her. She has truly won my heart. Let a solicitor be summoned to draw up the contract and the marriage settlements. And let a jeweler be called. A ring. 'Od's blood, but I must have a ring!" (*Exit in haste.*)

Tender: (*Aside to audience: "By heavens, he's caught in parson's mousetrap now. Well, she's a pretty creature and has wit enough to hold him, by my oath. Would there were another such paragon for me!"*)

(*Scene five: Proudheart and Dazzle walking in a garden with their waiting women.*)

Dazzle: My dear Phoebe, you are agitated. Never say that roguish knave of a Lacklove has overset you! Attend him not, my dear, else he will play with you and desert you. Incline your affections toward Mr. Truly Constant. There is a faithful gallant."

Proudheart: (*Waving her fan about*) "You advise so? Yet you do not incline toward Mr. Constant, my dear Margery. Do you not find him a trifle . . . dull?"

Dazzle: (*Aside: "She takes not the bait. How to prevent her from stealing away Lacklove?"*) "He is a sober gentleman, 'tis true, yet one who will honor you, and cause you no heart burnings, not even a moment's unrest."

Proudheart: "I fear I am a restless being, Margery. I could not favor a gentleman who would send me to sleep. I need a sharp, stimulating kind of gallant to keep me awake, to keep my wits alive."

Dazzle: "I think you will do yourself great harm if you settle on Lacklove. Beware, my dear Phoebe, of this rake, least in two months time you be his leavings.

Proudheart: (*Walking about agitatedly*) "Oh, I am not fit company today, my dear Margery. I pray you, leave me to settle my restive spirit in my own way."

Dazzle: "As you wish." (*Exit, frowning angrily, with her serving woman.*)

Proudheart: "Go you, too, Faithful, and fetch me a book—No, no. My stitchery—No! My drawing things. Yes, my drawing things—Go. Fetch them."

Faithful: (*Aside to audience: "My lady's in a tizzy! It's that handsome gentleman rogue put her there, I'll be bound!"*) (*Exits.*)

(*Enter Lacklove dressed in all his finery. Sees Proudheart walking alone in her garden.*)

Proudheart: (*Agitatedly slapping her fan against her palm*) "Fie, sir. Why are you come here? I have requested that you cease pestering me. Must I call for assistance and have you forcibly removed from my presence?"

Lacklove: "My proud love! I give you leave to do anything to me that might please you, after you grant me leave to speak with you but for a brief five minutes."

Proudheart: (*Aside: "I mistrust that doting look upon his face. He has smoked me. Ah me, I am a lost thing if he means not well, for I've discovered, however unwisely, I love him most fiercely!"*) "Speak then, importunate creature."

Lacklove: "Madam, that your heart should be pierced as painfully as mine has been by that sweet, torturous shaft of love. 'Tis like a knife in my breast, this longing I have for you, to speak with you, to gaze upon you. I love you, madam. Violently, madly, consumingly, totally, completely. I will surely die if you refuse to be mine."

Proudheart: (*Breathlessly*) "I have inspired these violent feelings? Surely I am not so praiseworthy, nor so desirable, an object. No, no. These lover's vows of yours are like to prove false."

Lacklove: "These lover's vows of mine are the truest thing I have ever uttered. Thy beauty, thy wit, thy virtue is my delight and I find that without you I shall cease to exist, for in you, sweeting, resides my heart. Will you be mine, my heart? I swear, no other shall ever have that organ, for it reposes in you."

Proudheart: "You have protested falsely ere now, sir, so I have heard, to a dozen ladies of the town. What proof can you give me that you will not prove faithless this time?"

Lacklove: (*He produces the marriage contract and shows it to her then places the ring on her unresisting finger.*) "There! I am pledged . . . I have surprised you, I see, sweetheart."

[The ring was the Wexford family engagement ring

which Vicki recognized instantly as the one she returned
to Ned one year ago. She was speechless, forgetting her
lines for the moment. She stared at him disbelievingly.
"Will you, Vic?" Ned whispered for Vicki's ears alone.
She could only nod mutely.]

(*Lacklove sweeps Proudheart into his arms and kisses
her most thoroughly.*)

Lacklove: "Is there not a man of the clergy about?
Let him be called, for I've a mind to be married today.
(*Kisses her again.*) I long to be a husband before night-
fall. We shall be the veriest pair of turtledoves that ever
twined together on Valentine's Day."

Proudheart: (*Vicki recovers herself somewhat to be
able to recite her lines.*) "Well, perhaps I may endure
you for some little time, sirrah."

Lacklove: "Not for some little time, *wife*. For all
time."

Proudheart: "Wife—how strangely the word issues
forth from your lips. Alas, shall I truly dwindle into a
mere wife, then?"

Lacklove: "You shall dwindle into a wife only if I
enlarge into a husband. 'Tis the way of things in our
world, my dear and only love."

(*He sweeps her into his arms, kisses her briefly and
carries her off stage.*)

Thunderous applause greeted them as they left the
stage. While the audience continued to clap and roar with
laughter after the actors had departed, Vicki stood in the
little alcove outside the library with Ned. He immediately
removed his wig and ran a hand through his wet hair,
leaving it in thorough and charming disarray.

After she had recovered somewhat from her own breathless excitement at the completion of a successful performance—and at Ned's unexpected, whispered words during the last scene—she began to pull the ring from her finger so that she could hand it back to him.

"No, no. Leave it where it is," he murmured, lifting her left hand and pushing the ring back into place. He lifted her hand to his mouth and kissed her fingers, then turned her hand over and pressed his lips to her palm for several long seconds, gazing intently into her eyes. "The ring should stay there always," he whispered, "and, if you'll let me, my dear, I would like to add a gold band to join it. Soon."

Vicki looked down at the Wexford family engagement ring glittering with diamonds and emeralds where it rested on her finger. "Can it be that you are proposing to me again, Ned?" she asked breathlessly, looking up into his eyes.

"What do you think I've been trying to do for the past several days, Victoria Colefax, if not proposing to you!"

"Well, I thought you were trying to make me see what I had missed by foolishly calling off our engagement last year. I thought you were trying to pay me back for rejecting you. I never thought you would ask me again."

"Vicki Colefax! I never took you for a widgeon before! Of course I wasn't trying to 'pay you back' for last year. I've had marriage in mind since we got here. No, long before that. Since you threw me over last year. I was trying to do things differently this time."

"Oh, Ned, were you? In what way?"

"Well, I was trying to court you properly, romantically."

"Courting me romantically? Hmm. What you were,

doing didn't seem to be leading to a proposal of marriage, though, you must admit, Ned."

"But you enjoyed it?" he asked with a grin.

"Did I? I don't recall."

"My coy mistress is toying with me," he said with a sigh. "Expect you want something more formal, *Miss* Colefax, before you will admit a thing?"

"A formal declaration? Umm, yes . . . but something more romantic would be nice, too." She tried to restrain her giggles—and her excitement. "After all, it *is* Valentine's Day!"

"So be it then." He got down on one knee, took one of her hands in his and looked up at her with a light shining in his eyes. "Miss Colefax, I would be honored beyond my just desserts if you would agree to be my wife."

When Vicki didn't say anything, but just looked at him expectantly, Ned burst out, "Dam—dash it, Vic, what else do you want me to say? Ah, you are waiting for your romantic declaration, are you?" He jumped to his feet and pulled her into his arms, and growled into her ear, "I love you, Vic. I will always love you and there is nothing I desire more in this world than for you to be my wife. Will you?"

"Yes."

Then he kissed her ruthlessly. When they emerged from their embrace disheveled and breathless some minutes later, Ned murmured, "Is *that* romantic enough for you, my Valentine's heart?"

"Oh, yes, Ned. It is a girl's fondest dream to be proposed to in such a manner, hearing her lover's vows of everlasting devotion." There was a distinct gurgle of laughter in her throat.

"Do you dare to tease me about my lovemaking,

madam?" He nuzzled her neck and ear with his mouth and teeth.

"Oh, no, only you are such a slowtop. . . . I'm just breathlessly waiting for my next kiss."

"Are you, indeed? Well, turn about is fair play, madam. First, I'll hear *your* true lover's vow, dear heart."

"Oh, Ned, do you doubt that I love you truly, utterly, completely. More than life itself, my dear. More than life itself, my own true love."

The twins, peering out from behind a curtain where they had concealed themselves, ready to take action if it were needed, grinned at one another, and took themselves off to spread the good news.

Before she asked the cast to return to take their bows, the Countess Sutcliffe, dressed as a page in a costume that showed off her perfect figure even after four children, strode onto the stage to recite a brief epilogue.

"My dear friends, before our players come out to bid you adieu, allow me to borrow a few words from the Bard's own Rosalind: 'I charge you, O women, for the love you bear to men, to like as much of this play as please you. And I charge you, O men, for the love you bear to women—as I perceive by your simpering none of you hates them—that between you and the women the play may please. If I were a [free] woman I would kiss as many of you as had beards that pleased me, complexions that liked me, and breaths that I defied not.' "

"Ho, if there's to be any kissing, lady wife, then I insist that the beard, the complexion, and the breath that please you be mine, and only mine," Charles called out from his front row seat.

A roar of laughter rose from the audience at the earl's words. Clementina looked momentarily abashed, then laughed along with the rest, giving her husband a look that said she would have something to say to him later for the interruption.

She continued when the clamor died down, "The lady author of the play has given me leave to add a small rhyme of mine own composing. With your indulgence, dear friends, I'll begin:

Lacklove's pretense and Proudheart's disinterest
  were no armor,
For love would pierce their hearts, such is the
  power of amour.
Cupid's darts will land where they may,
Especially on this, good Saint Valentine's Day.
May your lover's vows ever prove true,
Bringing nothing but joy your life through.
Our Valentine's play is done.
We trust with offense to none.
If these our players have pleased you,
Good friends, give us your hands with no more
  ado."

When the players returned to take their bows and the audience had clapped until their hands were stinging, the Marchioness of Wexford turned to Margaret Colefax and observed, "From the look on our children's faces, not to mention their linked hands, I would say that we shall soon be given the job of planning a wedding, my dear Margaret."

"I believe you may be right, Barbara," Margaret replied with a wide smile lighting up her face. "They look so happy, it brings tears to my eyes."

The marchioness reached over to pat her friend's hand, feeling rather like shouting for joy than crying for happiness, now that it seemed her dear son was to wed, and to such a wonderful girl as Victoria Colefax, too. And Vicki would be *such* a help in settling those madcap twins of hers next year, she thought with some relief.

Joan Hadleigh was leaning over to whisper to her husband, Henry, "My dear, to think that our son Richard will soon be married to Lady Jane Fenners. Why, I was never more surprised than when he came to us this afternoon and told us he had just spoken to Jane's mother, and her guardian and received their permission to pay his addresses. And he had already proposed to that sweet girl and been accepted!"

"Well, well, I didn't expect that the boy would settle down for a few more years yet. But it seems he's been felled with one of those arrows shot by that naughty Cupid, just as I was at about his age."

"Oh, Henry, you've always been the most romantic of husbands," Joan said, blushing at her husband's teasing remark.

Lady Jane's mother, the Dowager Countess of Sutcliffe, smiled as she saw her daughter's happy face. She had greatly feared that Jane, with her quiet ways and shy manner, was doomed to remain a spinster all her life. Now to see her on the arm of that handsome rascal Richard Hadleigh, filled her with joy. Her daughter would have a happy and fulfilled life after all. And she was getting what she had always insisted she wanted—a love match.

The dowager tapped Lady Martindale on the arm and imparted the exciting news to her through her ear trumpet.

And on stage, several couples had walked off in a daze, leaving two dark-eyed sprites dressed as serving wenches to smile and wave and blow kisses to the audience. Their sorely tried mother had to blink twice to be sure her eyes weren't deceiving her. Cynthia and Delia had managed to alter the plain and simple serving costumes they wore for the play into something infinitely more alluring. In fact, Lady Wexford thought, they had lowered the bodices, tightened the skirts, and raised the hems, so that now they looked as though they had just played the part of doxies rather than waiting women.

"Those girls will be the death of me yet!" she murmured under her breath. "Thank heaven I shall have a strong-minded daughter-in-law to help me manage them next year in London."

"Well, my love, well?" Charles, Earl Sutcliffe, grinned at his countess when she joined him that night in their bedchamber.

Clementina ran up to her husband and threw herself into his waiting arms. "Oh, my dearest Chas, not only do we have a wedding to prepare for our dear Jane, but we shall have Vicki wed to Ned at long last!"

"And all thanks to your loving machinations. What a little matchmaker I've married."

She twisted one of the frogged closings of his dressing gown, "Well, my love, you've known *that* since I tricked you into falling in love with me."

He kissed her briefly. "Hmm. You may think you manipulated me, Tina, but believe me, darling dear, I had quite determined to have you for my countess from the first moment I laid eyes on you."

She blushed and looked directly into his bright blue eyes that were shining with love and humor into hers. "Oh, Chas! You've never told me that before."

"Just saving it for Valentine's Day, my dear. After all, must have something more to offer you than fancy bouquets and silly rhymes," he murmured against her lips. "Why, you might even consider it a new lover's vow of your very own."

Music of the Heart

by
Olivia Sumner

One

Though the Burlington ballroom had been completely
redone for this year's Valentine's Day Ball, the four
young ladies gathered on the steps nearest to the hall
took little notice of the new crimson flock wallpaper or
the alternating red and gold panels. All of them had
paused to gaze at their images in the mirrors when they
had passed one or the other of the newly imported twin
Portuguese trumos, but not a one had noted the gold and
marble beauty of the trumos' elaborate and unusual combination of pier table and looking glass.

"Did you ever see so many red roses?" Cassandra
Bowen asked. " 'Tis a veritable bower, though perhaps
the slightest bit overdone."

" 'Tis well known Lord Burlington maintains the finest greenhouse in London," Estelle Redrick put in. "As
well as an unusually fine conservatory."

Georgianne Bates showed no interest in roses, green-
houses, or conservatories, her gaze being fixed on a group
on the far side of the ballroom. "What is it about Juliet
Grant the gentlemen find so interesting?" she wanted to
know. "I daresay any one of us is more attractive. And
certainly we are all dressed far more in the mode."

"Juliet Grant is the most outrageous flirt in all of London," Cassandra said with an over-the-shoulder glance

at the circle of admirers gathered around Juliet. "Why else is she able to hold court as though she were the Queen of Hearts?"

"If the gentlemen of the *ton* chose the Queen," Estelle said, "I imagine she would be."

Cassandra raised her eyebrows as though to challenge the comment but said nothing to Estelle, speaking instead to the youngest member of the group. "Do stop gawking, Mary Margaret. While such rudeness might go unnoticed in Glasgow, we are not so rag-mannered here in London. Come away, do."

Not only her Scottish cousin but also Estelle and Georgianne followed Cassandra, making their way from the ballroom toward the anteroom set aside for the ladies to refresh themselves.

"I expect the gentlemen's Queen of Hearts vote might well be unanimous," Georgianne said with one last glance back at the admiring ring around Juliet.

Cassandra frowned at her. "I cannot understand why, when she is so constantly inconstant. In December, if you recall, Juliet seemed to favor Jeremy Bright, while in January, at least according to the tittle-tattle, Lord Beechley was the one who happened to catch her eye."

"And now, at the Valentine Ball, Mr. Drabney appears to be leading the field," Georgianne said, gazing with sly innocence at Cassandra. "Was it not Mr. Drabney I saw dancing attendance on you at the New Year's *fete?*"

Cassandra stopped below one of the small, partially enclosed balconies set at intervals around the hall, balconies that were entered from the mezzanine. Staring down her nose at Georgianne, she said sharply, "That does not pertain, not in the least. I care not a whit what Mr. Charles Drabney does or does not do."

"I should lower my voice, if I were you," Georgianne warned with a significant glance at the balcony they stood underneath.

Cassandra sniffed. "No one is occupying that balcony at the moment, I particularly noticed. In any case, I always speak softly, not to mention melodiously. My voice has been compared to the notes from a harp plucked by an angel."

"I, for one," Estelle put in, "like Juliet more than a little. I find her most amiable and consistently cheerful despite the tragedy in her life and her rather lowered circumstances."

As Estelle spoke, a plump, attractive lady of a certain age was being seated in the balcony above her by a younger and dashing dark-haired man. Since neither woman nor man said a word, the four young ladies underneath were not aware of their presence.

"I have the strangest suspicion," Georgianne said, "that Juliet Grant will never marry." When the others stared in surprise, she added, "You were quite on the mark, Cassie, when you mentioned her inconstant heart, always seeking but never finding, like a butterfly flitting from flower to flower. One must feel sorry for her."

"Better an inconstant heart," Estelle said with feeling, "than no heart at all."

"No heart at all?" Mary Margaret Taylor, visiting from Glasgow, spoke for the first time. "Pray how is that possible?"

Cassandra smiled at her. "I believe Estelle refers to Lord Talland."

Estelle raised her fan to hide a blush. "I was making a general observation with no particular gentleman in mind," she protested.

Georgianne reached to cover Estelle's hand with her own. "I suspect each of us has harbored feelings of tenderness to a greater or lesser degree for Talland at one time or another. Hopeless feelings, I might add. As yet no amount of warmth has succeeded in melting the ice encasing his heart. If indeed, he actually possesses one."

"Who, pray tell, is Lord Talland?" Mary Margaret asked.

"Who is Lord Talland?" the others repeated in unison, much as though Mary Margaret had never heard of the Tower of London or St. Paul's Cathedral.

"Lord Talland is Malcolm Rothwell, Viscount of Talland," Cassandra said, "and shall one day become, God willing, the fifth Earl of Midhurst."

Estelle added, "Lord Talland lives in *the* town house on *the* square in Mayfair, Grosvenor Square, besides having an estate in Surrey and, I believe, another, smaller holding at Hart's Hill in Sussex. His stable is one of the three best in England. His bay, Lion Heart, placed first in last year's Derby."

Georgianne sighed. "Lord Talland is tall and darkly handsome with eyes as green as Irish shamrocks. Since he is also a mysterious, brooding man, his mere glance is enough to send shivers down one's spine."

Cassandra sniffed. "Not *my* spine. He quizzes the young ladies of the *ton* as though we were cattle for sale at an auction at Tattersall's, raising hopes only to finally wrinkle his nose and turn away without offering a bid. If pride precedes a fall, Lord Talland will one day take a mighty plunge."

With the exception of Mary Margaret, the others shook their heads. "You sang a somewhat different song last year," Estelle reminded Cassandra.

"If only I could see this Lord Talland," Mary Margaret said, "so I could judge him myself."

"He was not in the ballroom when we left it," Georgianne said. "Although an excellent dancer, he seldom ventures onto the floor. I believe I glimpsed him earlier this evening in conversation with the Chancellor of the Exchequer. He was wearing a coat of green, the color of his eyes, and black breeches."

"The hue of his heart," Cassandra murmured. "If he has one. No doubt bored to distraction by the Valentine's Day Ball, I venture to say that by now Lord Talland has undoubtedly left for White's. Or to visit Marylebone."

"I know White's is a gentlemen's club," Mary Margaret said, "but Marylebone?"

"Marylebone," Estelle told her in a lowered voice, "happens to be where Mrs. Chauncey Lowell has her residence. Mrs. Lowell, some say, is the most recent object of Lord Talland's attentions."

"You have painted such a fascinating picture of this man without a heart," Mary Margaret said, "that I confess to being disappointed I shall not have a chance to view him." She sighed. As if her sigh was a signal, the four young ladies, without a backward glance, moved on.

It so happened, however, that Malcolm Rothwell, Viscount of Talland, had not made his way to White's nor was he in or near Marylebone. He was, in fact, at that moment seated in the balcony with Lady Ashcroft, his maternal, and only blood-related aunt.

"Shame on you, Malcolm," she said, tapping his knuckles with her fan as she watched the young ladies walk away. "I had not realized you were such a heartbreaker."

He shrugged. "No more so than this Juliet Grant they

spoke of. I don't believe she and I have ever met. If we have, I must own it has slipped my mind."

"Juliet Grant," Lady Ashcroft repeated the name thoughtfully. "I do believe she must be Catherine Pender's granddaughter. The Grants died some years ago—a tragic accident of some kind, as I recall."

Letting that pass—he had no idea who she meant—he said, "You look most charming tonight, my dear aunt."

"Save your compliments for the young ladies," she told him with mock severity. Almost immediately she sighed. "You really must leave town tomorrow?"

Talland nodded. "By the first light of dawn. My orders are to report to Major Eustace in Portsmouth the following morning."

"Have you tired of London? Of all your friends?"

He leaned toward his aunt. "The truth is nothing seems to spark my interest anymore. I feel as though I spend my life on a round-about with the same people doing the same things coming into view, disappearing, then coming into view again. I need a change. A new challenge. Adventure."

"I realize this is advice you must have heard from me before, Malcolm, but I feel I must repeat it for your own good. You should marry."

He smiled. "I tell you I seek excitement and you immediately suggest the exact opposite."

"How wrong you are."

"I realize, my dear aunt, that your marriage to Uncle George was the exception. The young ladies of the *ton*, I fear, either bore me with their chatter or tire me with their brilliant repartee. When I marry I want someone who has, besides the usual social and, perhaps, monetary attributes, the ability to make me comfortable. That is what a husband should be, comfortable."

She raised her eyebrows. "Are you funning me, Malcolm? I strongly suspect you are."

"Not in the least. I consider marriage a venture of the greatest importance and thus have given the matter of choosing a wife considerable thought. She should be someone who is adept at entertaining, who manages the household, and leaves the husband freedom to pursue his interests. In other words, the ability to make him comfortable."

"Then I have the ideal candidate for you."

"Oh? And who might that be."

"Heston, my butler. Other than being of the wrong sex, he fulfills your requirements to perfection."

"Now you, Aunt Elaine, are funning me."

"Perhaps I am." Her smile faded almost at once. "I worry about you," she said. When her nephew started to speak, Lady Ashcroft raised her hand to silence him. "Not about your marrying, that will have to take care of itself, but about your buying a commission in the cavalry. I never have seriously worried about you before, but somehow this time is different."

"Beaumont and I have been close since we were boys and, as you know, we joined up together. You could not expect I would allow him to go off on such an adventure without me. Besides, I happen to lead a charmed life, Aunt Elaine, I always have and I suspect I always will. Let me tell you what happened to me at White's on Thursday. I was losing steadily when suddenly—"

"I understand about Beaumont but the lucky turn of a card or the fortunate throw of the dice means nothing."

She shook her head impatiently. "Do you believe in omens, Malcolm?"

He smiled one-sidedly. "Only the favorable ones; the others I ignore."

"You always were inclined to be flippant."

"A bad habit, I own. Pray tell me of your omen."

"It was a dream I had last night, one of the strangest, most disturbing dreams I ever had." His aunt closed her eyes as she remembered. "I was at Hart's Hill," she went on softly, "walking along the entrance hall looking for you, Malcolm. Of a sudden, a roaring gust of bitter cold wind swept through the house, rattling the shutters, blowing out the candles and leaving me in pitch darkness."

"Hart's Hill *is* a rather drafty old pile."

"Almost at once," she went on, ignoring his comment, "I heard someone sobbing so I followed the sound, groping my way up the great staircase to the balcony and then along the east corridor to the open door of a bedchamber. The sobs stopped the moment I crossed the threshold. Still in total darkness, I made my way across the room to the bed. When I reached out I touched someone lying there."

Malcolm, feeling the intensity in his aunt's voice, took her hand in his. "And?"

"In dreams you often know something without having any notion how you came to know it. In my dream, I knew the person on the bed was you, Malcolm, and I knew you were in great danger. 'Help me,' you cried, and I said, 'Tell me how to help you, what should I do?' and you said again, 'Help me, help me.' "

Lady Ashcroft opened her eyes.

"There was no more?" Despite himself, he felt a slight chill of apprehension.

"No more. I awoke to the echo of your pleas." His aunt stood, taking both of his hands in hers when he rose with her. "Oh, how foolish I am," she said, "troubling you with my meaningless dream on this, your last night in London." She raised herself on tiptoe and kissed his cheek. "You were kind to keep me company but I daresay you have plans for the evening and I must be getting back to the ball." She squeezed his hands. "May God bless and keep you."

"And you," he said.

When she released his hands and left the balcony, Malcolm hesitated and then hurried to overtake her on the mezzanine. Turning her to him, he hugged her, murmuring, "I love you, Aunt Elaine."

He saw tears in her eyes. "And I, you, Malcolm," she said softly.

Releasing her, he watched as she descended the steps toward the ballroom, thinking he might follow her but then he shook his head and turned away, instead going down the side steps. As he neared the bottom, he heard voices from the direction of the conservatory, a woman's voice followed by a man's, and he caught a glimpse of a yellow gown before the voices receded. He glanced into the conservatory with its lush display of winter-defying greenery and found it deserted, the far door ajar.

Still undecided whether to go to the ballroom for a few more farewells or to leave the ball and make his way to White's, he paused in the doorway to the conservatory. A sparkle caught his eye and, curious, he entered the warm, humid room and crossed to an orange tree. There, caught on one of the tree's thorny branches, he saw an emerald set in the center of a small golden heart.

How lovely, he thought, removing the ornament from

the branch and holding it to the light, admiring the deep green glint of the precious stone and the rich golden luster of the heart. Slipping the heart into his pocket, he turned, intending to give his find to Lady Burlington, this season's Valentine's Ball hostess.

Hearing the rustle of a gown he paused and a young lady, a stranger to him, appeared in the conservatory doorway. He stared at her, his heart pounding, vaguely noting her yellow gown but far more intensely aware of her curling brown hair, her deep blue eyes and the anguished expression on her exquisite face.

Catching sight of him, her eyes widened as though in recognition and she started to speak only to stop and shake her head, almost in annoyance. "My heart," she said at last, her voice breathless. "I have lost my heart." Her hand went to the bodice of her gown, touching a brooch with a sapphire set in a small heart on one side and an empty space on the other.

Still he stared at her. He should, he realized, say something to her, make a clever remark warning young ladies to be careful not to lose their hearts, but he discovered he was strangely speechless. This will not do, Talland told himself, this will not do at all.

"Several years ago," he found himself saying, for no reason he could discern, "I was walking west along Bond Street on an overcast day when all sound seemed to fade away, leaving a profound and eerie silence. After a few minutes, a few seconds more likely, the sun appeared from behind clouds, blinding me, and when I could see again I heard the rumble of the carriages and the cries of the hawkers."

He could tell by her puzzled expression that as far as she was concerned he was making precious little sense.

"As though for a short time the world had stood still," he said, trying to explain himself, "and then after a pause started whirling again. I had much that same sensation just now when you appeared from out of nowhere." She still seemed confused. "And you?" he pressed on, wondering if she felt at all the same.

Her gaze met his and he thought she was about to nod but instead she merely said, "How fanciful you are, Lord Talland."

So she knew who he was. "You have the advantage over me," he told her.

"Miss Juliet Grant."

Juliet, what a charming name, was his first thought, and then he remembered the conversation he and his aunt had inadvertently overheard. So this was Juliet of the inconstant heart. While, of course, he had none at all. Except, of course, for hers.

He smiled, telling himself this might prove to be an interesting evening, after all. "And so you have lost your heart," he said.

Again she touched her brooch. "The mate to this heart," she said. "It was my mother's gift to me, made shortly before she died."

"I have your heart." Reaching into his pocket, Malcolm brought forth the emerald heart. Stepping closer, he examined the brooch, conscious of the faint scent of violets mingling with the rather overpowering sweetness of the orange blossoms. At such close range he could hardly miss the delightful swell of her breasts.

Perhaps aware of this, Juliet took a step backwards.

"I was about to suggest I might reattach your heart," he said, "but I fear the brooch will need a goldsmith's attention." He held out the heart, offering it to her on the palm of his hand. "You must be careful not to lose your heart ever again. Once is quite enough."

She plucked the heart from his hand, unable to do so without touching him, which had been his intention. She blushed and averted her gaze.

"Have we met before?" he asked. "You did seem to know my name." Privately he decided that if he had ever been introduced to her he certainly would have remembered this enchanting creature.

She shook her head, meeting his gaze once more. "Thank you so much," she said, "for finding and returning the heart. The brooch was a wedding gift from my father to my mother, the entwined hearts a symbol of their love. She treasured it as do I."

"I think you were intended by fate to lose your heart tonight, and I was meant to give it back to you. Now you must beware or I shall be tempted to take it again."

Amusement glowed in her blue eyes. "Spoken like the gallant I have heard that you are."

"Not merely gallant, in this case," he insisted, surprised to realize he actually meant what he was saying. The inconstant-hearted Juliet Grant had somehow bewitched him, making him regret that he had only a few hours to spend with her before leaving for Portsmouth. He smiled ruefully as he recalled boasting to his aunt that he led a charmed life.

"Since our time together is to be so brief," he found himself saying to her, "please do me the favor of calling me Malcolm now, at once, and you shall be Juliet to me." Seeing her eyes widen, he cursed inwardly. For some reason he was completely off-stride. She must think him either mad or shockingly forward.

"I leave at dawn for Portsmouth," he explained hastily.

She nodded uncertainly, glancing from side to side, appearing torn between humoring his eccentricity and fleeing from the conservatory. He intended to do all in his power to keep her here. Was it possible she had felt nothing when their eyes met a few moments ago? No, impossible.

He frowned. Did she think he was wasting these precious moments engaging in glib repartee? In carrying on a meaningless flirtation? Somehow he must convince her otherwise, make her realize his sincerity. Time. What he needed was time and yet he had next to none.

"May I have the honor?" he asked. "Shall we dance?"

Again she hesitated, then nodded, taking his offered arm. He escorted her from the conservatory to the ballroom where a quadrille was forming. As they danced from partner to partner, he was oblivious to the whispers and the stares directed his way, his attention focused entirely on Juliet, searching for some sign, perhaps a sudden, surprised smile or a glance that lingered overlong, some acknowledgement that her feelings were at least partially akin to his.

That sparkle in her eye, for instance. What did it mean? Everything? Or nothing? That slight pressure of her hand on his as they passed one another in the dance. Was it mere chance or did it hold a secret meaning?

What a fool you are, Talland, he admonished himself. Have you of a sudden become mildly demented? Has the excitement of leaving for the Peninsula clouded your judgment? Or did this feverish feeling, this exultation, this fire in his blood, mean he was on the verge of falling ill?

When next they came together in the dance, he studied Juliet with all the cool detachment he could muster. She was not beautiful, certainly not, her captivating youthful bloom would soon fade. Curling brown hair, large blue eyes, there was certainly nothing remarkable about either. Gowned in the current fashion, of course, but without any special flair. So you see, Talland, this Miss Juliet Grant, by any objective measure, is a perfectly ordinary young lady.

Then why was he possessed with this overwhelming need to look at her, to treasure each of her small gestures, why this desire to hear her voice, to breathe in her violet scent, to learn all there was to know about her, however trivial, why did he long to touch her, to hold her in his arms? He considered himself a reasonable man, a thoughtful man, but he could provide no answers.

Perhaps it was fortunate he would be leaving London in the morning. In a few days, or a few months at the most, this unreasonable infatuation would pass much as a fever eventually cooled. By Midsummer's Eve he would be shaking his head and wondering what had afflicted him at the Valentine Day's Ball. And, by next Valentine's Day, he should have completely forgotten Juliet Grant.

The quadrille set ended and he led her not to the supper room but in the opposite direction, to a corridor adjoining the ballroom. Though she looked a question at him, she offered no objection.

"Do you waltz?" he asked.

"I never have."

"The steps are simple," he said, showing her.

"I have waltzed by myself," she owned.

He held out his arms. "Shall we?"

"But we have no music."

Realizing the orchestra in the ballroom was indeed silent, he said, "Then I shall supply some." He started to hum a popular French waltz and after a moment she joined in.

He took her into his arms where she fit as perfectly as he had somehow known she would. They danced along the corridor, the portraits on the walls whirling around them, the two of them alone together in a world of their own, caught up in the magic of the dance, one he hoped would never end.

Juliet gasped and stopped dancing.

"What is it?" he asked, stepping away.

"I have lost my heart again," she said, looking down. The golden heart with the emerald lay on the polished wood of the floor. "I had tied it into my handkerchief for safekeeping but I fear it will not be safe until the two hearts are linked together as they should be and secured to the brooch."

He frowned as he scooped the errant heart from the floor. A woman's notion: Linked hearts, secured by marriage, equalled a couple joined together for the rest of their lives. Women were always attempting to entangle men. He did not want entanglements, he wanted to be free, able to choose his own way in life. Best to end this here and now, before there could be any significant attachment.

"Let me escort you to your party," he said abruptly, nodding toward the ballroom. "As I mentioned I drive to Portsmouth in the morning and the hour grows late."

She stared at him. Did he sound as confused to her as he did to himself. Did he know his own mind?

Of a sudden, Juliet turned and ran from him, ran toward the ballroom, leaving him looking after her, awash both with relief and the fear he had made the greatest mistake of his life.

Two

Juliet hurried into the ballroom, side-stepping several young gallants who were eager to speak to her. Where *was* her grandmother? It was clearly impossible to leave without Grandmama and she must get away quickly, she could not bear to remain at the ball one moment longer.

She had not acted so foolishly since she was eleven years old and moon-eyed over her music teacher, a handsome young Frenchman. For a fortnight after Grandmama had replaced Monsieur Armand with a woman, Juliet had drooped dismally, returning to her usual cheerful self only after the cook's tabby, a favorite of hers, had kittens. She dearly loved both cats and kittens.

Still, she suspected there was a considerable difference between her childish *tendresse* and her sudden, overwhelming attraction to Lord Talland, jingle-brained as she knew it must be. Why, when she knew his cold-hearted reputation, had she allowed herself to be swept into a make-believe world where, clasped in his arms, she had wished to remain forever? Why had she imagined she'd seen not only admiration in his green eyes but the same bedazzlement she had so inexplicably felt?

It would not do, no, not at all. She had behaved like a shatterbrained gudgeon. And she no longer had the excuse of being a child. With a sinking feeling inside, she decided it would take far more than a favorite cat to make her forget this folly. Would she ever be able to completely eradicate Lord Talland from her heart?

Cassandra Bowen, accompanied by a younger, sandy-haired girl Juliet did not know, beckoned to her. Juliet forced a smile, shook her head and hurried on. She could not bear to go over and speak to Cassandra just now, to make polite conversation when all she wished for at the moment was to be safe at home.

Safe. That was certainly not a word that could be applied to Lord Talland. When she had waltzed with him, being safe was the last thing on her mind. Dangerous, was a far more applicable word in conjunction with him. Yet she had not been afraid. Far from it. While held in his arms, she had felt wonderful, felt as though nothing existed except the two of them. . . .

Why had he taken the trouble to make her feel that way, only to turn cold shortly thereafter? She blinked back tears she dare not shed. Not here and not now.

Thank heaven, there was her grandmother, chatting with an older woman whose dark hair had barely begun to gray. Though the woman looked somehow familiar, Juliet could not place her.

"Why, here is Juliet now," her grandmother said as she hurried up to them. "My dear, this is Lady Ashcroft. She and I were childhood chums but we have not seen one another in some time. Elaine had no idea my little granddaughter had grown up and become a fashionable young lady."

Juliet smiled at Lady Ashcroft, forcing herself to utter the required polite phrases, hoping she would soon be

alone with her grandmother so she could convince her
to leave the ball.

"I am delighted to meet you," Lady Ashcroft told
Juliet. "I do wish we could have the chance to become
better acquainted, but Catherine tells me you both are
leaving for the Hebrides tomorrow."

"Yes," Juliet said, "in the morning." Lady Ashcroft
seemed pleasant, in other circumstances she might enjoy
talking to her. But at the moment all she could think of
was getting away before *he* appeared. She could not bear
to see him again.

Not that he would come near her. He had made it only
too evident he was tired of her company.

"I seem to be one of the few people I know remaining
in town," Lady Ashcroft said. "You and Catherine are going to the Hebrides and my nephew is off to Portsmouth
at cock's crow."

Because Juliet was occupied in covertly scanning the
room, dreading that she might see Talland, it took her a
moment or two to realize what Lady Ashcroft had said.
Taken off guard, she blurted, "Portsmouth?"

Lady Ashcroft nodded. "I thought he might have mentioned it to you while you were dancing with him. I do
wish this dreadful war was over. Serving under General
Wellington is fine and noble, of course, but I am un-
commonly fond of Malcolm and I dread seeing him exposed to danger."

As Juliet tried not to show her dismay at the connection between Lady Ashcroft and Talland, her grandmother said, "Juliet, my dear, I had no idea you and Lord
Talland knew one another until Elaine came over to me
and asked if that could possibly be my granddaughter
dancing with her nephew."

Since Juliet did not want to distress her grandmother by admitting she had never been introduced to him, she searched for a answer close to the truth that would be more palatable. "I had the misfortune to lose one of the linked hearts," she said finally, her fingers touching the brooch, "and Lord Talland found—" She stopped abruptly. He had not returned the heart with the emerald to her!

At that moment she saw him standing on the top of the steps leading from the hall to the ballroom and her heart stood still. He would not, she realized, appear to any more of an advantage in an officer's uniform than he did at the moment, for he already eclipsed every other man present. Even in the drabbest of country-wear, Lord Talland would stand out.

He turned his head and his gaze met hers. She could not look away, she could not breathe. As he strode toward her, the music, the laughter, the voices all vanished and the world stood still.

The world did not start whirling again, as he had put it, until he stood before her. "I wondered where you had got to," he said, as though his dismissive words in the corridor had never been uttered. As though she had left him by her own choice instead of being driven away by his coolness.

He nodded to his aunt, politely acknowledged his introduction to her grandmother and then offered Juliet his arm. "I believe you promised me a waltz," he said.

She had already granted him a waltz as he was well aware but with the two older women smiling at them, what could she do but place her hand on his arm and allow him to lead her away? Since she refused to lie to herself, she had to admit that she wanted to go with him, that she longed to be held in his arms again while they waltzed—not that she intended him to know.

"Where is my heart?" she asked him when they had passed beyond earshot.

"Rest assured your heart, inconstant as it may be, is safe in my keeping," he told her as he placed his arm about her waist and whirled her into the waltz.

Inconstant? What could he mean? She had never met a man who spoke so continuously in riddles, just as she had never met a man who fascinated her so completely. He danced superbly, as graceful as a cat, although the shameful truth was she enjoyed being in his arms quite as much as the dancing.

With such a clear warning signal, she should remain on her guard. But then again, why? For them, there was only tonight before they parted, heading in different directions, not to meet again for at least months, perhaps years. Or possibly never. No! She refused to believe they might never meet again.

When he murmured in her ear, "We have but a few hours," he seemed to be echoing her thoughts. She did not object when he paused at the steps on the far side of the room from his aunt and her grandmother and led her up them. Nor did she refuse when he collected her white velvet cape with the ermine trim, draped it over her shoulders and escorted her from the hall into the moonlit night, even though it crossed her mind that her reckless behavior might well leave an irrevocable stain on her reputation.

Evidently this had also occurred to him because, as he handed her into his curricle, he said, "I shall say you were smitten with a sudden illness and I was obliged to see you safely home."

She gazed at him frankly. "Is that what you intend to do—see me safely home?"

He paused in pulling on his gloves to touch her cheek with the back of his hand. "I am beginning to understand I have no choice but to do the proper thing. Surely you know by now this is no ordinary flirtation. Since we must have some time alone together, though, be warned that I intend to take the long way to your home."

The truth is, she told herself, I *have* been smitten by a sudden illness, one I may never recover from, an illness named Malcolm Rothwell. "Malcolm," she murmured, saying his name aloud to see how it sounded on her tongue. His pleased smile made her heart turn over.

"Juliet. Have you noticed how melodic your name is?"

To hear him say her name was music to her ears but it would not do to tell him so. "Why did you say I had an inconstant heart?" she asked instead.

He slanted her a quick glance. "I was led to believe you have been known to flit from admirer to admirer like a butterfly to one flower after another."

Juliet, taken aback, could provide no ready reply. She had no idea she had become an object of gossip.

His gloved hand covered hers for a moment. "I hope, my lovely butterfly, you will tell me that the reason you hesitated to settle on any flower is because you were searching for the right one and had not yet found it. Or found him. Found the right man. If I make any sense. Meeting you has addled my wits."

"If you're asking me whether I have given my heart to any man, indeed I have not."

"Ah, but you are wrong. I am a man and I do believe I have your heart."

She stared at him a moment, then smiled. He was not

the only one whose wits were addled. She had completely forgotten that he had not returned her emerald heart.

"Have I mentioned how delightful your smile is?" he asked and then shook his head. "You must have heard similar compliments from any number of gentlemen. Words! How can they convey what has happened to me? Yet words are all I have to try to tell you how I feel. I have never before realized how limiting words are. Ah, Juliet, I cannot think why we have never met before."

"I spend much of my time in the country with my grandmother," Juliet said. "My parents were killed in an accident when I was eleven and she has been my guardian since then. We live rather modestly."

"I, too, lost my mother when I was eleven," he said. "Of course my father remarried and my stepmama is truly the perfect wife for him. I don't dislike her but she has never taken the place of my mother."

She thought she remembered that, like her, he had no siblings. So, as a boy, he had been left with no one to share his grief after his mother's death. Feeling a certain kinship, Juliet covered his hand with hers.

"Damn propriety," he muttered, swerving the curricle around a corner so abruptly she fell against him. He wrapped an arm about her, holding her next to him as he urged the horses on.

Juliet tried to edge away but, when his grip tightened, she gave herself up to the enjoyment of being close to him. She had already broken the rules by leaving the ball with Malcolm and, as she had heard her grandmother say, if one is to be hanged, it may as well be for a sheep rather than merely a lamb.

"Aunt Elaine will not mind," he said as he directed

the horses into a narrow drive and then halted them in what seemed to be a mews. "Or rather what she don't know will not do her, or us, any harm."

Releasing her, he alighted, secured the horses, then came around to help her from the curricle. Stripping off his gloves, he took her gloved hand, crossed the mews, opened a wooden gate and ushered her into a tiny enclosed back garden. Moonlight silvered plants and bushes while the familiar scent of thyme and basil spiced the night air.

"This is my aunt's herb garden," he said, leading her to a wooden bench, though neither of them sat down. "My secret place when I was a boy since no one ever thought of looking for me here. I realize now my aunt must have known where I was, but she never gave me away."

"Now *I* know your secret," she teased, hoping he would not notice how breathless she was.

"So you do. Fair is fair. In return, you must forfeit one of your secrets by telling it to me."

How did he expect her to think, much less speak when he stood so close, gazing so intently at her? "Your eyes don't look green in the moonlight," she said, immediately wishing she could retract the words. How terribly birdwitted she must sound.

"Nor do yours look blue, as blue as the sapphire in your brooch, as I recall. But the color of your eyes and mine are no secret. Surely you have at least one small one to confess."

She could think of no secret except for her childish folly. "At eleven," she said reluctantly, certain he would label her a silly goose, "I developed a *tendresse* for my French music teacher. I have never told a soul. Though

I do believe my grandmother surmised the truth because he disappeared from the scene overnight, to be replaced by a stern mistress of the pianoforte."

"Ah, these Frenchmen," he said. "Always causing problems." He cupped her face in his hands, bending his head until she felt his warm breath against her lips as he spoke. "Shall I kiss you or do you believe it may prove too dangerous for us both?"

Her pulses quickened and her knees took on the consistency of currant jelly. "Dangerous?" she whispered.

"Dangerous," he repeated, "but inevitable," and lowered his mouth to hers.

Though more than one had tried, she'd never allowed any man to kiss her on the mouth. Malcolm's lips, warm and questing, were the first to touch hers. Her eyes drooped shut with the intensity of her pleasurable excitement as she gave herself up to his kiss.

Thrills ran along her spine. When his lips grew more demanding, deep inside her a fire sparked into life. Without her willing it, her arms came up to hold him to her. How could anything so enjoyable, so wonderful be wrong?

Even in her bemusement she understood it was not the kiss that caused her ardent response but the man who was kissing her. Malcolm Rothwell, Lord Talland. Who was leaving for Portsmouth at cock's crow. The mere thought of him going away from her caused her to cling to him and press closer.

His lips left hers. "We cannot keep on with this." He spoke against her throat, a strange and exciting hoarseness in his voice. "At least I cannot. For if I do . . ."

"But I want to," she murmured.

"As do I. You have no idea how desperately." He held her away from him. "Just as this is a special place, Juliet, what we feel for one another is special. So much so that I must bring you safely home, just as I promised I would."

She bit her lip. "Must you?"

He kissed the tip of her nose. "Unfortunately, yes. You are the sweetest, most delectable young lady in all of England and not taking advantage of you is most damnedably difficult."

At that moment she wanted nothing more than for him to do just that—take advantage of her. She was not entirely certain exactly what it might entail but she wanted, she needed, to have him go on holding her in his arms and kissing her.

He pulled her down onto the bench and peeled off one of her gloves, finger by finger. When her hand was bare, he brought her palm to his mouth, kissed it and then curled her fingers over the kiss.

"Save that until I return so that you can give it back to me then," he said.

"Yes," she whispered, barely able to speak for the tumult within her. The warmth of his lips on her palm had traveled all the way down to the tips of her toes.

"I wish it were possible to take you to Portsmouth with me so we could spend a few more hours together but, of course, that is completely out of the question."

"You are going to fight under General Wellington," she said, repeating what his aunt had told her. She was unable to voice her fear that he might be injured in battle and she refused to entertain even for a moment the idea that he might be killed. "You *will* come back," she said fiercely.

"Certainly. I have always led a charmed life. And my luck has definitely not deserted me—did I not meet you this very evening?" He spoke with such assurance that she could not help but believe him.

"I trust you will become better acquainted with Aunt Elaine while I'm gone," he added.

"I would like to. Perhaps the chance will come when Grandmama and I return from visiting her cousin in the Hebrides. We leave in the morning."

"So you are going away, too." He caught her hand again, pressing it between both of his. "Please believe me when I say I have never felt this way before. I cannot and will not say more, the circumstances being what they are."

"I shall never permit another man to kiss me," she said solemnly. "Only you."

His laugh was tender. "How sweetly young you are, after all."

"I am not a schoolgirl!" she exclaimed indignantly.

"I did not mean to imply you were. What I meant was that your innocence charms me, as does everything else about you. But it would be unfair of me, as a cavalryman, to hold you to any promise. Except one."

Anticipation tingled through her. "What may that promise be, pray tell?"

"Without fail, you must attend next year's Valentine's Ball. Attend, and look for me there. I will do all in my power to be at that ball and, when we meet there, we shall take up where we, regretfully, must now leave off."

He rose and pulled her to her feet. Would he kiss her again? She longed for him to. For a moment she thought her wish would be granted but then he stepped back, asking, "Do you have any idea how tempting you are?"

Since there was no reply she could possibly make, she remained silent, gazing up at him, so caught up in the spell he cast that she was unable to move.

He grasped her shoulders. "If any other man does kiss

you while I'm gone," he growled, "I swear I will call him out and kill the bastard."

He didn't say another word as they left the garden and returned to his curricle. Nor did they speak during the short ride to where she and her aunt were staying. He halted the horses and was about to jump down when he paused.

"I almost forgot to return this," he said, reaching into a pocket, pulling out the heart with the emerald and offering it to her.

"No," she said. "I have come to believe it was meant that you should find my heart—after all, your eyes are as green as the emerald. Therefore you must take my heart with if you on your journey to keep you safe."

He smiled at her as he returned the heart to his pocket. "I shall take care not to lose this. As some would have it, since I have none, your heart is the only one I possess."

He stepped down, came around and lifted her from the curricle. She raised up and, greatly daring, kissed him quickly on the lips. Before she could draw back he caught her to him, holding her, prolonging the kiss until she was certain her knees would buckle.

She had not dreamed a kiss could be so pleasurable and at the same time promise more, promise caresses that would assuage the sweet ache inside her. She retained barely enough reason to understand she must not make a spectacle of herself in public, where anyone might see.

Drawing back, she said breathlessly, "I promise I will be at next year's Valentine Ball."

He released her and again she noted the thrilling huskiness in his voice as he spoke. "As I will be, if it is within my power. I have promised to meet you at the Valentine's Day Ball and Rothwells never break their promises."

Three

Juliet stared at herself in the looking glass over her dressing table and bit her lip. Why, when her hair had given her no difficulty for twelve months, must it choose tonight to curl in all directions at once, ends sticking out here and there like an untidy hayrick?

"I don't know, Miss Juliet," Adele, her grandmother's maid, said as she struggled to tame the wild disorder. "It do seem to have a mind of its own."

Which was more than Juliet had. She had looked forward to this evening with eager anticipation but now that it was here she was in a veritable quake, her thoughts running between post and pillar, becoming more and more muddled.

Because she had been wearing a gown of pale-yellow when they met, she had chosen a white gauze gown over a silk petticoat of jonquil yellow, the thin material of the gown allowing the yellow to show through. But was the color *too* bright? She could not decide and wondered if he would even remember the color of her last year's gown.

Watching Adele insert another brass hairpin in an effort to hold her hair in place, she prayed that she would not start shedding the pins during the evening—they cost the earth and Grandmama had already spent more than she should have on clothes for this occasion.

"We cannot have the gossips whispering that you don't have a feather to fly with," her grandmother had insisted when she objected to the cost.

To own the truth, she did not. And Grandmama herself was far from plump in the pocket.

Adele affixed the circlet of yellow silk roses onto Juliet's curls, stood back and surveyed her work. "You'll do," she announced, which for Adele was high praise. A moment later she whirled around, hissing, "Shoo! Scat!" at the striped tabby sauntering into the room.

"Never mind," Juliet said. "Let her be—Mab is doing no harm."

"Why you gave that great ugly beast the name of a fairy queen is beyond me," Adele said. "And you know very well my lady don't approve of any animal being above-stairs."

"I think Mab is as beautiful as any fairy queen could possibly be," Juliet insisted, bending to rub the tabby behind the ears.

"What I think is she's getting ready to kitten again," Adele observed, eyeing the cat's bulging sides, "and like as not looking for a cosy spot to have them."

Juliet smiled. "I dearly love kittens."

"I expect you'd find you wasn't so fond of them if she chanced to drop her litter in your bed." Adele stooped, lifted Mab into her arms and left the room.

Juliet turned back to the looking glass. Because her mother's brooch, lacking its second heart, was un-wearable, she had chosen to eschew jewelry entirely. Examining her mirror image critically, she wondered how Malcolm would see her. Plainer than he remembered? She could not bear to think he might be disappointed.

Perhaps he had forgotten her altogether—after all, a

year had passed, a long lonely year for her. A year of fighting Napoleon for him. Though he had not written her, Lady Ashcroft had received several letters and in each he had requested his aunt to give his greetings to Juliet Grant and her grandmother.

She knew he was abiding by the rules, but how she would have treasured a letter of her own from him. At least she knew he was well and was safe. In his last letter, written at the year's end, he had told his aunt he expected to be back in England before February and Juliet had prayed he would return in time for the ball.

Now she wondered if he would remember to come to the Valentine's Ball. But of course he would; he had given his solemn promise.

His image was still vivid in her memory—his emerald eyes, coal-black hair, wry smile, and tall, commanding figure. She would never forget the glow in his eyes when he gazed at her, a warm brightness that stirred her just to recall it. He had mentioned that he quite liked the violet scent she used—what else might he remember about her? The forward way she had kissed him when they parted? She found herself flushing at the memory and pressed her hands to her hot cheeks.

"My dear child," her grandmother remarked from the doorway, "do cease prinking. You already look charming, as fresh as a spring flower. I daresay you will find yourself the belle of the ball."

Juliet smiled at her. The truth was she aspired to be the belle of only one man.

Once they were seated in the carriage, Grandmama said, "I do hope Lady Ashcroft will be at the ball. I have not seen as much of her as I would like." She sighed.

"Alas, it cannot be helped since we cannot afford to spend much time in London."

"Lady Ashcroft has been unfailingly kind to me," Juliet said.

Grandmama patted her hand. "No one could fail to become fond of you, my dear Juliet. I do believe she entertains high hopes that her nephew will offer for you once the two of you have the chance to become better acquainted. She is eager for Lord Talland to wed. Fortunately your antecedents on both sides are impeccable and, since the Rothwells have no need for the heir apparent to marry a heiress, you should be quite acceptable to them, even with a meager dowry."

Juliet had not dared to carry her fantasy of being reunited with Malcolm as far as the possibility of becoming his wife. At the moment she merely longed to see him again, to bask in the glow of his green eyes and feel his arms enclose her as they waltzed together. Surely that was not too much to hope for. Or was it?

A dark shawl of anxiety settled over Juliet, vexing her to the extent that, as they entered the hall she hardly noticed how fancifully the Polders had decorated their home for the Valentine's Ball—red hearts of every kind hung everywhere. She gave up her white velvet cape, murmured a polite greeting to Lady Polder and assured her grandmother that yes, she would remember to take particular notice of the sienna marble chimneypiece in the anteroom to the left of the hall.

After fending off a young man of her acquaintance who clamored for a dance, she was greeted by Cassandra, who had a young cousin in tow.

"Mary Margaret Taylor, from Glasgow," Cassandra said. "I made every attempt to introduce you to Mary

Margaret at last year's ball but, of course, you were otherwise occupied."

"With Lord Talland, for one," Mary Margaret put in. "I had been informed that he rarely deigned to dance so I took particular notice when he partnered you in a quadrille." She sighed. "He is most dashing, do you not agree?"

Before Juliet had a chance to reply, Cassandra spoke again. "Gossip has it Lord Talland has recently returned to England." She gave Juliet a sly look. "Pray tell me, will he be here tonight?"

Juliet tried not to show this was the first she had actually heard of his return. Forcing a smile, she said, "We can but hope so."

Cassandra had never been more than a rather sharp-tongued acquaintance and, given Cassandra's proclivity for gossiping about others, she did not wish to become over-friendly with her. She especially did not want to discuss Malcolm with Cassandra. Or with Mary Margaret Taylor. Or with anyone, for that matter. What had happened between them was her secret, hers and his, and she did not wish to share any part of it with others.

Glancing about for an excuse to leave, she caught the eye of Jeremy Bright. He had evidently been waiting for her to acknowledge him because he hurried to her side.

"Do say you will dance with me, Miss Grant," he begged, after a polite but scanty greeting to Cassandra and Mary Margaret.

"I should be delighted," she told him, welcoming the chance to escape.

As she passed from partner to partner in a country set, she scanned the ballroom. In vain. Malcolm was nowhere in sight. 'Tis still early, she assured herself. He will arrive later, as I have been told is his habit.

After the dance ended, she found herself surrounded by gentlemen who wished to be her partners for the dances yet to come. To pass the time, she accepted several offers, but, when the orchestra struck up a waltz, she asked to be escorted to where her grandmother sat. She would waltz only with Malcolm. Grandmama immediately dispatched the young man to bring them two glasses of lemonade, colored pink in honor of St. Valentine.

When he was out of earshot, she leaned close to Juliet and whispered, "My dear, I regret to tell you that Lord Talland is back in England but will not be attending the ball."

Juliet stared at her in surprised dismay. "How do you know?"

"Pray keep your voice down, child. It will not do to attract attention."

"Is he ill?" Juliet's concern furrowed her brow.

"No. That is, not in the ordinary sense of the word. Lady Ashcroft was unable to be here but, knowing we would be, she took the trouble to send me a note." She slipped a folded paper to Juliet.

"Dear C.," Juliet read silently. "For no reason I am able to discern, my nephew has immured himself at Hart's Hall and intends to remain there. He refuses to see anyone. Though he claims nothing is amiss, I own I am worried. Your friend, E."

Without realizing what she was doing, Juliet crumpled the note in her hand. Her grandmother extracted it and slipped the paper into her handkerchief pocket.

"You are understandably concerned," Grandmama said, "but I insist you put a good face on the matter, thus giving no cause for gossip. I am certain several people noticed the footman hand me the note so we will not leave immediately lest a connection be made between the note and our going. We must remain at least one more hour."

"I cannot," Juliet whispered, the strange, disquieting emptiness inside her expanding alarmingly, making her feel queasy.

"You can and you will." Grandmama's firm tone left no room for argument. "We shall accept the lemonade, make a show of sipping it and you will agree to at least one more offer to dance. After the passage of the hour, I will make our excuses. Everyone believes ladies of a certain age tire easily so my departure will not be unduly remarked upon and, of course, you would be expected to leave with me."

That hour was the longest Juliet had ever experienced. When she was finally seated in the carriage with her grandmother, she realized she had no idea what she'd said or done during those sixty minutes.

She sighed, twisting her gloved fingers in her lap. "I cannot think what could have gone wrong. He promised to meet me at the ball. He assured me his family has always honored their promises."

"You must accept that there is always a first time for everything, even in families who pride themselves on their honor," Grandmama said, covering Juliet's restless hands with one of hers.

"I shall try. I shall also do my best to accept the possibility he may no longer be interested in resuming his acquaintance with me," Juliet's voice quivered as she spoke. Though she felt her heart would surely break if that happened, she could not deny it *was* possible.

Trying to swallow the lump in her throat, she added,

"Even should it prove true, I don't believe that his indifference to me can be the entire reason for his absence.
He is behaving most oddly, do you not agree? By all
accounts Lord Talland is a man who enjoys the pleasures
of town life. Why would he suddenly shut himself away
in Sussex and refuse all company? I believe something
is amiss despite his assurances to the contrary. I intend to
call on Lady Ashcroft on the morrow and discuss the matter
with her."

After a moment her grandmother nodded. "I do believe you ought to do just that, especially since Elaine
herself admits she is beside herself with worry."

A fortnight later, Juliet, accompanied by Prudence,
one of Lady Ashcroft's maids, and traveling in an Ashcroft carriage, set off for Hart's Hall.

"If my sciatica was not plaguing me, I would go with
you," Lady Ashcroft had told her. "Still, perhaps 'tis as
well, since Malcolm's letter to me stated in no uncertain
terms that I was not to visit him. I told you about my
dream, did I not? The dream I had before he left England."

Juliet nodded. "A prophetic dream, you feared."

"As it proved to be, alas. I fear he needs my help
whether or not he will admit he does. Listen carefully
now. You must not send word ahead that you are coming
to Hart's Hall. What you must do is simply pop in and
confront poor, dear Malcolm before he realizes he has a
visitor. We shall hope the sight of you will bring him to
his senses." Lady Ashcroft's brow had furrowed. "If your
presence doesn't move him, then I shall really begin to
worry."

Juliet tried to believe it was possible that after his initial surprise Malcolm would be delighted to see her, but more and more doubts assailed her until she sought distraction from the gloom they brought. Noticing Prudence staring wistfully out the carriage window, she followed her gaze. There was naught to see other than a line of low rolling hills covered with grass and bushes.

Hazarding a guess, she asked, "Are you from Sussex?"

Prudence turned to her. "Born 'n' raised here, I was, miss, 'tween the Downs 'n' the Weld. Seeing the Downs again makes me feel right to home."

"Have you ever been to Hart's Hall?"

"Not to say been there but all us Downsfolk knows where 'tis—closer to the Weld than the Downs 'cause the Hall's got trees 'round and about. Got more'n trees, come to think on it."

"I don't quite understand," Juliet said when Prudence didn't continue.

"Be a tale about the Hall in these parts. Heard it as a wee 'un, I did. Fair give me the shivers till me auntie spoke up. Worked at the Hall as a girl, she did. Nothing scary at Hart's Hall, nay, nothing, says she. 'Tis just an old rhyme about them ruins at the foot o' the hill."

Intrigued, Juliet leaned toward her. "Do you recall the rhyme?"

"I does, miss." Prudence sat up straight, closed her eyes and intoned:

> "A man who cannot see
> A beast within a tree
> A crone who crippled be
> A maid trapped in the scree
> These four together hold the key."

Her eyes opened and she blinked at Juliet. "Don't no-body know what the words mean, Auntie told me."

"Not even what the key might unlock?"

"Nay, miss."

"What about the ruins?"

"Me grandda says he heard 'twas some sort o' tower there afore his time. Afore they built Hart's Hall atop the hill."

Juliet pondered the rhyme. "Scree," she repeated be-cause the word was unfamiliar to her. "Is that a local saying?"

Prudence nodded. " 'Tis like a heap o' stones. Grandda spoke o' some kind o' celebration at the ruins come each 'n' every July. Bonfires 'n' dancing 'n' all. Said no one remembered why 'twas done."

Later, as they neared their destination, Juliet watched for the ruins, thankful for something to occupy her thoughts other than her meeting with Malcolm. The closer they came to the Hall, the more anxious she grew over her welcome by Malcolm.

"Look, miss, there 'tis," Prudence cried, pointing.

Thinking she meant the ruins, Juliet craned her neck to look. What she saw instead in the light of the late afternoon sun made her draw in her breath. A magnifi-cent house perched at the top of the highest hill in the vicinity, a house crowned on the corners by domes and cupolas. Tall oaks thrust up their mighty limbs behind what could only be Hart's Hall.

The knowledge Malcolm waited inside that house made her heart pound with uneasy anticipation. What would he do when he saw her? Would his green eyes glow with warmth as they had when first they met? Juliet's hand crept up to touch the flawed, single-hearted brooch she wore as though it were a talisman to ward off ill fortune. Though Malcolm had not come to the ball as he had promised, he could not have forgotten her—not with her emerald heart to remind him of their meeting.

A white-haired butler—Ames, Lady Ashcroft had told her—opened the door to her knock and, as he ushered her into a vast cube-shaped entrance hall, she handed him the note as she had been instructed to do.

"I am Miss Grant," she told him. "Lady Ashcroft asked that you read what she has written to you before announcing me."

Without comment, Ames did so. When he finished, he folded the paper neatly, slipped it into a pocket and regarded her with pale-blue eyes. She thought he looked dubious but he said only, "If you will follow me, please, Miss Grant."

Juliet, her entire attention fixed on meeting Malcolm, was scarcely aware of the Ionic columns and Greek statuary she passed nor the tapestries lining the walls of the corridor. As Ames entered a room with beautiful Venetian windows overlooking an arbored garden, she realized he meant to lead her outside via the glass doors at the far end of the room.

Pausing, she asked, "And where is Lord Talland?"

"He is in the arbor, Miss Grant. He spends much time there."

Once outside, she noticed that late afternoon shadows darkened the area under the rose-covered trellises forming the arbor, the sweet smell of the blooms drifting on the cool breeze.

"Ames?" Malcolm asked from the shadows.

"Milord," Ames replied, halting. "By Lady Ashcroft's request, I have brought Miss Grant to see you. She is with me now." He gestured for Juliet to go past him into the arbor and promptly returned to the house.

As she entered the arbor, Juliet found she had to swallow before she could speak. "Malcolm?" she said tentatively. Seeing his tall figure standing before her made her suddenly shy. Perhaps she'd been too forward in venturing here uninvited, even though Lady Ashcroft had encouraged her to make the trip.

Why did he not greet her? She stopped and waited expectantly, wishing it were not so gloomy under the roses because the dim light concealed his expression. As it was, she could barely see his face.

"Juliet," he said finally. Hearing her name on his tongue made her breath catch. She took an involuntary step toward him, eager to touch him, to feel his arms close around her. If he embraced her, surely all would be as it had been at last year's Valentine Day's Ball.

His next words, formal and cold, froze her in place. "You should not have come. Had I known you were here, I would have refused to see you."

Pain pierced her heart, followed by a wave of humiliation. Tears stung her eyes, tears she blinked back desperately lest he see them. When she regained control of her voice, she said, "I confess I was concerned when you did not appear at the Valentine's Ball. Then your aunt, who is not well, told me she was troubled by your absence from town, and so I thought perhaps a visit here—"

Malcolm cut in abruptly. "You have wasted your time as well as mine. Lady Ashcroft has no cause for worry, nor you for concern. She will have to accept that I prefer solitude for the time being and you must realize that promises made during the heat of the moment are, more often than not, broken."

Each word was another nail driven into her heart but pride stiffened her spine. She refused to show how stricken she was. "I am sorry to have disturbed you," she said stiffly.

Malcolm reached into a pocket of his waistcoat. "Actually your visit offers me the opportunity of returning this without the bother of sending it to London." He pulled out a small object and balanced it on his palm. "You may have your heart back," he drawled without moving from where he stood. "I have no further use for it."

Choking back a sob, Juliet took the necessary few steps to reach him, snatched the emerald heart from his hand, turned on her heel and fled from the arbor, running across a lawn and around the house until she reached the drive where she paused in distress. She had forgotten the carriage would not be there since the driver would have gone on to the stables. As for Prudence, she undoubtedly was in the kitchen having tea with some of the Hart's Hall servants. Though Juliet dreaded to, she had no recourse but to return to the house.

As she approached the front door, it opened. "Miss Grant," Ames said, "I have taken the liberty of sending your maid to the stable to tell your driver to bring the carriage around to the front of the house."

Even as she thanked the butler, Juliet realized with bitterness that Ames had known all along she would not be welcomed by Malcolm. No, not Malcolm. No, nay, never no more, as the old song went. From now on he was Lord Talland to her. Lord Talland, the man without a heart.

* * *

When he heard the carriage pull away, Talland slumped onto the iron bench in the rose arbor, his success sour on his tongue. Juliet was gone and they would never meet again. He had driven her from him, exactly as he had meant to—there had been no choice. Devoid of all hope, he covered his face with his hands.

Standing unseen on the terrace above the arbor, Ames sighed when he heard the troubled sounds from the shadows beneath the roses. True, Lord Talland had made him swear never to divulge the reason why he had come to earth at Hart's Hall, but milord was expecting too much of even the most devoted of butlers. He had known milord, boy and man, for twenty-six years—a boy full of mischief who had matured to become a nonpariel, what the *ton* called top-of-the-trees. And now Lord Talland could not so much as bring himself to mount his favorite horse.

It was more than he could bear, more any man could be expected to bear, to watch and listen and remain silent. Ames fingered the note in his pocket as he told himself this could not, must not be permitted to go on. . . .

Four

Standing on the threshold of the open doors of the morning room, facing the new day, Talland felt the warm sun on his skin, heard the twitter of birds and smelled the mixed sweet and spicy perfume of flowers. He did not need to see the brightness of the sun, nor the flitting birds, nor the vivid hues of the flowers to know spring was well established. As it should be, of course, since this was, with a hey and a hie and hoe-down-derry, the merry, merry month of May. A bitter smile twisted his mouth.

Juliet had come to Hart's Hall soon after Valentine's Day. He had not needed to see her to know who she was, the music of her voice and the subtle scent of violets was enough to identify her. How ironic that only in his dreams could he actually see her. Or anything else.

His deliberate coldness had hurt her, he knew, but it had been his only recourse because he did not intend her to learn what had happened to him. Perhaps she believed she loved him but if he had told her the truth, her love would turn to pity. How could it not? No woman could truly love a blind man and he could not bear to be the object of Juliet's pity. Never!

In any case, her heart would quickly mend. Their acquaintance had been so ephemeral that he felt sure she would soon forget him. Was not she known as a butterfly who flitted from one conquest to another? Yes, she would someday recover and wed another but he doubted that he would ever be able to forget her. The heart he was rumored not to possess ached with his longing for her.

Dismissing these futile ruminations, he stepped down onto the brick terrace and, using the cane he hated, felt his way to the steps leading down from the terrace onto the flagstone path to the arbor, his favorite place. Under the fragrant roses he was safe from observation, alone except for the bees that buzzed among the flowers. The servants knew better than to venture anywhere near, so no one and nothing disturbed him except his own thoughts.

He could also have gotten away from everyone by having Lion Heart saddled, gotten away by riding the bay across the Downs until they were both spent. He grimaced. Even the thought of the bay, once his favorite mount, made fear clench his guts. The truth was he had not even been able to visit the stables, much less Lion Heart, since his return from the Continent.

Dr. Lancer had urged him to at least try to greet Lion Heart and, once he had accomplished that, perhaps feed the horse a lump of sugar, working his way gradually to the point of being able to mount the bay. Talland shifted his shoulders uneasily. He had not even been able to manage the first step. The mere idea of approaching any horse threw him into a panic. He had not the slightest idea why.

Enough! If he dwelt on horses much longer he would soon begin to sweat and tremble and God knows he did not want to embarrass himself or his staff.

The one person whose presence he might have tolerated was Beaumont. His old friend had been the one person who might have understood and accepted his blindness without pity. But he had been told Beaumont was dead,

killed in the battle where he had been injured. No one
seemed to know any details. The news of Beaumont's
death had so distressed him that all these months later he
did not allow himself to think of his friend because he
could not do so without falling into a deep melancholia.

All he knew about his own injury was what Dr. Lancer
had told him, for when he awakened from a stupor, blind,
in a field hospital, he had no memory of what had happened to him.

Talland had come to realize it did not do to dwell on
the past, on what might have been, so he resolutely
sought to focus his mind on something else. For long
moments he could not find a way to distract himself,
then he fastened on his first thought of the day. It was
spring, it was May. Words from a madrigal began to circle in his head and, humming the tune, he concentrated
on remembering them.

> "Now is the month of Maying
> When merry lads are playing
> Each with his bonny lass
> Upon the green, green grass . . ."

Damn and blast, this would not do, either. He would
never be a merry lad again nor did he expect to find
himself a bonny lass. Grimly, he began to conjugate
Latin verbs until the boredom of the task calmed him.

When, later, he heard the muffled clop of horses'
hooves and the distant rattle of a carriage, he cursed and
rose from the bench. The drive to Hart's Hill was private;
if he heard a carriage, the vehicle was headed here.
Emerging from the arbor, he tapped his way up the terrace steps, intent on reaching the house and holing up

in his rooms before the misguided visitor arrived. Visitors had become rarer and rarer since his strict orders to Ames that no one except Dr. Lancer or his father was to be allowed into the house, no matter if they did carry notes from his aunt. So far his father had respected his request to stay away.

He wondered who this visitor might be. Some arrogant bastard who had the temerity to believe Talland might agree to see him? He smiled without humor. He literally saw nobody.

Shutting himself in his upstairs suite, he paced back and forth, no longer having to count the steps lest he bump into furniture or a wall. He had learned to know every inch of these rooms very well—not so difficult when one had nothing else to do.

He heard the carriage pull up in front and stop, heard the squeak and clank of the steps being lowered, heard someone get out. Or try to, something seemed amiss. He frowned and, stepping closer to the drawn curtains of the window, he listened carefully, aware his hearing had grown more acute as if to compensate for his loss of sight.

"Very well then," a familiar voice said, "there is no help for it. Since I am unable to alight, two of you will have to lift me from the carriage and set me on my feet. Mind you, I will need the aid of a strong arm to make my way to the house."

Talland groaned. He might have known that, despite his insistence she not visit him, Aunt Elaine would finally arrive on his doorstep. Juliet had mentioned his aunt was ailing and obviously she still was. Ames would, of course, be obliged to admit Lady Ashcroft and he was sure the butler was well aware Talland would give no order to send her away. How could he in good conscience turn off the aunt he dearly loved, especially when she was not well? He had no choice but to let her stay.

Though he might try to avoid being in her company while she was here, he realized he would be unsuccessful. Aunt Elaine had never been one to take no for an answer. Even if she had to be carried, she was quite capable of tracking him to whatever lair he chose to hide in and confronting him there.

Since this was true, he must put a good face on it, admit to his blindness and enlist her aid in keeping his affliction a secret. He rang for Biggs, the man who had been his batman in the army and was now his valet, to make certain his appearance would past muster.

"Got a look at 'er ladyship, I did, sir," Biggs told him as he brushed his master's jacket. "Wouldn't care t' cross swords with 'er, so to speak."

"Very wise," Talland muttered.

Biggs knew better than to offer help unless it was asked for so he did not assist Talland when he left his rooms and walked toward the stairs alone. He had descended seven of the first fifteen steps leading to the landing when he was suddenly attacked. Sharp claws pierced through his breeches as something—some kind of animal—climbed his left leg.

"Bloody hell!" he exclaimed, reaching down to detach whatever it was. He encountered soft fur. As he held the animal away from him it yowled. A damned cat.

"Oh, dear," his aunt said from the hall below. "I fear Nimue is being naughty again."

"This—this creature is yours, Aunt Elaine?" Talland's words were tinged with irritation.

"Not exactly, dear boy, although I admit she came with me. Pray do her no harm, she is but a kitten."

"I am not in the habit of harming animals," he said gruffly, resuming his descent of the stairs. "I am also not accustomed to kittens using my leg as a climbing post. Pray relieve me of this—what did you call her?"

"Nimue," his aunt replied. "Merlin's nemesis, if you recall. The sorceress who tricked him."

The scent of jasmine filled his nostrils as hands plucked the kitten from his grasp. Not his aunt's scent, nor her hands, he decided. Aunt Elaine's abigail was most unlikely to be wearing scent so who the devil was this woman with her?

Before he could ask, he smelled his aunt's lemony scent and then she embraced him. "Oh, my dear Malcolm," she said as she let him go, " 'tis so good to see you. I have been worrying about you immured all alone here at the Hall. Then when Dr. Ellis warned me that my sciatica—I have been suffering most dreadfully from it—would only grow worse if I did not remove myself from London and spend some time in the fresh air of the country, quite naturally I thought of Hart's Hall. So here I am. Rather," she corrected, "here we are."

"We?" he said with some annoyance. Aunt Elaine couldn't mean her abigail because she would understand he took it for granted the maid would accompany her. Who else did she intend to foist on him?

"Don't look down your nose at me, there is no reason to get on your high-horse. Due to my ailment, I was in desperate need of a companion and had been searching high and low for one I could rub along with. Do you have any idea how difficult it is to locate a gently bred lady with sufficient intelligence to make a suitable companion? By chance someone mentioned this poor little afflicted orphan, we met and, as luck would have it, took to one another instantly."

"Afflicted?" Talland repeated the word, despite himself.

"Why, yes. Dear Celia—Miss Fletcher, that is—happens to be a mute. Though she cannot speak a word, fortunately she is not deaf and understands all that is said to her. She suits me in every way and I am sure you cannot object to her presence here."

"No, of course not," he muttered, embarrassed by the discourtesy of discussing the poor girl's disability in front of her. "You are welcome at Hart's Hall, Miss Fletcher."

Since it was obvious his aunt would soon realize exactly what was wrong with him, he knew he could not put off the admission much longer. Perhaps it would ease the humiliation the girl must be feeling if he made his confession here and now.

Taking a deep breath he said, "I quite understand, Aunt Elaine, since I, myself, am afflicted, though in a different way. I have hesitated to distress you with such unpleasant news, but the truth is I returned from the Continent blind."

Braced for an outpouring of shocked sympathy, he was taken aback when she said quite calmly, "You must hate it most dreadfully. I am certain I would."

Regaining his voice, he exclaimed accusingly, "You already knew!"

"You do recall Harry Thompson?"

"Are you referring to General Thompson?" he asked, wondering what she was leading up to. The army doctor who had taken care of Talland had sworn to keep mum about his blindness.

"As it happens my old friend Harry is a general," Aunt

Elaine replied. "When Dr. Lancer refused to discuss your condition with me, naturally I appealed to Harry and it seems that once a soldier, always a soldier. Dr. Lancer, though no longer in the army, felt he must obey a general's direct command."

Damn and blast. He might have known his aunt would find a way to ferret out the truth. How much had Lancer revealed? Talland could only hope the doctor had offered no details about his blindness. The tinkling of a stringed instrument startled him from his uneasy musing and he turned his head toward the sound, forgetting as he sometimes did, that he could not see what he looked toward.

"Celia uses her dulcimer as her voice," his aunt informed him. "I believe she is telling you how pleased she is that you have welcomed her to Hart's Hall."

As she spoke, Talland felt the kitten's claws stab into his leg. Swallowing a curse, once again he detached the animal. What a devil of a coil. All he had asked for was to be left alone and here he was not only saddled with his ailing Aunt Elaine, but also a mute damsel with a dulcimer who smelled of jasmine and a climbing cat with the ridiculous name of Nimue. Irritated as he felt about the situation at the moment, perhaps it was as well he couldn't see a bloody one of them.

"If the cat is not yours, Aunt Elaine," he said through clenched teeth as he held the animal away from him, "then I assume it must belong to your companion."

The dulcimer wailed briefly and unmistakably mournfully, making Talland raise his eyebrows. Did the girl think he meant to throw her Nimue to the foxhounds?

"I trust you will do all in your power to keep the creature under control, Miss Fletcher," he said. "I am not overly fond of felines."

The faint scent of jasmine grew stronger and soft hands brushed against his as she took the kitten from him. To his annoyance, he found himself relishing the sensation. Good God! For all he knew she was a mere child.

"It was remiss of me to have kept you standing about in the hall," he said stiffly. Certain that the butler was hovering nearby he added, "Ames, do have Lady Ashcroft and Miss Fletcher shown to their rooms."

"At once, milord," Ames assured him.

With relief, Talland escaped to his hideaway in the arbor. He would, he supposed, be forced to appear for dinner. After weeks of practicing with the help of Biggs, he managed quite deftly at the table but he definitely preferred to dine alone. He sighed, deciding it would not do; some amenities must be observed. Very well, he would bear their company at dinner—he imagined the companion would be with his aunt—but at no other meal. He also intended to avoid them as much as possible.

He did not begrudge his aunt's houseroom but, while he admittedly loved her, she was not a person who valued peace and quiet. Nor did she approve of what he had heard her refer to as "the dangerous habit of too much solitude." For some reason she seemed to regard it as she would a particularly pernicious illness. Talland scowled. If he preferred solitude that was his own affair. He bloody well meant to go on just as he had been, aunt or no aunt.

Dinner proved to be as he had feared, an awkward affair. His first mishap occurred when he turned to his left, where he knew Miss Fletcher had been seated and, making an effort at polite conversation, said, "I do not believe I have ever seen a dulcimer. I know from the sound it must be stringed, but does one play the instrument with one's fingers or with a bow?"

Silence greeted him, causing him to remember too late that the girl was mute.

"Neither," Aunt Elaine finally said. "I believe the dulcimer originally came from Persia. Celia's is made of chestnut wood, is shaped like a trapezoid and has eighteen quadruple bass strings tuned by pegs. She plays it with two light sticks that end in a broad blade. And plays it exceedingly well, I might add."

"Yes, of course," he said. Feeling he owed the girl something more because of his gaffe, he came up with, "I hope to hear you play for me sometime soon."

"Not this evening, dear boy," his aunt said. "We are far too fatigued from the journey."

"Another time," he agreed readily. Actually he truly enjoyed music, although from what he had heard of the dulcimer it did seem particularly designed for mournful ballads. While he did not play any instrument, as a boy he had quite liked to sing. As he recalled, his mother had told him he had a pleasant voice and carried a tune well.

As though she was privy to his thoughts, Aunt Elaine said, "Do you know, I have never heard you sing since Rowena died." In what he realized was an aside to her companion, she added, "She was Lord Talland's mother, his father's first wife and my older sister. We all adored her but, alas, the familiar adage is far too true—the good all too often do die young, leaving us old reprobates to live on and on and on."

Talland could not help but smile at his aunt's fanciful description of herself.

"There, you see, Celia," she said, "he has not forgotten

how to smile. I cherish the hope that he also still remembers how to sing."

Why the devil would she—or anyone—believe he wished to ever sing again?

"Oh, dear, that ferocious scowl is meant for me," Aunt Elaine said. "Even when he was still in skirts, he was a most formidable scowler and quite cowed his nursemaids."

"I cannot conceive that Miss Fletcher would have the slightest interest in how I behaved as a child," he said stiffly, wondering with some annoyance if his aunt meant to tell this companion of hers—a stranger—every detail of his life.

Miss Fletcher laughed, a delightful, musical laugh, unlike the high-pitched giggle of some young women. Evidently it was possible for her to make some sounds. But what had she found so amusing? Him? Or Aunt Elaine's prattle? Not that it made any difference.

When he retired that night, he found himself recalling the music of her laughter and shook his head as though to drive it away. He slept poorly but that was nothing new.

In the morning, while Biggs was shaving him, Talland found himself saying, "It occurs to me I don't have the slightest idea how old my aunt's companion is."

"Eighteen at least, sir," Biggs said. His batman had grown accustomed to addressing him as "sir" in the army and rarely remembered to use any other term, which was perfectly all right with Talland, though upsetting to Ames.

"Mousy sort o' dresser," Biggs went on as though he'd been asked to describe her. "Not what ye'd call a real looker. Still 'n' all—" He paused to wipe Talland's face with a warm, wet cloth.

"What is it you mean to say, man?" Talland urged when Biggs finished with the cloth.

"Dunno exactly. Got something, she 'as, ain't sure what. A gent just might give 'er a second gawk."

"A gent?"

" 'E'd 'ave t' be a gent on account've 'er being a lady. Can't miss that, no sir."

Since Aunt Elaine had mentioned that her companion was gently bred, Talland wasn't surprised. But Biggs's other comments about the girl interested him. What was the unusual "something" she had that Biggs wasn't able to identify?

What the devil did it matter? Why was he wasting time speculating about Celia Fletcher, a girl he could not even see—whom he would never be able to see?

Talland broke his morning fast and went on to the arbor without encountering his uninvited guests. He would not go so far as to call Aunt Elaine an unwanted guest, though 'twas a near miss.

Recalling the prophetic dream she had related to him before he left England, a dream of Hart's Hall, darkness and himself crying out for help, he shook his head. Prophetic up to a point, certainly, but he definitely did not want nor need help. Not from his aunt or from anyone else. As he saw it, there was nothing that *could* help him. He would live in darkness forever. His life, as he had been accustomed to live it, was over.

A new sound thrust itself into his brooding. Not the twittering song of birds but a sprightly melody, a tune played on a dulcimer. He barely stopped himself from looking around, the habit was difficult to break. Instead, he concentrated on locating the source of the music by careful listening.

The player was near. Very near. How had she approached so close without him hearing her? He had not realized the dulcimer could sound so cheerful. The tune was familiar, something about a fair, Johnnie being so long at the fair. He began to hum.

As the words of the song's title came to him, without willing it, he started to sing: "Oh, dear, what can the matter be? Dear, dear, what can the matter be? Oh, dear, what—?" He broke off as the meaning of the words penetrated.

Damn and blast! She had come along and seen him sitting on the bench sunk in thought. Did she imagine he was wallowing in self-pity? Was it possible the chit could be mocking him with her song?

He rose abruptly and took a step toward the arbor entrance. His booted foot came down on something soft and a frightful screech froze him in place. After an instant he realized he must have stepped on Nimue's tail.

"Sorry," he muttered. Though the cat had annoyed him the previous day, he would never knowingly harm it.

The dulcimer music ceased. Listening, he heard a crooning and realized she, Miss Fletcher, Celia, must have picked up the kitten to comfort it. Her croon was as musical as her laugh.

"I was not aware the cat was near," he said. He meant to go on, to tell her that the arbor was private, for his use only but the words remained unsaid. For some reason, he felt a bond with Celia Fletcher, no doubt because of her affliction. Who knew better than he how painful the loss of a taken-for-granted ability could be?

Now that he thought about it, she would have no conceivable reason to mock him with her choice of a song—what had led him to entertain such a notion? To make up for his unwonted suspicion, he gestured to the bench opposite the one which he customarily used, saying, "Perhaps you might like to sit there and play for me again. I should like it above half if you will."

The scent of jasmine surrounded him, then, to his surprise Celia grasped his hand and stroked his palm with one of her fingers. After a confused moment or two he realized she was tracing the letter S on his palm. "S," he said. She then wrote an invisible "i," "n," and "g" before letting go of his hand.

"I take it you want me to sing while you play," he said, pleased that she had found a way to communicate with him. His hand still tingled from her unexpected touch. To refuse her naive request would be churlish, indeed, so he decided to agree and nodded his assent.

When he heard her begin to play, he sat on the other bench. No sooner had he done so than the kitten sprang into his lap. Nimue, apparently well aware that he was not a cat lover, with feline perversity insisted on his company. Not wishing to disturb the cat's mistress by pushing the animal off, Talland allowed Nimue to remain on his lap.

Recognizing the tune as "The Blue Bell of Scotland," he began to sing: "Oh, where and oh, where has my Highland laddie gone. . . ."

By the time he finished singing and the dulcimer fell silent, he found he was stroking the cat's soft fur, fur no softer than the gentle touch of Celia's hand. The company of his aunt's companion soothed him, perhaps because she could not speak except with her dulcimer. He had always enjoyed music and she did play delightfully well.

There was, he remembered, a love song dedicated to a girl named Celia. When the words came to him, he stiffened, taking his hand off the cat.

Drink to me only with thine eyes and I will pledge with mine. . . .

He was blind, unable to see, much less pledge with his eyes. In any case, what woman would want a blind man to pledge anything to her? He was within an ace of making an utter sapskull of himself over a girl he could not even see. As he scowled at his own foolishness, he heard the faint rustle of Celia's gown as she rose, then the soft scuff of her slippers as she left the arbor. Nimue jumped off his lap, leaving him alone.

Being left to himself was exactly what he had wished for. Why, then should he feel he had been deserted?

Five

As May ended and June began, Talland began to look forward with increasing eagerness to having Celia Fletcher appear in the arbor during the day to serenade him with her dulcimer. He even accepted Nimue's presence with equanimity. How fortunate that Aunt Elaine did not demand all of Celia's time and that Celia seemed to enjoy his company.

The days no longer dragged past, without realizing what was happening, he spent less and less time brooding while more and more Celia came to occupy his thoughts. He did not realize where this might be leading until one morning in late June.

Talland had no more on his mind than how fine and warm the day was until, as he approached the arbor, he heard the tinkle of Celia's dulcimer begin and suddenly he felt as though she was welcoming him home. His heart seemed to turn over in his chest and he increased his pace, stopping beside the bench where she sat.

"I recognize 'Black Is The Color Of My True Love's Hair,' " he said, doing his utmost to conceal how moved he was, "but I fear I don't know the words." He eased down beside her uninvited and offered his hand. "Will you teach them to me?"

Letter by letter she traced the words on his palm while

he closed his eyes, relishing her touch. He did not have to see to know how close she was to him, so enticingly close that if he leaned to her, their lips would meet. He ached to wrap his arms around her, to kiss her, to hold her and never let her go. When, in the midst of a word, she ceased forming the letter and then he heard her catch her breath, he felt she sensed his need and, perhaps, shared it.

For a moment that stretched into eternity, neither moved. Then he rose abruptly and strode to the other bench, standing beside it with his back to her, fighting to damp down his desire. He had no reason to suppose she would welcome any advance from him and only a clodpole would force himself on a defenseless young lady.

"Play something," he said huskily, hoping the music would distract him. "Anything."

Instead of obeying, she fled from the arbor. Was she frightened of him? he wondered. Or could it be she was afraid of how she had felt?

Come to that, what exactly were his feelings for Celia? God knows he desired her. Was there more? He didn't know but it occurred to him that in the past few weeks he had been so preoccupied with Celia's presence that the thought of Juliet Grant had rarely crossed his mind. How was it he could so easily forget Juliet when he had been so certain he loved her?

"What a shame Celia cannot speak," he said to his aunt that afternoon as they strolled arm in arm along the paths of the formal Italian garden his maternal grandfather had commissioned. Aunt Elaine always leaned on him during their walks, claiming she needed assistance because of her ailment. She had, he noticed, needed less support of late so she must be improving. Which meant that any day now she might announce she was returning to town and, of course, taking Celia with her. A muscle twitched in his jaw.

"Celia has her own methods of communication," his aunt said somewhat tartly.

He knew that very well. In the beginning he had enjoyed having Celia write words on his palm with her fingertip. Now he feared having her touch him would be sweet agony. He wanted, he needed more than the feel of her finger writing on his palm.

"She is also most obliging and accomplished," Aunt Elaine added. "I've come to believe she would make some fortunate gentleman an excellent wife—if only he could overlook her affliction. And, of course, her lack of any dowry." She sighed. "Alas, men being what they are, I fear Celia is doomed to a lifetime of spinsterhood."

About to protest his aunt's jaundiced view of gentlemen, Talland paused as it occurred to him for the first time to wonder exactly why Aunt Elaine had come to Hart's Hall with Celia in tow. While he did not doubt his aunt had been suffering from sciatica, all that blather about the doctor saying country air would be good for her might or might not be true. Given that it was, why had she chosen Hart's Hall? Though the place had once been her home, she cared little for the Downs and once had confided to him that even as a child she had considered the Hall gloomy and had much preferred her father's town house.

He could not deny she was fond of him and no doubt she had worried excessively about his welfare once she discovered he was blind. Perhaps that had been enough to make her to come here, despite not being any too fond of the Hall. She may well have used her ailment as an excuse, fearing he might try to turn her away otherwise.

Thinking on it, he recalled her sciatica was no new ailment, she had complained of the problem off and on for the last few years. Never before had she felt it necessary to leave London and never before had she sought a companion when she was suffering. Why had she this time? Considering the way her abigail cosseted her, Aunt Elaine should have little need for a companion—if indeed Celia Fletcher had been actually chosen to be her companion. For someone who supposedly had been hired to provide company for his aunt, he belatedly realized Celia did, in fact, companion him at least as much as she did Aunt Elaine.

His aunt was a wily woman and, though she tried to conceal it, she was also exceptionally brainy. It was certainly possible that she had deliberately sought out and found this mute young lady for the express purpose of bringing her to the Hall. To him? Perhaps that was a bit too much to swallow. On the other hand, after he'd whistled Juliet Grant down the wind, rejecting her completely, Aunt Elaine could have reasoned that, because he was blind, the only woman he might find acceptable was one who was also afflicted in some way.

The devil take Aunt Elaine! She had hit the bull's eye with her very first shot; he had played into her hands, been enough of a looby to prove her right. He *had* grown fond of Celia. But if his aunt thought she had a match in the making, she was very much mistaken. He had no intention of marrying anyone.

"As I believe I have mentioned before," he said to her at last, giving no hint of his conclusions, "the truth of the matter is that women wish to marry and men do not.

Therefore, we can always find logical reasons to postpone the act."

"You are an only son," she reminded him. "You cannot put off producing a heir forever."

"Ah, but I can. If you recall, my father has a brother who, with the aid of his formidable high stickler of a wife, has managed to produce two sons. Which means the earldom will continue in the direct Rothwell line whether or not I ever marry."

Talland smiled crookedly when his aunt did not reply. "I may not be able to see it but I do believe I can feel that famous speaking look of yours."

"Celia is a sweet girl, Malcolm," Aunt Elaine told him, a warning note in her voice. "I do not scruple to remind you to remember that."

He sobered. "I do not need to be reminded to behave like a gentleman." Even if such behavior was already becoming difficult.

That night he dreamed he was strolling in the Italian garden with a girl on either arm. Though he could see neither, he knew from the scent each wore that Juliet was on his right and Celia on his left.

"Why is *she* here when you have told her you do not want her?" Celia asked him.

Juliet said nothing. Taking her hand from his arm, she reached for his palm and wrote on it with her finger, "I am your love."

Bewildered, he told himself that Celia was the mute, not Juliet. He must be wrong about which girl was on which side. How could he have confused the violet scent with that of jasmine?

Then they stopped, forcing him to a halt and both wound their arms around him, jostling for position as they stood on tiptoe to kiss him. But instead of the soft sweetness of women's lips, theirs were inexplicably rough. . . .

Talland woke to find Nimue licking his face. "Bloody hell!" he exclaimed, pushing the cat away but holding onto it as he sat up. He was about to ring for Biggs to come and get the animal when he heard a whisper of a footfall and smelled the faint scent of jasmine.

His breath caught. Celia was in his room. He could tell by the lack of daytime sounds that it was still night, so she had come to him in the darkness and what could it mean but that she felt as he did?

Don't be so caper-witted, he told himself sternly. The likelihood is she has only come to retrieve Nimue. But whatever the reason, his heart continued to pound in anticipation.

"I have the cat," he said softly.

He heard her, felt her, approach his bed. Soft hands touched his bare arm. Was she reaching for Nimue or for him? He breathed in not only jasmine but her private woman's scent and lost his head completely. Unable to help himself, he released the cat and caught her hand, pulling her to him, into his arms, his bed.

She fell against him, warm and enticing, wearing only a thin nightshift and he kissed her with all the pent-up passion of a man who has been too long denied the embrace of the woman he desires.

Celia did not struggle but responded so ardently that he was well nigh overwhelmed. He desired her, he needed her, he must have her.

Her eagerness all but convinced him she had come to his room knowing what the result would be. She wanted what he wanted.

Celia is a sweet girl. His aunt's words echoed in his head. He tried not to listen but in vain. The truth was that Celia was also an innocent. Her caresses, though eager, were unschooled, inexperienced. Though this made him all the more hungry for her, it also reminded him that he was taking advantage of that innocence.

Using more will power than he had known he possessed, Talland grasped her shoulders and held her away from him. "I must not," he said hoarsely, as much to himself as to her.

He heard Celia sob as she freed herself, slipped from his bed and left his room. Sweet Celia. She could laugh and she could cry and she fit into his arms the way no other woman ever had.

Talland shook his head, troubled by something familiar in that last thought. He tried to trace what bothered him to its source but, unsettled by his still rampant need, he failed. Though he did not expect to fall asleep for the rest of the night, he was wrong. When he woke, he realized by the sounds he heard that it was morning. Next he discovered that the purring near his left ear came from Nimue who was curled up on his pillow.

Letting the cat be for the moment, he lay considering what had happened in the night, finally making up his mind to what must be done. Rising from the bed, he picked up the cat, absently cuddling it against him, and walked to the window that he could never look from again. Whether he wanted to act or not, he had no choice.

Later that morning, he took Aunt Elaine aside. "I do not mean to turn you out," he said bluntly, "but I believe your ailment is considerably improved and I know you must miss the excitement of town."

"What you really want is for me to remove Celia from

Hart's Hall," she replied, as usual one step ahead of him. "From within your reach."

"It would be best if you did."

"For whom?"

"For her!" Exasperation edged his voice.

"But not for you, is that what you mean?"

"You must know she tempts me, since you deliberately brought her here for that very purpose."

He heard her breath hiss out in indignation. "Malcolm William Rothwell! What a shagrag you are, accusing me of being a—a procurer. I am quite beside myself."

"You know very well that is not at all what I meant, my dear aunt. If anything, I am accusing you of trying to be a matchmaker. No matter how I feel about Miss Fletcher, I do not mean to marry her. This being so, her presence here is a distraction to me and may prove to be worse for her."

"Just yesterday you were assuring me that a gentleman such as yourself could be trusted to behave properly."

"That was yesterday. I am no longer so sure."

"Has this fit of conscience come on because you are still in love with Miss Grant?" his aunt asked. "Or is it now Celia you favor?"

"How the devil do I know?" he shouted. Lowering his voice with considerable effort, he added, "I have already made it clear to Juliet there is no longer anything between us. As for Celia, what I have decided to do is to provide a handsome dowry for her."

For a long moment Aunt Elaine remained silent. Had he finally managed to advance one step ahead of her?

"How noble of you, dear boy," she said at last. "I shall, of course, abide by your wishes and leave Hart's Hall as soon as possible, taking Celia with me. However,

I refuse to leave before the celebration because I have made plans I do not care to cancel."

"Celebration?" he repeated, trying to sort out what she could possibly be referring to.

"Don't be so ninny-headed. Have you completely forgotten Hart's Day? Forgotten the celebration at the ruins on the tenth of July? The servants and the locals certainly have not forgotten, they expect the usual fete."

"My mind has not been on celebrating," he said shortly.

"How fortunate you are that mine *has* been," she told him with some asperity. "Especially since I am only a guest at Hart's Hall and an unwelcome guest, at that."

"Never unwelcome, Aunt Elaine," he protested.

"Humph! Be that as it may, since this was once my father's estate, I feel an obligation to keep the family ritual alive. As you should, Malcolm, since he was your grandfather."

Talland's possession of Hart's Hall had come through his mother Rowena, Elaine's older sister. Since his mother had died, leaving him to inherit the Hall, he had visited here rarely, but he did know of the celebration and he was ashamed of not having made plans for it.

"I own I have been remiss," he told her.

She squeezed his arm. "I have never been able to long remain vexed with you, Malcolm, imp that you were and stubborn creature that you have become."

He could not deny that he and Aunt Elaine had always rubbed along well. He was grateful that, despite his blindness, she offered him no unwanted sympathy, treating him much as she always had with mixed affection and exasperation.

"In truth, I don't wish you to leave Hart's Hall," he admitted.

"In truth, I admit I long for the liveliness of town," she admitted in turn. "I was not cut out to be a country dweller. Yet I shall remain a fortnight more to see the celebration through, 'tis no more than my duty. Celia shall, of course, stay here with me until then and you, my dear Malcolm, must make do with that as best you can."

For the next several days, Malcolm avoided the arbor, choosing instead to walk along other garden paths. One path meandered through what had once been the kitchen garden and the scent of thyme and basil rose around him, evoking a memory of Juliet and how he had kissed her among the herbs of his aunt's garden in town. He had believed then he could never forget her. Strange how seldom he thought of Juliet of late. . . .

He continued along the path, aware that it came to an end at a low stone wall, marking the descent that led down to the ruins. He stopped beside the wall, looking down. Though he could no longer see what was there, he pictured the rubble scattered among the grass and bushes and the scanty remains of what might have been a stone tower.

"A proper tower should be built at the top of a hill, not the bottom," he had insisted to his grandfather as a boy. "I expect it fell because they could not defend it from their enemies."

"Our ancestors were not paperskulls," Grandfather Lang had said gruffly. "Though we have no records, I expect the tower was built for another purpose entirely."

"For walling up prisoners?" he asked eagerly.

Grandfather's lips twitched as though to suppress a smile. "Have you not noticed the dry stream bed that runs past the ruins? More than likely a mill once stood there in ancient times."

Trying to hide his disappointment, he said, "But everyone says it was a tower."

"I don't," Grandfather Lang had pointed out. "Since there is no way of discovering exactly what the ruins once were, no one can state with any authority 'twas a tower—or a mill, for that matter. Perhaps 'twas no more than a folly, not meant for any real purpose except to indulge the fancy of the man who ordered it to be built."

A folly, Talland thought, staring unseeingly below. 'Twas certainly folly to build a tower at the lowest point of the terrain. Possibly he had inherited *his* folly from that particular Lang ancestor. How could he have indulged himself to the point where he had all but bedded an innocent like Celia?

Engrossed in his brooding, he was late in hearing the slight scuff of a woman's slippers on the path. He waited, listening for the plaintive tone of the dulcimer. Though it did not come, he knew Celia approached. Indifference was the key, he counseled himself. He must not allow himself to be tempted.

She came to stand beside him. Not close, because the scent of jasmine was faint. A raven flew overhead, croaking, otherwise there was silence except for the hum of summer insects. Apparently she had not brought the dulcimer along. Did that mean she did not care to communicate with him? But if that was true, why was she here?

"Those are the ruins below," he said finally for lack of anything else to say. "The Lang Folly. My grandfather was the last of the Langs; he was my mother's and Lady Ashcroft's father, as perhaps you are aware. In any case, that is where the celebration will take place next month."

Despite his best intentions, his heart thudded when he felt her tentative touch on the back of his hand. Obligingly he turned his palm upward.

L-e-g-e-n-d, she spelled out.

The legend, so simple it was difficult to forget, was no more than a five line verse that had never made much sense to him when he was young no matter how long and hard he probed the words for meaning. He had not thought about it in years. "As I recall, it goes like this:

"A man who cannot see
A beast within a tree
A crone who crippled be
A maid trapped in the scree
These four together hold the key."

He paused, blinking, as the first line echoed in his head. *A man who cannot see.* A blind man. Himself.

Celia took his hand. C-a-t, she traced. T-r-e-e.

Presumably she meant that Nimue, like all cats, climbed trees and therefore could qualify as the beast within a tree. He smiled at her, pleased at her interest. "Perhaps we are on our way to solving the riddle. The next line might be interpreted as referring to my aunt. She does limp a bit yet, though I doubt she would appreciate being called a crone. That leaves the fourth line." He shook his head. "You are a maid but certainly not trapped anywhere and I trust you never will be. I fear we have further to go before we understand what the key may be."

They would, he realized, never have the chance. Gloom as dark and heavy as a many-caped driving-coat settled over him as he realized in a fortnight she would disappear from his life, off to London with his aunt.

She reached again for his hand, tracing, G-o t-o r-u-i-n-s.

"Are you asking how to get down to them from here? Just beyond this wall there is a winding trail cut into the side of the hill. Or at least there used to be, it may not have been kept up. The long way is to take the drive and go around the hill."

N-o-w, she traced.

Folly, he told himself firmly, even as his pulse leaped at the thought of being alone with her at the ruins. Far too dangerous. In any case he had not attempted the climb down the side of the hill since he had returned blinded, so he had no idea of what obstacles might lie in the way. He would be helpless, she would have to lead him like a child. Unable to bear such a notion, he shook his head. No, definitely not.

An image formed in his mind of himself as a boy riding his pony down the drive and around to the ruins, but he blotted it out quickly before the unreasonable panic began to rise within. He had not been near a horse since his arrival at the Hall. How could he when the very thought of mounting a horse terrified him?

Dr. Lancer had tried to discuss this unusual and recent fear with him—after all, Talland had been in the cavalry—but in vain. Talland could not. Even thinking about horses sent him into a cold sweat. An involuntary shudder rippled through him.

He did not realize what a spectacle he must be making of himself until Celia's arms came around him and she crooned soothingly, obviously seeking to comfort him. Even though her touch and her closeness helped to banish the unknown ghosts that haunted him, humiliated by his show of weakness, he pulled free. As he did so, his hand inadvertently brushed over her breasts, scraping across something hard and sharp that was pinned to her gown.

The thought that she might believe he had deliberately caressed her breasts added to his upset. Turning from her, he stalked back along the path toward the house, retired to his rooms and spent the rest of the day pacing. The tenth of July could not come and go soon enough to suit him. He bloody well did not want or need any woman's pity.

Not until Biggs came in to help him change for dinner and exclaimed over the bloodstains on his shirt did Talland realize he had been bleeding. Tracing a shallow scratch on his hand, Biggs said, "Cat got you, did 'e, sir?"

Talland shook his head. "Nimue has not come near me since early morning. I don't know how I got it."

" 'Tain't much o' a scratch," Biggs assured him. " 'Tis scabbed over already."

As he left his bedroom, Talland recalled his hand brushing across the front of Celia's gown. At the time he'd been more aware of the softness of her breasts than anything else, but now that he thought about it there had been something sharp—probably a piece of jewelry pinned to her bodice.

A vision of Juliet Grant at last's year's Valentine's Ball sprang into his mind. Juliet, gazing up at him with her beautiful blue eyes. At the bodice of her yellow gown she wore a brooch with a sapphire heart, a brooch missing the emerald heart that had been linked with the other, the emerald heart he had found. He paused. Why was he suddenly reminded of Juliet? Was it because she had fit into his arms as though she belonged there?

As did Celia.

"Deuce take it," he muttered. "I cannot possibly be right." Yet what if he was?

Turning on his heel, he reentered the bedroom. "Biggs?" he said.

"Yessir."

"You did tell me the color of Miss Fletcher's eyes, as I recall."

" 'Appen I did, sir. Ain't no sky I ever seen's been any bluer."

"Thank you."

Walking slowly along the hallway toward the staircase, Talland shook his head. At least half the women in England must have blue eyes. Many wore brooches. Besides, Celia was a mute. Celia played a dulcimer, surely a most unusual instrument. Celia wore jasmine scent, not violet.

She also fit into his arms in exactly the same way Juliet had done. He knew he was not mistaken about that.

As he reached the stairs, his aunt's voice floated up from below. "Oh, there you are, Celia. How thoughtful of you to bring my shawl. Come, we shall have Ames serve us sherry while we wait for Lord Talland in the parlor."

Talland hesitated for a moment, then turned and walked quietly and quickly to the opposite corridor, well aware of which room was Celia's. Running his hand along the wall, he counted the doors. Reaching the third, he pushed open the door and entered the room, using his cane to feel for obstacles in his path.

She would not dare to wear it even though he was blind lest someone comment in his hearing, but he was sure she must have it with her. In her jewel case? He nodded. The case would be atop the dressing table or in a drawer.

He paused again, uncomfortable at the thought of prying into her private belongings. A gentleman did not lower himself to such behavior. But the turmoil within him drove him on, forcing him to break his own rules. He might abhor what he was about to do but he bloody well was going to do it!

He understood he might be wrong, might be conjuring up a conspiracy where none existed. Right or wrong, it made no difference. His suspicions gnawed at him and would not easily be put to rest. He must, he had to make certain, one way or the other.

Feeling along the top to the dressing table, his hand encountered a small case, his fingers found the lid. Because the case was not locked, the lid raised easily. Taking a deep breath Talland reached inside. . . .

Six

Talland had never possessed an unreasonable fondness for drink; he had rarely been foxed to incoherence. Even after purchasing his commission in the cavalry, he refused to subscribe to the notion that how many bottles it was possible to consume in one evening was the measure of a man. But he also knew that there were times in a man's life when drink proved to be the only solution, temporary though it might be, to an untenable situation.

His aunt was aware of his moderation. When, before dinner, he downed four brandies in quick succession, he heard her sniff progressively louder—some might even go so far as to say snort—as Ames poured each drink for him. Talland told himself her eyebrows must have risen to record heights. Though blue-devilled almost past bearing, he found himself bitterly amused by her inarticulate disapproval.

Once in the dining room, over the soup he turned to Aunt Elaine, seated at his right. "If you don't mind," he said, pleased to note that he was not slurring his words, "I should be pleased if you would deign to describe your charming companion's costume for this poor blind man."

After a moment of silence—he hoped it was shocked silence because he had mentioned his affliction in a far from tasteful manner—his aunt said sharply, "Do keep the line, Malcolm."

"Pray don't be such a high stickler, my dear aunt. I deny that I have in any way crossed the boundary of acceptability. Why should a man who cannot see be forced to imagine how those who dine with him are dressed? I cannot believe that I have put Miss Fletcher to the blush by my modest request."

Reaching carefully for his glass of wine, he sipped it before turning to Celia. "I realize you cannot say so, but perhaps you might care to indicate in some way to Lady Ashcroft that you are not unduly overset."

In the quiet that followed, he finished the wine in his glass and set it back onto the table, motioning to the footman he knew waited behind him for a refill.

"Since you insist on being told, Miss Fletcher is wearing a blue gown," Aunt Elaine said at last, her tone chilly.

"To match her eyes?" Talland asked. "I understand the color of Miss Fletcher's eyes rivals the bluest of skies. Perchance do her slippers match the gown? And what of her accessories? Are they a similar color or a delightfully contrasting one?"

"Do cease, Lord Taland." His aunt's voice was stiff with outraged formality.

"If I have offended I am curst sorry," he said, belatedly realizing he had not only come up with less than felicitous phrasing, but that perhaps his pronunciation of s was not quite precise.

"I don't believe you are quite yourself this evening."

"How perceptive of you, dear aunt," he said mockingly.

"It don't take much wit to observe that you are the worse for drink."

"A ramshackle fellow, all in all, you think? No doubt

'tis so. I do not scruple to tell you that I feel I have made a cake of myself, which is enough to bring a pang to the stoutest heart. If, indeed, I possess a heart. I have been told 'tis doubtful."

"Whatever else you may or may not have done," Aunt Elaine said, "you have certainly caused me to lose my appetite completely. Come, Celia, we shall leave my nephew to the solitude he deserves."

He raised his wine glass to toast their departure, drained its contents and motioned for more. Just as well those two crafty ladies had left, he thought, because he was rapidly becoming too foxed to be careful what he said and he did not wish to reveal too much. Not yet.

" 'Ere's me arm, sir," Biggs's voice said sometime later, he had no idea how much later. Talland made no protest when Biggs helped him rise from the chair and led him up to his rooms.

"Never trust a woman," he told Biggs solemnly as the valet got him ready for bed.

"Learned that when I was but a wee lad," Biggs assured him.

"Deceivers one and all." Talland struggled to enunciate clearly.

" 'Tis the bloody truth," Biggs agreed.

Talland fell into a profound sleep immediately, only to rouse sometime later with a viciously throbbing head. Listening carefully, he tried to determine the time. The lack of any of the familiar early morning sounds convinced him that darkness still shrouded the earth. Since he was too uncomfortable to permit sleep to overtake him, he rose and began pacing the room in his bare feet.

What had he accomplished other than to give himself a frightful headache? Aunt Elaine, of course, had been

driven into a veritable miff but he doubted she suspected
what he had learned. As for her companion . . . Talland
paused in his pacing and sighed. What was he to do?
Certainly not drink himself into another state of outrageous intoxication. What then? He would have to wait
to decide, since at the moment his headache prevented
him from coming up with a viable alternative.

Too restless to return to bed, he decided to go downstairs
where he padded soundlessly through the rooms until he
came to the French doors leading to the terrace. Opening
them as quietly as he could, he stood on the threshold,
letting the cool night air flow around him, hearing the
country sounds of frogs and night insects. And something
else—the plaintive plinking of a dulcimer.

So she could not sleep either. He started to step down
onto the terrace, then hesitated, listening. The tune she
played was "My Love Will Ne'er Forsake Me." It might
be argued he had done exactly that. He clenched his fists.
Devil take her—in the circumstances, what else could
he have been expected to do? Live with her pity?

He grew so choked with frustrated rage that he was
tempted to march straight to the arbor and expose her
flummery. Talland shook his head, immediately regretting the motion when the throbbing intensified. This was
not the right time, nor was he in any condition for a
confrontation. Carefully closing the doors, he retreated
to his rooms where he found a drowsy Biggs waiting.

" 'Ave a bit of a 'ead, do ye, sir?" Biggs asked.

Talland admitted he had spent more comfortable nights
and submitted to Biggs's ministrations which finally re-
sulted in him sinking into a morass of dream-plagued sleep
where, during a fearsome thunderstorm, coal-black horses

ridden by invisible spirits rode the night skies. Instead of fear, a savage grief gripped him.

He woke with tears drying on his cheeks and no idea why the nightmare had affected him in such a strange way. Making an effort, he dismissed the dream from his mind.

Talland sat up, finding to his relief that his headache had all but vanished. The sounds he heard told him morning was far advanced. He grimaced as he recalled his loose-in-the-haft overindulgence. What a cork-brained notion that had been. At least he had retained a grain of sense, enough to avoid an awkward confrontation. He needed to have his wits about him to deal with her. What he should have done and what he would do now was to plan a deceptive undergame of his own.

He came down to the dining room in time to join his aunt and her companion for the midday meal, sensing their surprise at his unexpected appearance. "My most abject apologies," he murmured. "I am not usually so rag-mannered. Rest assured you shall not be subjected to such bad *ton* at Hart's Hill again."

"You *were* rather deep in your cups," Aunt Elaine said with a sniff.

"I pray you will forgive me."

"Don't I always?" she asked wryly.

"Always. Which is why you remain my favorite aunt."

"As well as your only aunt. By blood, at least."

"Had I a hundred, you would still trump them all."

"Don't be excessive, dear boy," she reprimanded but he detected a smile in her words.

Talland took care to keep the conversation light and inconsequential during the meal. When they were preparing to leave the table, he turned toward Celia. "I shall not be convinced you have forgiven me unless you promise to join me at about three this afternoon and play your dulcimer for me. Always providing, of course, that the time set does not conflict with your other duties."

"If Celia wishes to grant you this favor," Aunt Elaine informed him, "I have no objection to the time you have set. There, she has nodded her agreement so she will join you, though I am not entirely certain that she ought to forgive you."

He bowed slightly, first to his aunt, then in Celia's direction. "Shall we meet in the arbor?" he asked.

After a moment his aunt said, "Celia has signed to me that she would prefer to meet you by the stone wall."

Though he had no notion why, he had no objection. "I yield to her choice. I shall ask Ames to see that benches are placed near the wall."

As he left the room he congratulated himself on how well he was handling everything. He was disabused of that notion when Aunt Elaine caught up with him near the music room, urged him inside and closed the door.

"I have sent Celia upstairs to fetch a handkerchief," she said, "so she cannot possibly overhear while you explain to me exactly what flummery you are up to."

Talland did his best to feign a look of astonished innocence. "Me?"

"You should know by now I am not easily taken in."

"I am making no attempt to run a rig," he insisted. "You do me an injustice."

"I wish I could believe you."

"I wish you will," he said fervently, not wanting to have her thrust a spoke in his wheel.

She sighed. "I thought I detected a certain similarity in your impeccable behavior at the table and the I-am-a-very-good-boy act you were wont to don as a child when you were up to something particularly pernicious. Perhaps I am wrong. I do hope so."

"I am, after all, no longer a child."

"No, not in some ways, I grant you that much." She sighed again. " 'Tis against my better judgment but I shall try to believe you are not playing some deep game."

"If there is anyone devious in this room, my dear aunt," he could not resist saying, "you would qualify long before I would."

She chuckled briefly. "How well you have me pegged." Then she gripped his arms and he knew she was searching his face. "The eyes may be windows to the soul," she murmured, "but yours tell me nothing."

"Blind eyes can neither see nor speak," he said, bitterness creeping into his tone.

Releasing him, she said, "Dr. Lancer told me that your eyes are not damaged in any way. While he does not question your blindness, he admitted he was puzzled by your inability to see."

"I *did* have a head injury," he blurted, taken by surprise that Lancer had broken his word about discussing details.

"So the doctor said, but not, apparently, in an area that should have affected your vision."

"The fact remains I cannot see." Talland spoke with finality, hoping to end the conversation. So much for trusting Lancer. He should have known better.

He heard his aunt open the door. "Celia is waiting for me," she said. "Do be a good boy. Blindness doesn't excuse bad behavior."

Her words made him realize she still suspected he was up to some sort of hum.

She was right.

As he let himself out through the French doors, shards of his dream returned to clutter his mind with visions of a foam-flecked horse galloping through the night, as red-eyed as the mount of the Wild Huntsman in the tale that had frightened him as a child. He found himself trembling and forced the image from him.

I should go to the stables, he told himself firmly. Go now and conquer this irrational fear of horses that has me by the throat. I will go. I may not be ready to mount a horse, but Lion Heart will not have forgotten me. I certainly ought to be able to make myself touch him, perhaps even stroke his neck.

He turned in that direction and began to walk toward the stables. When he was, by his reckoning, no more than halfway there, his steps became slower and slower until at last he came to a complete halt. No matter how he urged himself on, he could go no farther.

More disgusted than angry with himself, he whirled about and retraced his steps.

"Sooner or later you must conquer this fear," Dr. Lancer had insisted. "Until you do, you will be at its mercy."

What a deuce of a coil it was, being afraid of one's own favorite steed, a bang-up horse who had once outraced the Duke of Orford's prized Windrunner. He loved Lion Heart, damned if he didn't, and yet he could not make himself go near the bay.

He banished that thought from his head as forcefully as he had the nightmare beast and began humming a tune to distract himself from brooding about what was wrong with him. He smiled wryly when he recognized that he'd chosen "The Lass with the Delicate Air." After a moment he began to sing it aloud as he walked toward the arbor. She would not be there to greet him, he would be quite alone. Until later. He quite looked forward to their *tête à tête*.

When the time came to meet at the stone wall overlooking the ruins, Talland found himself possessed of a lowering presentiment, a feeling that doom hovered, waiting to descend. He hesitated to set off on the path, wondering if he was about to make the mistake of his life. He shook his head. No doubt the residue of that bloody nightmare was still troubling him. He walked on, the scent of marjoram following him.

Biggs had supervised the placing of the bench and reported to his master exactly how many paces away from the wall and off the path it was, to the left, under a hawthorn which had been trained to grow as a single-trunked tree. So first to the wall, Talland was telling himself when he heard the music of her dulcimer join with the twittering of the birds.

He listened carefully and determined she was at the wall rather than sitting on the bench. In a matter of moments he stood beside her, saying nothing to interrupt the music, an Irish tune he recognized as "The Minstrel Boy."

. . . To the war has gone. . . . How appropriate. For war it was to be.

Something brushed against his lower leg—apparently Nimue had followed her. Not caring to be surprised by a sudden decision of the cat to climb his leg, he reached down, picked up the animal and held it a moment. What an appropriate choice the cat's name was, after all. Had she seen him as Merlin and herself as Nimue, the nymph who tricked Merlin into a fatal enchantment?

She would soon discover just who was tricking whom. He set the cat atop the wall, thinking that before he'd become more intimately acquainted with Nimue than he at first had wished, he had never realized how fragile and delicate cats' bones felt under the thick fur of their coats.

As fragile as Juliet had felt in his embrace.

As delicate as Celia had felt when he held her.

Cats were actually quite sturdy creatures, noted for insisting on having their own way no matter what, being eminently capable of reaching that goal by slyness and trickery.

And women? He smiled thinly.

He waited until she finished the tune, then reached for the dulcimer, politely asking, "May I?" She released the instrument and the fingering sticks to him without question. He set the dulcimer and the sticks carefully on the grass beside the wall.

Without another word, he pulled her into his arms and captured her mouth with his. Holding back with difficulty the savage passion that leaped inside him the moment he touched her, he fought to keep the kiss a pledge rather than a declaration of possession.

"Celia," he whispered against her lips. "I must confess my feelings for you." He felt her start of surprise with grim satisfaction.

Holding her pressed to him so she could not see his face, he said, "I have hesitated to tell you because I believed I loved another. Perhaps my aunt has mentioned Juliet Grant, whom I met at a Valentine's Ball more than a year past and formed somewhat of a *tendresse* for. I know now what I felt for Juliet was no more than momentary attraction. You are the one, the only one. She was nothing; you are everything."

Was he overdoing it? he wondered when she seemed to be trying to free herself. He kissed her again, longer and more deeply than he meant to. However he truly felt about her, there was no doubt he desired this woman intensely.

"You have quite brought me round your thumb," he murmured against her throat. "I see no choice but to offer you—" he paused, his voice breaking as though overcome by emotion. "No, perhaps 'tis too soon to speak of that," he went on. "But I do want you to know Juliet could not hold a candle to you. She was no more than a pretty butterfly while you are—ah, I cannot begin to tell you, I can only show you."

When his lips found hers again, the combination of his own throbbing need and her increasingly ardent response came close to being his undoing. His hands molded her breasts, sliding down over her hips and pressing her hard against him.

Too much by half! he warned himself. Much more of this and he would be rolling in the grass with her, oblivious of anything but his own desire.

With some difficulty he managed to pull back slightly. "Tell me you will be mine," he begged, the hoarseness of real passion in his voice. Had she nodded? He couldn't be sure but he hoped so. "You will never need to worry about money," he told her, "for as my mistress I will protect you with a lifetime trust that cannot be set aside, even in the unlikely event that I ever do decide to marry."

She gasped in outrage, then thrust him aside with all her strength. He had little time to relish his revenge. From below rose a high-pitched, desperate caterwauling. Hearing her begin to scramble over the wall, he grabbed for her, catching a fold of her skirt. She tore it away from him and was over the wall, out of his reach. He knew she believed Nimue was in trouble and meant to plunge down the twisting path toward the ruins to rescue the cat.

"Juliet!" he shouted. "Be careful!"

She didn't answer. He desperately wanted to go after her, despite the madness of a blind man trying to negotiate an unseen, no longer familiar trail. No, impossible. But there was Lion Heart. He could easily and quickly get there mounted on Lion Heart. Provided he *could* mount him. A vision of the red-eyed horse thundered into his mind, freezing him in place.

From below Juliet cried, "Nimue!" her voice a despairing wail.

"Are you all right?" he shouted.

She made no response. His jaw clenched. "For the love of God, answer me!" he called.

A choked-off scream, a rattle of stones, then silence. *A maid trapped in the scree* . . .

Jolted by the sudden knowledge that if he lost her there would be nothing left for him, Talland whirled and ran along the path, heading for the stables, his fear of losing the woman he loved sweeping all else aside. In his haste, he tripped and fell more than once over obstacles he could not see. But he sprang up each time and rushed on.

"Milord!" a man cried and he recognized the voice as belonging to one of the grooms.

"Bring Lion Heart to me," he ordered. "Never mind a saddle."

He had not ridden bareback since he was a lad but, when the groom led out the bay, he grasped the reins and sprang onto Lion Heart, guiding the horse with his knees to the drive. As they pounded down the hill, Talland was seized by the uneasy conviction he was repeating an action that had taken place before, an action that had ended in unimaginable horror. Shaking off the uncomfortable feeling of *déjà vu,* when he judged they'd reached the right place, he urged the horse off the drive and around the hill toward the ruins, shouting Juliet's name.

Why had he clung to the bird-witted delusion that he must pay her back in her own coin for having played such a miff-maff May-game with him? She could hardly have connived at such an elaborate hoax without his aunt's co-operation. For all he knew, his wily Aunt Elaine might well have concocted the entire addle-brained scheme in a misguided effort to "help." Yet he had chosen to punish only Juliet, the woman he now realized he loved more than life itself. Damn and blast!

Talland knew there were scattered stones and rubble hidden in the grass, but in his eagerness to reach Juliet he did not allow Lion Heart to slacken his pace. When he felt the horse stumble and begin to fall, the world seemed to spin wildly. He clung to the bay's mane, suddenly no longer aware of where he was, transported back to the past, hearing the rumble of cannon and shells exploding around him, the stench of gunpowder acrid in his nostrils.

The horse went down, he was flung from the saddle and struck his head but was not knocked out completely. Dizzy and confused, he tried to get to his feet and found he could not because his left leg was pinned under his dead horse, a black named Nightshade. Try as he might, he could not extricate himself and was forced to lie there helpless while shells burst around him. My luck has run out, he thought bleakly. I shall die here. So much for leading a charmed life.

A horse pulled up nearby and his old chum Beaumont dismounted, saying, "Have you free in a trice, Talla—"

A bullet cut him down before he finished the word. He slumped across the dead Nightshade, his blood running down to soak Talland's uniform while his brown eyes, glazed in death, stared accusingly. Talland's mouth opened in a soundless scream of denial and then everything went black. . . .

Talland sat up, shaking his head, completely disoriented. He blinked in disbelief at the ragged wall to his right. The ruins? He stared at the bay horse who was scrambling to his feet in front of him. Lion Heart! But how could that be? Only moments ago he had been in the thick of battle, only moments ago Beaumont, who would never have been in the cavalry except for him, had stopped to rescue him, then died within his arms' reach.

Died because of him.

Seven

Talland sat in the grass by the ruined tower, blinking in confusion. Dazed, disbelieving the evidence of his own eyes—that he was back in England on the grounds of his estate—he struggled to understand, but his mind was still fixed on Beaumont's death.

A yowl from somewhere above him drove him to his feet. Gazing up into a small ash tree, he saw a cat. Saw Nimue. *Saw.* Good God, he could see!

Before he could make head or tails out of how that had happened, the reason he was at the ruins came to him. Juliet! Where was she?

He looked quickly around; she was nowhere in sight. Since she would never go off leaving her cat trapped in a tree, she must be nearby. He shouted her name. No answer came. He pictured her lying somewhere injured, unable to call for help and his jaw clenched.

Forcing his way through the rank growth of grass and bushes he searched for her, calling, "Juliet! Juliet!" while pausing now and again to listen for any faint response.

Distracted by his fear for her welfare, he failed to notice the cave-in until he stepped into the half-hidden hole and plunged down and down, showered as he fell with dirt and pebbles from above. His jolting landing stunned him.

* * *

Juliet came to in darkness, unable to make out where she was or how she had gotten there. Then she remembered Nimue and that she had seen a fox chasing the cat. She recalled plunging down the hill in an attempt to rescue Nimue—but then what had happened? Why was she lying on her back in this dark and disagreeable place?

Slowly, cautiously, she sat up and, as she did, small stones slid off her. As she brushed at her gown, she discovered she was covered with tiny pebbles and dirt. Fighting back panic, desperately wishing she could see, Juliet tried to stand and found she was in a room—if that is what it was—so low her hair brushed its ceiling. Feeling to either side she encountered large stones set unevenly into the dirt walls.

It was more like a passageway than a room, she decided, striving to remain calm as she bit her lip in an effort to keep from screaming. If she could manage to keep her wits about her she might have a chance to find a way out but if she gave way to the terror simmering inside her, she might well stay trapped.

Setting herself to think as clearly as she could, she reasoned that she must be under the ruins where, apparently, tunnels had been dug for some long-ago purpose. While she did not understand how she came to be in one of those tunnels, she definitely was and so must use her wits to free herself.

Malcolm! she thought with a sudden leap of hope. He knows I came down to the ruins, surely he will come after me. Then the entire ghastly, humiliating scene by the wall atop the hill flashed into her mind. Reminded how he'd called to her as she climbed over the wall,

called her by her true name, called her Juliet, tears stung
her eyes. He had somehow penetrated her disguise and
had deliberately lured her into displaying her affection
for him, only to stab her to the very heart. How cruel
he was!

Why had she ever thought she loved him?

A faint sound from somewhere above caught her attention. Was someone calling her name? She listened,
but the sound was not repeated. Maybe Malcolm had not
followed her, maybe he did not intend to rescue her.

How she hated this darkness! It seemed to press in on
her from all sides until she began to believe she could
not breathe and in desperation stumbled forward, blindly
groping her way along the passage as she gasped for
breath. Eventually she realized she was, in fact, breathing
quite normally and some of her fear subsided.

Having no idea whether she was heading toward a possible exit or into a dead end, she blundered on because
moving was preferable to huddling motionless in the
threatening darkness. When she finally spotted a ray of
light in the distance, she cried out in relief. At last!

While she made her way as fast as she could along the
passageway toward the light, it occurred to her that the
darkness of the tunnel was what it must always be like for
Malcolm, darkness with no hope of seeing the light. Her
heart ached for him. In his own way, he had come to terms
with being blind, braver than she would have been in the
same circumstances. To admit the truth, she still loved him,
cruel as he had been to her. She always would love him.
But she would never, ever, tell him.

Keeping her gaze fixed on the light that grew brighter
and brighter, she failed to watch her footing and stumbled over an obstacle on the floor of the passage. She

fell onto something soft, something that groaned and moved. Juliet screamed and tried to scramble away.

Hands caught her, held her. "Juliet!" Malcolm cried hoarsely.

His arms came around her, shifting her until she fit against him. Neither spoke, lying together on the dirt floor of the ancient tunnel with dirt and pebbles still slithering down at intervals from the hole above them.

"A maid trapped in the scree," he murmured finally, pushing himself to a sitting position and pulling her up with him.

"These four together hold the key," she responded, freeing herself from him and rising. "But what the key may be, I am sure I don't know." She started to brush dirt from her gown but, realizing it was hopeless, gave up.

"There is light up above," she told him. "We are at the bottom of a hole."

He rose. "I know, I fell down it. Is that what happened to you?"

She hesitated. "I did not fall into this hole. I don't really remember how I came to be in the tunnel, but I must have fallen through an opening in some other place because when I came to myself there was no light at all." She shuddered.

He touched her shoulder briefly as though realizing she needed comfort but that she did not want him to hold her again.

"I came galloping like a true knight to the rescue of his lady fair," he said, "but then the tale went awry. Instead of the knight finding the lady, you found me. And now we are both in need of rescuing. Which I expect will come soon, once word reaches Ames that I rode off on Lion Heart without waiting for him to be saddled."

"You really did ride?" she said. "I thought—" She broke off, belatedly remembering she was not supposed to know about his strange fear of horses, information that Lady Ashcroft had wormed out of Dr. Lancer and shared with her.

"I rode." The grimness in his tone startled her.

She waited for him to explain but he said no more. He did not look at her but stared down the maw of the tunnel into darkness that she told herself matched his own.

"Nimue!" she cried, suddenly recalling the cat's plight. "A fox was after Nimue."

"Your cat is at the top of an ash tree," he said. "Clever as they are, foxes cannot climb trees so Nimue is safe. I would hazard that many generations of fox families have known and used the underground passageways of the ruins over the years. I cannot think why the tunnels might have been dug in the first place."

"Yet we supposedly hold the key," she reminded him. "Might there be hidden treasure?"

"I will have the passageways searched. But, somehow, I doubt the meaning is that simple. Of late I have been discovering that nothing is as simple as it seems on the surface."

So far he had avoided any mention of what he had said and done at the wall and she decided this was his way of introducing the matter. She waited, expecting him to begin an apology but he said no more. Was he waiting for her to open the discussion? If so, he had all eternity because she had no intention of doing so.

When she had first fallen over him here at the bottom of this hole, her only feeling was an overwhelming relief that he had come for her and she had welcomed the comfort of his arms. That warm feeling had gradually faded.

He still had much to answer for and, apparently, he did not mean to so much as make a start.

"Captain!" A man's voice shouted from somewhere above. "Where are ye, sir?"

"Biggs!" Talland called back. "Here! I seem to have fallen down a hole, along with Miss Fletcher."

"Not Miss Grant?" she could not help but ask.

"Ames is the only one who might have recognized you as Juliet Grant but apparently he did not. Biggs thinks of you as Celia Fletcher and so do the other servants. I see no point in confusing the issue at this time."

"Lady Ashcroft says Ames is too proud to wear the glasses he needs," Juliet said. She found herself disturbed at the idea of having to continue her masquerade. What was the point now that Malcolm had unmasked her?

Biggs's face appeared at the top of the hole as he peered down at them. "Found ye!" he cried.

"Good man. You will need a rope to—"

"Rope's on hand, sir." Biggs sounded faintly offended, as though Talland should have realized he would come prepared for any eventuality.

Juliet, at Talland's insistence, was the first to be pulled up. Not only Biggs but three grooms and two footmen were in attendance by then and she was borne off to the Hall immediately.

When she reached the house, Lady Ashcroft took one look at her and began issuing orders right and left. A copper tub and heated bath water were carried to her room with a maid to wash her hair while she scrubbed the dirt from her skin. As she was donning her robe, a kitchen maid brought in Nimue.

"Mr. Ames thought ye'd be wantin' t' see yer cat," the girl said.

Juliet clutched Nimue to her and nodded her thanks to the girl. With so many servants about, servants who still believed she was Celia, the mute, Juliet did not dare speak.

"After such a dreadful experience you must not even think of attempting to come down for dinner," Lady Ashcroft insisted. "You shall be served in bed and I shall have a tray brought up for myself so we may dine together in cosy comfort."

Understanding Malcolm's aunt would expect to be told everything while they ate, Juliet nodded. By forming two words: H-e k-n-o-w-s, on Lady Ashcroft's palm, she had already passed on the most vital information, the rest could wait.

Talland refused to wait for a bath. He washed the worst of the grime from himself while Biggs laid out a change of clothes, then he hurriedly donned them with his valet's assistance.

"Never mind how the cravat is tied," he muttered when Biggs showed a tendency to fuss. "We must be off. I want to be in London by first light. And mind you, not a word about what you, and you alone, have discovered. I mean to keep it a secret for the time being."

"Ye should know by now, sir, I keeps me mummer dubbed," Biggs said.

Talland nodded, certain he could trust Biggs to keep his mouth shut. As he started for the door, Biggs handed him one of his canes, winking as he did so.

Talland accepted the cane, aware it was important, for the moment, to keep up appearances.

* * *

"Is Lord Talland all right?" The question burst from Juliet when, later, she and Lady Ashcroft were finally left alone in her bedroom.

His aunt shrugged. "I can only assume so since I understand from Ames that he and Biggs rode off to London as soon as Malcolm changed clothes. I had no chance to speak to Malcolm at all. You say he actually knows you are Juliet Grant?"

Juliet nodded, having made up her mind what she meant to tell Lady Ashcroft and what she felt must be left out. "I have no notion what made him suspect, but I did discover what convinced him of my real identity. When I looked through my jewel box a short while ago, I discovered my heart brooch, as well as the unattached emerald heart, were missing."

Lady Ashcroft stared at her. "Are you quite certain Malcolm took them? It is possible one of the servants has light fingers, you know."

"I thought of that. When I asked Annie, the upstairs maid who does for me, if she knew of anyone who had entered my room in the past few days when I was not there, she stammered and carried on for a bit, then finally admitted she had seen Lord Talland go in last evening before dinner."

"That would explain his overindulgence later. I am still confused, though. Because they are heart shaped, I understand he would have had no difficulty identifying what he was searching for but I still do not grasp his reason for taking the brooch. Would not simply finding it among your possessions be enough?"

"Evidently not. Perhaps he meant to confront me with

the brooch. He was, let us say, considerably upset by my pretense of being Celia Fletcher."

Lady Ashcroft smiled wryly, a smile so like Malcolm's that Juliet was taken aback for an instant. "Men so resent the discovery that women can and do outsmart them. Once he regains his wits, though, I don't doubt I will be the one accused of masterminding the ruse."

" 'Tis no more than the truth," Juliet pointed out. "I take full blame for my willingness to participate, but I doubt I could have conceived such a brilliant plan."

"Yes, I do not scruple to tell you that idea was one of my better efforts along such lines."

Juliet blinked. "You have done this kind of thing before?"

"When circumstances call for a *soupçon* of deviousness to make everything come out right, I admit that I cannot always resist providing it. But enough about my fondness for meddling. Tell me exactly what happened between you and Malcolm and how you both managed to fall into what I understand may be a positive labyrinth of tunnels under the ruins."

Juliet, who was propped up on a chaise longue rather than in bed, sat straighter. "Pretending he believed I was Celia, he told me how fond of me he had grown, at the same time saying that he was no longer the slightest bit interested in Juliet Grant, that she had been a mere passing fancy." Anger rose in her as she relived the scene. "Everything was Celia, Celia, Celia—Juliet was less than nothing."

"But, my dear, you were, you are, both."

"I know, but the way he seemed to be so lightly dismissing what I believed we had between us—when I was Juliet, I mean—infuriated me. I am sure this makes me sound like a goose-top but I could not help resenting what he said. Of course he knew I would, which was why he was doing it."

"Men do tend to favor revenge."

"He certainly does! About then I noticed that Nimue, who had wandered down to the ruins, was being pursued by a fox. Forgetting all else, I rushed to her rescue. I heard Lord Talland shout, 'Juliet!' after me and realized with considerable bitterness how he had hoaxed me. The next I knew I woke up in the darkness of the tunnel."

She reached to Lady Ashcroft, who sat next to her in a slipper chair, and touched her hand. "The darkness so frightened me that, when I thought about how he was always in darkness, I could almost forgive him for what he had done to me."

"You must not forget that, in order to come to your rescue, he conquered that strange fear of horses he brought back with him from the war. The groom told Ames that Malcolm actually rode Lion Heart bareback."

Juliet nodded, biting her lip. She had not confessed everything to his aunt—how could she!—which made it impossible for her to admit how the revenge game he had played on her still rankled, festering within her heart like an embedded splinter in a finger. Yes, he had ridden to her rescue but he had not bothered to apologize for what else he had done. Make her his mistress, indeed!

When Lady Ashcroft took her leave, Juliet found herself too restless to try to sleep. She took up her dulcimer but, recalling how often she had played for Malcolm and how beautifully the words he had sung blended with her melody, she could not bring herself to pluck even one string. He had become such a part of her she feared that without him she could never again be whole. How much better it would have been if she had accepted his abrupt dismissal when she came to Hart's Hill for the first time.

But once she learned of his blindness from Lady Ashcroft, she had thought she understood why he had turned her away without admitting the reason—his pride had forced him to. And then, of course, his aunt had come up with her fateful scheme.

"Deceit rarely brings happiness," Grandmama had warned, but in the end she had reluctantly endorsed the plan.

Eventually Juliet climbed into bed and sleep claimed her. She woke to morning light from a dream where Malcolm dangled a golden key in front of her, saying, "If you can tell me what this unlocks, the key is yours forever."

She slid out of bed, wondering grumpily if he would have given her three guesses as they did in fairy tales. But after she drank her morning tea, brought in by Annie, her mood lightened a trifle. She decided that she would don her most becoming gown, never mind that Malcolm was in London and that he would not be able to see the gown if he were here. Indulging herself in a fit of the sullens would not accomplish anything, and she knew looking as well as she could always lifted her spirits.

But her spirits did not improve perceptibly until, sitting on the terrace with Lady Ashcroft in midafternoon, she heard the unmistakable rattle of a curricle. Since the drive could not be seen from this side of the house, she could not know whether or not it was Malcolm returning but her heart leaped anyway.

"That must be my errant nephew," his aunt said, rising. "Who else could it be? By his orders, we have not had anyone visit Hart's Hall since our arrival. Come, we shall await his presence in the parlor."

Though she was not at all certain she was ready to meet him or whether he would care to speak to her, Juliet followed without protest. She may not be prepared for the encounter but she had to admit that, despite everything, she wanted to see him, though she was determined not to reveal her eagerness in any way.

Malcolm did not appear until she and his aunt had been settled in the parlor for some time, Lady Ashcroft with a bit of embroidery and she with a book whose pages she had been staring at rather than reading until Lady Ashcroft asked her to read aloud. "For there is no need to pretend any longer that you cannot speak," she added.

" 'Tis but a book of old poems and ballads," Juliet said.

"I have no objection to poetry or ballads. Pray do read to me."

Glancing at the opened book, Juliet said, "This is called 'Lady Isabel and the Elf Knight.' " She recited the first verse and then came to the chorus:

"He followed her up, he followed her down
He followed wherever she lay.
And she had no wings to fly from him
And no tongue to tell him nay, nay, nay.
And no tongue to tell him nay. . . ."

"Poor Lady Isabel," Talland said from the entrance to the parlor. "Unlike pretty Juliet, she cannot speak and so discourage the wicked Elf Knight."

The book slid from Juliet's hands onto the floor. She made no effort to retrieve it, looking anywhere but at him, completely undone by his unannounced and unnoticed arrival.

"Why must you creep about startling people?" Lady

Ashcroft chided him. "We had no idea you were even in the house."

He nodded to her, crossed to where Juliet sat, bent, picked up the book, and offered it to her. Numbly, she took it, clenching her hands around the small volume.

"What did happen to Lady Isabel?" he asked. "Did she meet her doom at the hands of the evil-intentioned knight?"

"Actually, I believe she drowned him," Juliet managed to say.

"No doubt it served him right," Lady Ashcroft said. "Why did you not tell me you were going up to town, Malcolm? I could not imagine what had happened to you until Ames informed me. Why ever were you in such a hurry?"

"I wished to consult with Dr. Lancer as well as having other urgent business." He leaned against the mantelpiece and drove his hands into his pockets.

"Are we to be allowed to know what Dr. Lancer had to say?" his aunt asked.

"He admitted he was amazed."

"About you overcoming your fear of horses, I assume," Lady Ashcroft said.

Instead of replying, he turned toward Juliet. "Why?" he asked.

She gazed at him helplessly, as mute as if she were still pretending to be Celia.

"Don't bedevil the child," Lady Ashcroft ordered. "As you must have deduced by now unless your brains have become addled by your recent mishap, I conceived the nefarious plot. Someone had to rattle your cage lest you spend the rest of your life behind bars that you yourself had fashioned."

He glanced at his aunt. "I am perfectly aware it was your idea. What I am asking Juliet is why she aided and abetted you." Again he focused on Juliet, his gaze as intent as if he actually saw her.

"I—I don't believe I can answer you," she faltered. Anger at herself and at him stiffened her spine, giving her the courage to add, "Or perhaps the truth is I don't wish to reply."

She was glad she had taken the trouble to pick out a becoming gown and take special pains with her hair. Since he insisted on dueling with her, she needed every bit of spirit she had to counter his expert thrusts.

"I cannot think why you kick up such a fuss," Lady Ashcroft said to her nephew. "No harm was done. Just the opposite. Having us here enabled you to conquer your unreasonable fear of horses."

"That may be true," he admitted, "and I own I ought to be properly grateful. Still, I am quite certain that was not what you had in mind when you arrived."

"What I had in mind was your welfare!" Lady Ashcroft set aside her embroidery, rose and marched to where he stood. As she approached, Juliet saw Malcolm remove his hands from his pockets and straighten to face her. It occurred to her that he was not using his cane.

"I have known you since you were a puling infant," his aunt said, "and even then you exhibited an extreme stubbornness. The other evening you accused me of being a high-stickler when I objected ever so mildly to your rudeness due to overindulgence in drink." She paused to take a breath or two before returning to the attack.

"But you—" Lady Ashcroft shook her finger in his face and Juliet clearly saw him wince and jerk his head back, "you in your stubborn arrogance, insist there is nothing wrong with setting up your own high-handed rules, rules you refuse to clearly define. How dare you take offense when others fail to abide by them? Blind or not, 'tis past time for you to take a good, long look at yourself, Lord Talland."

Juliet quashed her momentary impulse to applaud as Lady Ashcroft stalked from the room. Malcolm watched her go and then swung around to face Juliet. She sprang to her feet, glaring defiantly at him.

"Put your sword away," he said mildly, "and we shall call a truce for the nonce."

His behavior had driven her into such a fury that she raised her hand, ready to fling the book of ballads at him. When she saw him duck aside, a sudden conviction froze her in place. He carried no cane. He had easily recovered the dropped book. He had known Aunt Elaine was crossing the room toward him and then had tried to avoid her wagging finger. He had ducked when she made a motion suggesting she meant to throw the book at him.

Lowering her hand, she placed the book carefully and precisely in the middle of the small table near her chair. "How long have you been able to see?" she demanded.

He spread his hands. "I thought you might catch me out. My blindness lifted after Lion Heart stumbled in the ruins and I fell off. Before then I had no memory of what had happened to cause me to lose my sight, I knew only what I had been told by those who had not been present when I was injured. But when I fell off Lion Heart, for a time I found myself back in the midst of the battle instead of in the ruins." He took a deep breath and let it out slowly. "I cannot yet bring myself to discuss the details but everything came back to me and, after I remembered, I found I was no longer blind."

Her anger faded as she listened, hearing truth ring in his words. "So that is why you hurried off to see Dr. Lancer," she said.

"I was afraid to tell anyone until he examined me, afraid the blindness would return as suddenly as it had lifted. You can imagine my relief when he assured me that it will not. I came into the parlor to announce the good news but when I heard you reading about Lady Isabel, some devil took me over and led me astray. In any case, I am at fault."

"You must find your aunt immediately and let her know you can see."

"I shall, as soon as I attend to other unfinished business."

"Nothing can be as important as telling her!"

"You are wrong." Four strides brought him to where she stood and, in his green eyes she saw the warm glow she remembered, a glow that began to melt her resentment of what he had done to her.

"You hurt me," she told him.

"I admit to it and I am ashamed. In so doing know that I wounded myself even more cruelly for I believed I had lost you forever." He cupped her face in his hands, gazing at her with such intensity she could not move.

"I think," he said, "that I must have known deep in my heart from the very moment Celia first touched me that she was Juliet in disguise. Else I could never have grown so fond of her so quickly." He brushed his lips across hers lightly, speeding her heartbeat and making her yearn for more.

"You are my love," he said huskily, "you have been from that moment in the conservatory when I found your lost heart and made it mine."

He let her go and reached into a pocket, pulling out a small red velvet-covered box. Opening it, he offered the box to her.

Juliet stared down at her brooch, at the two hearts once again entwined as they had been originally. She raised wondering eyes to him.

"My other reason for hurrying to London was to find a goldsmith to mend the brooch," he told her. "The sapphire heart and the emerald heart were meant to be linked together in the same way, my Juliet, that you and I were meant to be together. Say you forgive me for I want you for my wife, want you by my side until the end of time."

She opened her arms to him, murmuring, "Yes, yes, yes, Malcolm," and he kissed her properly, a tender kiss, yet one filled with the same passion she felt for him.

When their lips parted, he said, "Though 'tis June instead of February, you are, and always will be, my valentine." He swung her into an impromptu waltz, humming the same French tune they had danced to when they met at the Valentine's Day Ball.

As they moved around and around the parlor, Juliet suddenly cried, "I know what the key unlocks!"

He paused, still holding her close. "Will we find a treasure?"

She smiled up at him, her heart brimming over with happiness. "The greatest treasure of all, for what we found at Hart's Hall was the key to love."

ELEGANT LOVE STILL FLOURISHES –
Wrap yourself in a Zebra Regency Romance.

A MATCHMAKER'S MATCH   (3783, $3.50/$4.50)
by Nina Porter
To save herself from a loveless marriage, Lady Psyche Veringham pretends to be a bluestocking. Resigned to spinsterhood at twenty-three, Psyche sets her keen mind to snaring a husband for her young charge, Amanda. She sets her cap for long-time bachelor, Justin St. James. This man of the world has had his fill of frothy-headed debutantes and turns the tables on Psyche. Can a bluestocking and a man about town find true love?

FIRES IN THE SNOW   (3809, $3.99/$4.99)
by Janis Laden
Because of an unhappy occurrence, Diana Ruskin knew that a secure marriage was not in her future. She was content to assist her physician father and follow in his footsteps . . . until now. After meeting Adam, Duke of Marchmaine, Diana's precise world is shattered. She would simply have to avoid the temptation of his gentle touch and stunning physique—and by doing so break her own heart!

FIRST SEASON   (3810, $3.50/$4.50)
by Anne Baldwin
When country heiress Laetitia Biddle arrives in London for the Season, she harbors dreams of triumph and applause. Instead, she becomes the laughingstock of drawing rooms and ballrooms, alike. This headstrong miss blames the rakish Lord Wakeford for her miserable debut, and she vows to rise above her many faux pas. Vowing to become an Original, Letty proves that she's more than a match for this eligible, seasoned Lord.

AN UNCOMMON INTRIGUE   (3701, $3.99/$4.99)
by Georgina Devon
Miss Mary Elizabeth Sinclair was rather startled when the British Home Office employed her as a spy. Posing as "Tasha," an exotic fortune-teller, she expected to encounter unforeseen dangers. However, nothing could have prepared her for Lord Eric Stewart, her dashing and infuriating partner. Giving her heart to this haughty rogue would be the most reckless hazard of all.

A MADDENING MINX   (3702, $3.50/$4.50)
by Mary Kingsley
After a curricle accident, Miss Sarah Chadwick is literally thrust into the arms of Philip Thornton. While other women shy away from Thornton's eyepatch and aloof exterior, Sarah finds herself drawn to discover why this man is physically and emotionally scarred.

Available wherever paperbacks are sold, or order direct from the Publisher. Send cover price plus 50¢ per copy for mailing and handling to Penguin USA, P.O. Box 999, c/o Dept. 17109, Bergenfield, NJ 07621. Residents of New York and Tennessee must include sales tax. DO NOT SEND CASH.

Taylor—made Romance From Zebra Books

WHISPERED KISSES (3830, $4.99/5.99)
Beautiful Texas heiress Laura Leigh Webster never imagined that her biggest worry on her African safari would be the handsome Jace Elliot, her tour guide. Laura's guardian, Lord Chadwick Hamilton, warns her of Jace's dangerous past; she simply cannot resist the lure of his strong arms and the passion of his *Whispered Kisses*.

KISS OF THE NIGHT WIND (3831, $4.99/$5.99)
Carrie Sue Strover thought she was leaving trouble behind her when she deserted her brother's outlaw gang to live her life as schoolmarm Carolyn Starns. On her journey, her stagecoach was attacked and she was rescued by handsome T.J. Rogue. T.J. plots to have Carrie lead him to her brother's cohorts who murdered his family. T.J., however, soon succumbs to the beautiful runaway's charms and loving caresses.

FORTUNE'S FLAMES (3825, $4.99/$5.99)
Impatient to begin her journey back home to New Orleans, beautiful Maren James was furious when Captain Hawk delayed the voyage by searching for stowaways. Impatience gave way to uncontrollable desire once the handsome captain searched *her* cabin. He was looking for illegal passengers; what he found was wild passion with a woman he knew was unlike all those he had known before!

PASSIONS WILD AND FREE (3828, $4.99/$5.99)
After seeing her family and home destroyed by the cruel and hateful Epson gang, Randee Hollis swore revenge. She knew she found the perfect man to help her—gunslinger Marsh Logan. Not only strong and brave, Marsh had the ebony hair and light blue eyes to make Randee forget her hate and seek the love and passion that only he could give her.

Available wherever paperbacks are sold, or order direct from the Publisher. Send cover price plus 50¢ per copy for mailing and handling to Penguin USA, P.O. Box 999, c/o Dept. 17109, Bergenfield, NJ 07621. Residents of New York and Tennessee must include sales tax. DO NOT SEND CASH.